M000190150

PRAISE FOR EXPIRED PROMISE

Sizzling romance and intense action coming in hot! *Expired Promise* is the perfect addition to the Last Chance Fire & Rescue series. In her romantic suspense debut, Emilie Haney *killed* it! You're going to love this story—and that's one promise that won't expire!

RONIE KENDIG, AWARD-WINNING, BESTSELLING AUTHOR OF
RAPID-FIRE FICTION

High-action and pulse-pounding intensity, Expired Promise breaks the mold and delivers a romantic suspense story you won't be able to put down. Emilie Haney doesn't hold back giving readers a twisty plot and memorable characters that prove she is an author to watch! 10/10 recommend!!

NATALIE WALTERS, BESTSELLING AND AWARD-WINNING
AUTHOR OF TARGETED, SNAP AGENCY, AND
HARBORED SECRETS SERIES

"Wow! The simple complexity of the story was masterfully composed by the talented Emilie Haney. I'm looking forward to more books by her in the future!"

LILY, GOODREADS

EXPIRED PROMISE

LAST CHANCE FIRE AND RESCUE | BOOK 3

LISA PHILLIPS
EMILIE HANEY

sunrise
PUBLISHING

A NOTE FROM LISA

Dear Reader,

When we brainstormed *Expired Promise* I knew this one was going to be a high-octane thrill ride, and Emilie certainly delivered with Jude and Andi's story. I hope you enjoy reading it as much as I enjoyed getting to participate in the creation process.

I love stories of family, in all their messy realistic glory, and I especially love twins. Andi's brothers are a force to be reckoned with and we knew that if they got wind of the danger they'd stop at nothing to take down the bad guy. Not one good guy FD lieutenant, but two! They really were tornados.

At the heart of *Expired Promise* is something unspoken until Jude comes to town and sees Andi again for the first time in years. Their history gave them as much hope as it did make them believe their situations couldn't change. Andi seems to fight her family's expectations with a determination that's similar to how Jude goes after bad guys. But together they make a soft couple who lean toward each other in the end, and seek out what God has for them.

I'll keep saying it with each book – but I love these

characters! I adore the FD crew we created, and I'm so excited for all the stories in this series. And maybe even more to come! (You probably want a Logan story and a Bryce story as much as I do.)

Emilie, it's so fun to find an author who instinctively reaches for the Lisa story beats. Haha. Let's blow more stuff up soon, and have a good time doing it. You brought your heart into this process and wrote a story that's exciting and heartfelt. I can't wait for the next one!

Creating a community of readers is something every author wants to do. My readers are amazing people who are so friendly and supportive. Chatting with each person lets me know I've been doing my job, and I will keep striving to grow and improve with each new story I write. Every book is for you guys. It's why I do this.

So, as always, Happy Reading!

Lisa

*To Alex for your unending love and
support of my dreams.
Here's to many more books!*

1

The scent of salt and sweat hung in the air as ATF Special Agent Jude Brooks waited, breath held, at the edge of the gated Sosa Compound. He could just catch the repetitive sound of crashing waves not more than three hundred feet beyond the cliff that the massive villa was perched on.

His team surrounded him, guns drawn and waiting for his go-command, but he hesitated. The op was clear. A quiet breach of the villa's perimeter, thanks to disabled security sensors and cameras. Four teams at infiltration points ready to go on his signal. His main command team focused on finding and capturing cartel leader Diego Ruiz Sosa.

Thanks to countless scenarios he'd run on paper and in his mind, the op would involve quick engagement of Sosa's security team and minimal danger to all involved. It was by-the-book perfect, but there was one piece of information he was waiting for confirmation on. He wanted to know where the tip had originated from. The one that had first alerted the San Diego ATF field office of Sosa's presence in their area.

No matter that his team's surveillance had the drug lord on camera numerous times since the tip had come in a week before. Jude didn't like open ends. They got people hurt. Best to dot your i's and cross your t's.

"Sir?" His earpiece crackled to life. The team was waiting for his signal.

"Hold."

He wiped away a bead of sweat slipping from beneath his helmet. The heavy tac gear made the warm evening temperatures seem desertlike. He had to make the call. One last check of his phone showed no reply from the agent researching the tip. A bit of a gut punch, but the info would only be a redundancy of the work he'd already done. An untraceable call from the greater Denver, Colorado, area—a location Sosa was known to frequent for its proximity to I-70. No identification on the person who left the tip. No credible leads.

He'd run the risk assessments. He'd checked every box. The intel was credible. He could see Sosa with his own eyes. It was go time.

"All units ready," Jude subvocalized.

He did a visual check of the line. His team intermingled with SWAT, guns ready and eyes out.

"Cameras off at my command." Jude resisted the urge to clear his throat.

"Copy," came the disembodied reply.

It was now or never. No way would Jude let Diego Ruiz Sosa slip through their fingers. While the cartel leader's enterprise had been hit significantly over the last several years thanks to an informant they'd successfully embedded, the agent had been injured six months ago and opted to take the out. End the operation.

Jude couldn't blame him. The Sosa cartel spent money faster than it could move product, but that hadn't taken Sosa out of the game. It did, however, provide a perfect opportunity to catch him unaware.

"On my count." Jude flexed his fingers around the grip of his M-4 and settled his mind. "Cut cameras."

"Copy that, sir. And...we're dark."

He kept his voice low and counted off, "Three. Two. One. Go go go!"

The team rushed ahead like a tidal wave of black tactical gear. The breacher took care of the locked gates, and Jude's unit headed toward the left side of the villa. Accent lighting glowed everywhere, politely showing them the way toward their entry point.

Surveillance had reported that every night, around eight, Sosa liked to smoke a cigar on the patio overlooking the ocean. After fifteen minutes or so, he would retire inside to watch a telenovela. Sometimes with a woman, sometimes alone. Their intel said he would be alone tonight. Jude hoped that was accurate. He didn't want any collateral damage.

He paused where the edge of the house and the clear glass barrier narrowed before expanding to the patio. Jude's back pressed against the rough stucco of the house, stored heat radiating back at him, and carefully peered around the corner.

Signaling his line of sight was clear, he made hand motions to direct his team. He would make his way straight to a rocky pillar as his cover while agents Jackson and Perry kept under the windows. He signaled for Vanessa, or "Wiley" as they called her, to hang back for cover. The minute he gave the order, he saw her anger flare.

"Jude," came her hushed whisper.

He didn't have time for this. "Wiley, channel three."

Vanessa was headstrong with a hero-complex she needed to curtail sooner rather than later. Despite what she thought, his directives weren't about gender. It was about leadership, and he needed her on their six.

Her reply was instantaneous. "Sir, I think I can—"

"I gave the order. You follow it. That's how we're playing this. Or do I need to send you out?"

She waited a beat. "Copy."

Their eyes met for a fraction of a second, and he saw the rebellion bubble beneath the surface. He'd be having a talk with her about proper conduct during an infiltration the minute they were on the other side of this.

"Unit 3 in position."

Jude shifted back to the window. He repeated the motion for her to stay, then clicked his mic to signal his response to Unit 3. He looked back at his agents, pointedly not holding Vanessa's gaze, then counted down with his fingers.

They rushed ahead in ducked position to clear the windows, and Jude reached the pillar without incident. His breaths came heavy now, more from anticipation than exertion. A snatched look around the pillar showed a glass-fronted view of Sosa with his feet propped up on a mahogany coffee table. He had a glass of wine in one hand and the remote in the other. He was alone.

Relief flooded through Jude. It didn't make this easy, since Sosa always had dangerous guests in addition to an in-house security team, but it meant an innocent woman wouldn't end up in the crossfire.

"Unit two in position." The unit leader's voice was barely above a whisper. "I've got visual on two armed hostiles in the poolroom."

Jude played through the positions in his head. Unit 3 was on the northernmost side of the estate. Two was ready to breach from the front to the east. Four flanked them all, and he was in charge of Unit 1, with the sole focus of capturing Sosa. Everything was in place.

Jude readied his mic. "On three." He took one more deep breath. "Three. Two. One. Go go go!"

A flurry of activity hit all at once. Wood splintered. Gunshots filled the night.

He moved from his position to the glass-fronted side door. Jackson and Perry reached it just before him. They were preparing to break in when shots exploded the wall near his head.

Jude whipped around to see a tall man wearing black and wielding an automatic weapon. Where was Vanessa? His gut clenched. Had this goon blindsided her?

He aimed and took three shots. They hit center mass and the man went down hard. Jude waited, but no one else came around the corner.

"Wiley, report." Jude spun back to the task at hand, awaiting her reply. Nothing.

Intel indicated all glass in the house was shatter and bulletproof, so Perry used thermite to break the door lock.

The door swung inward. On count, Perry went in first, followed by Jackson, then Jude.

"ATF. Warrant. Hands up!" Jackson roared.

The couch was empty, the wine glass spilled on the floor.

"He's gone." Perry's reply came out muffled by his black balaclava.

"Come on." Jude motioned to the hallway he knew led toward the rest of the house from the media room.

Jude led with his gun out. He paused at one doorway—a bathroom—to check. Empty.

"Book, where's Wiley?" Perry ran down the carpeted hallway.

Jude wondered the same thing. Why hadn't she responded? He tried again. "Wiley, report?"

"Back of house," came a soft, staticky reply.

Jude held back a curse. She'd gone off on her own? He was going to throw the literal book at her. His agents would love that—adding kindling to the flame of their favorite nickname for him. "Book" because he did things by the book. They could tease him all they wanted, but he'd learned that sticking to the rules provided guidance and saved lives.

"Hold your position, Wiley. I repeat, *hold*."

There was no reply. He motioned for the men to stop with his hand held up flat. He replayed the map of the sprawling estate in his mind. They needed to go left, then straight to reach the back.

Jude took off at a fast jog, and they cleared rooms as they went until they hit a long hallway that ended in a circular room with another glass-fronted door. That had to be the one leading to the back deck.

"I've got him!" Vanessa said over the coms, her channel clear now that they were in proximity.

"Hold your position. I repeat, hold." Jude motioned for his agents to follow, and they raced toward the door. Just as the hall ended, a shot rang out.

Jude slid to a stop. Had that been over the coms or in the house? "Wiley?"

Her silence pushed him toward the door.

He left the cover of the hallway, and a shot echoed in the small space.

A thudding pain sent Jude reeling back. The bullet lodged in his vest above his left shoulder. Jackson grasped Jude's vest and hauled him back behind the wall. Every movement increased the thundering pain.

"You okay?" Perry's face swam into view.

"Yeah." Jude gasped. His left arm had gone numb. "Wiley?" He shouted over the com.

More bullets ate into the wall opposite him. Why wasn't she answering?

They needed another plan. He looked around and caught his reflection in a mirror. A quick explanation, and Jackson and Perry had the mirror ready to go.

"On my signal." Jude stood. Both men looked at him like he'd grown a second head, but he was regaining feeling in his arm. He'd be bruised, but nothing worse. Jude swapped out his M4 for his Glock. "Go."

Jude kept his back to the wall. The mirror went out, and he spotted a man positioned behind a waist-high bar before more gunfire shattered the glass. Jude nodded to the other agents as he pulled a flash-bang from his vest.

The explosion of sound and light disoriented the shooter, and Jude took him out with well-practiced shots to center mass. Jackson used the distraction to reach the back door. "Book!"

The note of panic in his teammate's voice was unusual.

Jude rushed to the open door. Vanessa lay in a pool of blood. Her eyes were open, staring. Sightless.

The sound of an engine erupted into the night air.

"Check her." Jude rushed to a steep set of stairs at the edge of the deck. He took several steps down but slowed. Below him, illuminated by orange dock lights, a black-and-red cigarette boat jetted off into the dark ocean waters. He could make out the figures of four men. One in particular.

Diego Ruiz Sosa had just gotten away.

"This is Unit Command. I need air and water support stat. Sosa is escaping by boat."

"Copy that. Dispatching now. Over."

"Sir...Vanessa..." Jackson's voice came over the coms.

Jude took the steps three at a time. He burst onto the deck, his left arm anchored to his side to minimize the pain. The sight before him churned his stomach. Vanessa.

One look from Perry and he knew there was no hope.

"Call it in." He swallowed hard.

"Brooks, we need you in here." The voice of the Unit 2 leader came over their command channel.

Everything inside of him wanted to break down. Vanessa, only twenty-six, and with so much life left to live. Vanessa, who bucked the system at every turn. Vanessa, sweet and funny.

"Brooks?" His coms barked again.

As much as he needed to process, now was not the time. "On my way."

The air inside the villa was warm, scented with alcohol where they'd shot up the bar. He rushed past and followed the directions of the Unit 2 leader until he came into a room on the third floor set up like an office.

An agent stood behind the desk.

"What is it, Owens?"

The agent looked up. "We think this might be a clue to what Sosa is up to next. You're the most familiar with his recent actions. Do you recognize anyone?"

Jude stepped past the tall man to look at the images scattered across the desk. Black-and-white photos. Clearly surveillance images. A woman and—

His sharp intake of breath caused the agent to spin around. "Everything okay, Book?"

"Yeah. I just..." He lifted a photo and his gaze traced the soft, feminine lines of a face years older than he remembered. "Yeah."

The agent moved back to the computer he was attempting to hack, and Jude shuffled through more of the images. *Andi.* Her mother. Her brothers. Her father.

The faces, all in various candid states, yanked him to the past. To summers spent at his grandfather's house. Cookouts with friends, playing guitar on the back porch, fishing the river, and spending time with her.

His first kiss.

Jude blinked and stepped back.

Not all of those memories were pleasant. It was a good reminder to take in the full picture—not just her beauty or the blue eyes that were once so familiar.

Cartel lord Diego Ruiz Sosa had pictures of Jude's first love, the girl who got away, and her family. There were too many questions, but his biggest one eclipsed all the others.

How in the world was Andi Crawford involved in his case?

2

F lames rose into the sky, licking up dry wood and insulation. The heat was almost unbearable to probationary firefighter Andi Crawford, despite her protective gear and the fact they'd only just arrived on the scene.

Not good.

"Roll that hose out," Lieutenant Amelia Patterson shouted. "We need to knock this fire down before it jumps to other structures. Stephens, make sure you soak down the house to the north first. Foster, around back to vent."

Andi helped Zack Stephens pull the secondary hose toward the house to the north. Ridge Foster ran past them, axe in hand, to vent the back of the structure. The woven nylon and rubber made the hose bulky, but this was why she worked out six days a week.

When they were in place, she used her legs to heft the hose under her arm and braced as a powerful stream of water soaked everything in the fire's path. On the south side, the rescue squad worked on the structure itself.

Her focus zeroed in on helping Zack aim the powerful

stream of water. Every muscle burned in her back and legs. The pain reminded her of everything she worked toward. Not only the safety of civilians, but keeping her coveted spot on the firetruck. In her mind, every fire was a test. One she aimed to pass.

"We have no exposure here," Zack reported over the radio. "We're moving to the south side of the structure on fire."

Chief Macon James repeated Zack's report in acknowledgment, but radio chatter interrupted him. A neighbor had seen two occupants enter the house a few hours earlier. A mother and her ten-year-old son.

Andi's heart leapt into her throat. A kid. She radioed to Amelia. "LT, I'll go in—"

"Negative, Andi. Chief's sending in Rescue. Do you copy?" She did, and Amelia went on to bark more orders. "Stephens, get that hose down here. Focus on the entrance."

Andi wanted to scream but knew better than to clog the line with unnecessary—not to mention dangerously out of bounds—arguing.

When the chief made up his mind, it was set in stone, but Zack didn't need her to help with the hose now that Foster had joined them, so she felt basically useless at this point. She could do so much more, if only they'd let her.

"Andi." Chief James's shout jolted her focus from the flames licking up the building. "I need you to be ready when they come out. They might need medical attention."

Her brow furrowed. "Where's Trace and Izan?"

"Accident on Pine Street. They've got backup coming but have to wait to leave."

"Copy that." She took in a breath, the air tainted by smoke and ash.

Since she'd transferred from Ambulance 33 across town to Eastside Firehouse as part of Firetruck 14, Andi had been called on to use her experience as a paramedic multiple times. It was second nature, so much so she had to hold herself back when calls for Ambulance 21—Trace and Izan's ambo—went out, but she had to admit it was getting old.

She wanted to *do* something, not just stand here as a backup for the paramedics. Be the firefighter she'd trained so hard to be. Sure, she was a decent paramedic, but being a firefighter was a more active way to save people, and *that's* where she felt the most alive. The most useful.

Logan's voice came over the radio. "We're entering the structure."

Andi couldn't help the jolt of worry that coursed through her. That was her older brother, Lieutenant Logan Crawford, heading up the rescue squad after his twin, Bryce, had suffered an injury several months back.

He was out of the hospital now, but Bryce's recovery was taking longer than he'd hoped, as evidenced by the daily family group texts about how much he hated physical therapy. He'd even asked Andi to fake a doctor's note so he could get back to Rescue, but there was no amount of espresso chip ice cream he could bribe her with to equal the risk.

"Careful," the chief said. "The burn has migrated toward the garage, but you know how quickly that can change."

Amelia spun around. "Stephens, Foster, concentrate that spray toward the kitchen now."

"Copy that," Zack said.

Andi took a step.

"Don't even think about it." Amelia drilled Andi with a look.

Andi rooted to the spot with her fists clenched. She hated this feeling of helplessness.

"We've got the mother. Coming through the front door. Cover us." Jayson's deep bass thundered over the radio.

Zack and Foster adjusted their angle and drenched the front door. When it opened, the influx of oxygen would feed the flames. They just needed to make sure it didn't get out of hand.

"Do you have a read on the boy?" Macon asked.

"Negative," Logan replied. "Still looking."

Andi bounced on the balls of her feet, ready to help with the mother.

Trace and Izan rushed past her, their blue uniforms covered by turnout gear. Looked like she was off the hook.

Jayson kicked the door out. Splinters and ash flew as he and Charlie Benning ran through the spray with a limp woman held up between them. The next moment, Logan tripped from the now open front door. He ripped off his mask as he approached Macon.

"It's clear, Chief."

"There was a boy," Andi heard herself say.

"There's no one else in there, Andi." Logan pinned her with a stare. "Trust me to do my job."

She ground her molars. What he really meant was she didn't know what she was talking about and to leave the "real firefighting work" to him. She was sick of him and Bryce giving her a hard time for switching career directions. If this were a medical issue, they'd never have questioned her.

Why, now that it involved fire, did he ignore her instincts? Hadn't she proven herself through extra training sessions? She'd gone above and beyond, but the twins refused to see her as anything more than their weak little sister. She was anything but weak.

"What if he's hiding and—"

"Drop it, Andi," Logan said.

Chief James gave her a look that said the same thing. She stepped away, knowing she'd only put her foot in her mouth rather than convince anyone. She trusted Logan, didn't she? It was just that the report had said there was someone else and—

Her gaze stalled as a shadow shifted in the house. There

was someone in there. Whoever it was moved away from the fire to the right side of the house where the flames had yet to reach.

The boy.

Andi stepped behind Zack and Ridge, who had hold of the hose. Amelia looked on from behind them, pointing out where to direct the spray. On the other side of the house, the rescue squad worked to move items from the garage that could prove hazardous should the fire reach them. Logan and the chief were still talking.

Andi continued back the way she and Zack had first gone to spray down the house next door. Was it possible the boy was inside and hadn't heard Logan call out? Was he trying to get out through a window?

She saw that shadow shift again behind the curtains. She looked back to her squad. They were busy hosing down the flames.

Andi knew what Lieutenant Patterson would say. That she was seeing things. That there was no one else inside and she was looking for a way to show off.

But what if there was? Something or someone inside had moved.

Knowing she'd get the chewing out of her life and deciding not to care, Andi rushed toward the house. There was someone inside, and she was going to rescue them. If it proved to her LT and her brother that she was capable, all the better.

Andi reached the side door. She'd heard radio chatter say it led to a separate bedroom and appeared cut off from the primary source of the fire. It was an odd place for an exterior door, but it was an entry point—one she was going to take.

She ran the scenario through her training. With the vent Ridge had cut in the back of the house, she would be safe to open this exterior door. She settled her mask firmly in place, twisted the knob, and counted to three.

The door opened into a room clouded by smoke. Logan's team must have secured the interior door, or it had closed with the force of air through the house, leaving the room mostly free of damage. There was an unoccupied twin bed to the right, covers mussed, and a closet on the opposite wall, door ajar.

She checked the closet to find it empty and then faced the interior door. Another three count and she pulled it open. The sudden influx of oxygen fanned flames to life in front of her. The wall of fire rose and then tempered, but not before she saw movement again. A lamp teetered and fell, drawing her attention to the shadow under the couch.

"Fire department, call out!" She yelled into the space, knowing her oxygen mask would cut back her volume. She listened but heard nothing.

The shadow shifted again, and Andi rushed forward. Her knees connected with the thin carpet, and she bent to peer under the couch. Scared yellow eyes stared back.

"You've got to be kidding me. A cat?"

Her radio blared to life. "Craw—Andi." She recognized the chief's voice. "Are you in that house? So help me—"

"Hold on, Chief." She grimaced at the possible aneurism that response was going to give him.

Baring her teeth back at the scared animal, Andi pulled the cat out and clutched it to her chest before turning back the way she'd come. Her footsteps slowed as reality settled in. She'd left both doors open, and now the exterior room was on fire.

"Shoot."

The animal in her arms seemed to react to her worry and tried clawing free.

"No you don't, you little menace." She pulled it closer and dropped low. She was getting them both out of here. Somehow. She just needed a moment to think.

"Andi!" The chief bellowed through the radio line.

She flinched and spun around to exit through the front, but another wall of fire met her.

Andi shifted the cat and toggled her radio. "Need an exit." She didn't bother to explain. At least, not yet. She would be explaining this for weeks. "North side. Open door."

"Hold on, Andi, we're coming." She heard the tension in Logan's voice, but she couldn't think about that now.

The fire was coming up on all sides, and she and this darn cat needed to get out of here before they became barbecue. The cat squirmed in her arms again, and she wondered if it was having a hard time breathing. She was as low to the ground as she could get, but she didn't want to miss her chance to escape.

A powerful stream of water shot through the room she'd come in. The flames receded some. She was about to risk moving when shapes emerged through the flames. Logan and someone else coming to save her.

So much for her brave rescue.

Andi wanted the floor to open up and swallow her whole.

"Come on." Logan helped her up.

Charlie reached for the cat. "I've got it." He pulled it close against his chest.

They tumbled out of the room through a stream of water that mixed with the ash and clouded her vision. Andi yanked off her mask and came to a stop at Chief James's death glare.

"Chief, I—"

"Later," he growled.

The threat of an impending chew-out was almost worse than getting one right then. That, coupled with the look from Logan as he shook his head, said she'd be hearing disappointment twice.

"Hey, Andi. Nice rescue."

She spun at the laughter that followed Zack's jab. Her squad stood around Charlie, the soaked cat wrapped in a blanket in his arms.

"Definitely impressive, Probie." Eddie made a face that said he was anything but impressed.

"Knock it off." The weight of their teasing heaped onto the reprimand she knew she was going to get. From the chief *and* her brothers.

Zack didn't bother to hide his smile as he reached out to pet the cat. It hissed back at him, a feral paw swiping at his hand.

"Look, it's just like you." Ridge's smile was goading. "Touchy."

"Ease up, guys." Charlie stepped toward her with the cat. "She saved a life today."

He deposited the cat into her arms, but she wasn't sure if she should say thanks or ignore him like she did the other guys.

"Just make sure next time you do it the right way." Charlie kept his voice low.

"If there is a next time." She sighed.

The weight of that statement was too heavy to bear. As a probationary firefighter, or probie, her actions today could signal the end of her career as a firefighter.

"We've all got to learn." He winked. "I wouldn't worry about it. But I would suggest getting Ashes some food. She's too skinny."

"You named it? Can't I just leave it here?"

Charlie's grin grew, and this time he brought in the entire squad. "Nope. I'm afraid the rule states you rescue it, you're responsible for it, Probie."

"Fine." Andi clenched her teeth. They could reprimand her all they wanted, but she wouldn't back down, no matter what. "Looks like the firehouse has a new mascot."

3

D riving up to his grandfather's two-story, cottage-style home was like taking a step back in time. Late-afternoon light filtered through leaves of the now-towering oak trees flanking the house. Even from the car he could see the brick steps looked worse for wear, but nothing took away from the surfacing nostalgia of summers spent in Last Chance County.

Herman Brooks had been a quiet man who'd expected Jude to pull his weight while visiting each summer, but there had always been time leftover for fishing, swimming, and back yard barbecues with the neighbors.

Jude turned the car off and stepped out. The familiar scent of freshly mowed grass and the minty odor of crushed salvia greeted him as his gaze automatically shifted to the right. The blue craftsman next door looked the same, complete with the cheerful marigolds in oversized pots on the porch.

It was Andi's childhood home, and brought back the reason Jude was here like an unexpected uppercut. The whole Crawford family could be in danger if the photos from Sosa's villa were any indication. That, or like his boss had suggested, they were part of this somehow.

Jude had a hard time believing the family he'd grown up with could have any involvement with a drug cartel, but he had his orders. Get to the bottom of it all.

This wasn't a vacation. This was work.

Leather bag and briefcase in hand, Jude turned toward his grandfather's house and took the steps two at a time. His first order of business would be to talk to Elizabeth and Paul Crawford, Andi's parents. He knew they still lived next door, according to his mother, but he didn't know where Andi was now. He'd have to ask them for those details.

He could have easily looked at the files his team had compiled on the whole Crawford family—probably should have, according to procedure—but it felt like an invasion of their privacy. It was his job, and he had every legal right, but knowing that he'd be face-to-face with them all soon enough, he'd waited. Better to hear their side of things, then verify with the files.

An uncomfortable tightness settled between his shoulder blades. He told himself it had nothing to do with seeing Andi again. No, he blamed the black-and-white eight-by-tens from Sosa's office and the danger they signified for her and her family.

It shouldn't matter that they also showed just how much she'd grown up and turned into a beautiful woman. How much he'd missed by leaving Last Chance County for good the summer he turned nineteen.

The keys jingled in his hand as he searched for the worn brass one. With his mother living in Florida and his job requiring most of his time in Southern California, Jude hadn't been back to Herman's house since his teenage years. Then, after his grandfather passed five years prior, there'd been no reason to.

Jude had called and left a message for his mom, explaining that he'd be staying at the house, but he'd missed her return call while on his flight to Last Chance County. As a rule, Meredith Brooks didn't text, so he knew better than to confirm his presence with her that way. Besides, it was too late now on the East Coast. He'd just have to connect with her in the morning.

The key slid into the lock with a familiar *shunk* and drew back the deadbolt with a click. He pushed the door open, pausing to pick up his bags, and stepped inside. The lights were off, as to be expected, but rather than a musty odor, a sweet scent drew him up short. It was familiar and—

Instinct made him duck. A flying object narrowly missed his head to slam against the doorframe behind him. He squinted and his hand darted to the gun absent from his waist.

"Get out! I'm calling the police!"

His eyes hadn't adjusted from the bright outdoors to the darkened interior, but the voice registered in Jude's mind with equal parts excitement and trepidation. "A-Andi?"

"I said—" A moment's hesitation. "Jude?"

Toned, bare legs moved into the light, and his eyes followed them up to cotton shorts nearly covered by an oversized T-shirt. It was Andi all right, her dark-brown hair pulled back into a braid from which long strands escaped to frame her face. Her cheeks were twin pools of bright pink, and she held a baseball bat aloft, ready to swing at a moment's notice.

It looked like she'd tumbled out of bed, and he was fairly certain it was his fault.

"Uh, ya—yes." Now was not the time for his stutter to raise its embarrassing head. "It's me."

She blinked. "What are you doing here?"

"I could—" He paused. Took a breath. "Could ask you the same."

She relaxed her grip on the bat, fingers going from white to pink, and let it rest against her shoulder. "Didn't your mom tell you?"

He thought of the missed call. Shook his head.

"I'm renting this place."

"Renting?"

"Yeah." Now that she had identified the source of the intrusion, she relaxed. She dropped the bat to the floor and stood it up next to the door. "Sheesh. You scared me, Brooks."

Brooks. Maybe it was growing up with two older brothers or the fact that Andi had always been a bit of a tomboy, but she'd called him by his last name one day and it'd stuck. He'd missed that. Missed her.

Jude mentally clamped down on those thoughts. This wasn't a social call—this was work.

"So-sorry." He fisted his hands. Countless years of therapy for his stutter and it still plagued him—usually at the worst times. He needed to breathe, slow down, and relax. "Sorry. I didn't mean to."

Her head canted to the side as she took him in, her bright blue eyes clear and radiating curiosity. He couldn't help but reciprocate the action.

Her childish features, round cheeks and freckled skin, had sharpened and cleared with maturity. Before him stood a woman even more beautiful than the teenager he remembered. A woman he'd startled out of bed and who was in her pajamas. The realization sent heat racing up his neck.

"Sorry." He took a step back and nearly tripped over the leather satchel he'd dropped. "I didn't know you were renting." He really should've called his mother back, no matter the time difference.

"It's okay." She blushed and crossed her arms self-consciously. "What are you doing here?"

He detected a hint of hope coloring her tone, but it wasn't time to get into why he was here. Not yet, anyway.

"Thought I'd check in on the place." He took another breath. "It's been a while since my mom or I have been able to get back to Last Chance County. It was time." It was close to the truth, and she seemed to accept it.

"You can say that again." She studied him. "I guess, since I'm renting from you guys, that means you're kind of like my landlord, huh?"

He chuckled. "I suppose."

"Then it's about time you visited." Her expression shifted to the playful one he remembered, and memories from the past flooded in. Andi had always challenged him—in good and bad ways. She wasn't one to take no for an answer. He could see a flicker of that young girl in the woman she was now, but there was more than just time between them.

"Why is that?"

"I've got a list of things to fix. A whole list, Brooks. I hope you're better at fixing things than Logan, because believe me, this house needs it."

He flinched. "That bad, huh?"

"Worse."

A memory resurfaced. "Wait. What about your dad? I thought he was handy."

A flicker of sadness dimmed the light in her eyes, and he knew he'd said something wrong. Regret at not reading up on the Crawford files surfaced.

"He had an accident." She looked down, her bare foot digging into the wooden floorboards. "It was years ago. His car ran off the road, and he suffered a traumatic brain injury—a TBI. It's affected a lot of how he functions now."

"Oh, Andi, I'm really sorry. I had no idea."

"It's okay." She looked up, and he could tell she was reliving the events of the past. "He's just not himself anymore. Most of the time he's pretty calm, just forgetful and has trouble communicating. At times he has episodes where he's agitated or depressed, and that's hard, but we've got a great nurse who stays with him so Mom can work."

"She's still a lawyer?"

Andi nodded. "Still runs five miles every morning too. Elizabeth Crawford, the bionic woman."

Jude couldn't help but notice that her laugh had more bite to it than necessary, but now wasn't the time to get into that. "And your brothers?"

"The super twins? They're doing great. Well, kind of." Andi bit her lip. "Bryce was in the hospital a few months ago. A pretty traumatic rescue gone south. He's doing better though," she rushed to explain. "Just doing PT—and hating it."

"And Logan?"

"Took over as LT of rescue squad for Bryce. As if he needed the ego boost." Andi sighed and dropped her hands. "Sorry. I think I sound bitter. I've just been dealing with a lot recently."

"Yeah?"

"Yeah." Her attention shifted to the dying light through the door behind him. "It was a less than stellar day on the job."

"What are you doing? Last I heard, you were a paramedic."

"Moved to firefighter on Truck 14." The pride in her voice was clear.

"Congratulations. I bet your brothers are proud."

Andi's expression fell. "I'm not sure they're at the proud stage yet, but they'll get there."

A challenge—to herself, Jude guessed—laced her words, but her gaze shifted back to him, then to his bags.

"You're not staying here." Her chin jutted out slightly, daring him to disagree. "So where will you go?"

Her demeanor was so Andi-like he almost laughed. Straight to the point, wanting the facts and no fluff. It surprised him she hadn't asked more about why he was here after so many years. Andi had never been one to leave a stone unturned, but it was better this way.

He needed to get his feet under him. Do some research. Figure out the best way to approach the Crawfords. His boss had made it clear the only reason he'd allowed Jude to come alone was his prior connection to the family and the advantage that would afford him. It would stay that way as long as it didn't impede his investigation.

"I'm not sure," he finally admitted. He was about to suggest the local motel when the sound of a phone shattered the silence.

"That's Mom's ring tone. Hold on."

Andi rushed down the hall, her bare feet slapping against the wood, and Jude took a moment to look around the living room. Now that his eyes had adjusted to the low light coming in from the opened door, he saw a comfortable cream-colored couch filled with plush pillows. Two bookcases on one wall brimmed with books. A coffee table with an array of papers and a few empty coffee mugs. And an old clock on the mantel, the same one his grandfather had always kept there.

The sight tugged at Jude, enticing him to fall back in time to those summers before his final one, but the sound of Andi running back down the hall distracted him. Their eyes met and he saw unshed tears.

"What's wrong?"

Andi shook her head as if trying to understand. "Logan's in the hospital."

4

Andi's hands shook so badly she knew it was the right decision to let Jude drive them to the hospital, but being a passenger meant she had no control over how fast they went. Her foot pressed against the floorboard, and she clenched and unclenched her hands.

"We're almost there." Jude made a sharp right turn.

"We just worked a fire together today." She thought about how he'd been right and she wrong about the house occupants. Not that it mattered when he'd been in an accident, but still, her thoughts toward him after shift hadn't been as sisterly as they should have been. "What if he's not okay?"

"What did your mom say, exactly?"

His question caught her off guard. "I don't know. That he'd been in an accident. That was it."

"Nothing else?"

Andi's jaw clenched. Jude was being so...Jude. Always calm, collected. A thinker. She'd hated that when they were younger, because he thought through *everything*, whereas she believed it was better to do first, think later. Where was the fun—the excitement—of doing everything by the book?

"Andi?"

Pulled from her memories, she recalled something else her mother had said. "He's being taken to a room."

"That's good." Jude's tone was even as he pulled into a parking space near the emergency exit of the hospital. "A room means he's not in surgery or the ICU."

Why hadn't she thought of that? In her haste to get to her big brother, she'd only heard "Logan" and "accident" and gone into focus mode. Get to the hospital. Be with him. Help her family.

"You're right." She shoved her door open. "I didn't think of that."

They locked gazes across the top of the gray car, and Andi allowed herself a moment to marvel at the man Jude had grown into. He'd always been good-looking as a teen, with thick, dark hair, and skin tanned by hours in the sun working in his grandfather's yard. He'd worn these tank tops that had every girl swooning over his muscular biceps, but until she was sixteen, she hadn't really seen him like that. At least, not until—

"Ready to go in?"

"Yeah. Let's go." She snapped back to reality just as a cool gust of night air tossed the freed strands of hair around her face.

She moved around the car and fell into step with Jude. She'd thrown on a pair of firehouse sweatpants and a hoodie, but walking next to Jude in his dark-washed jeans and black leather jacket, she felt childish. Perhaps it would have been better to take a few minutes to change.

Andi mentally slapped herself.

Her brother was in the hospital, and she was worried about what she was wearing. It was ridiculous. She wasn't some lovesick teen who wished the cute guy—who'd also happened to be her best friend—would notice her.

The minute they stepped into the hospital, Andi caught

sight of Bryce. The scruff on his jaw and the disheveled look of his dark-blond hair made him look untamed despite the fact he stood propped against a wall with his cane covertly stashed next to his leg.

Andi rushed to him. "Bryce, where is he? Is he okay?"

"Andi Bear." Bryce pulled her into a hug, and she stopped herself from chiding him about the nickname. "He's okay. Shaken and cut up, but he's going to be fine."

She pulled back. "What are you doing out here? Shouldn't you be sitting?"

"My physical therapist says standing is perfectly fine. I wanted to wait for you so I could take you back." Bryce looked up and behind Andi, and his expression morphed to surprise. "Jude?"

"Hey, man." Jude extended his hand. "It's been a while."

Bryce shifted his weight, using the cane for support, and shook Jude's hand. "It has. What are you doing here?" He looked at them, confused.

"He was at the house." Andi cut her gaze up to Jude's.

She didn't know why he was really in Last Chance County. She'd been caught off guard to find him in her doorway and hadn't thought to dig past the initial answer he'd given her about checking up on the house. Then the call had come in and—she needed to see Logan first. This could wait. "Where is Logan?"

"Okay, okay." Bryce didn't look satisfied by the response but shifted away from the wall. "I'll take you to his room."

Andi paused to look up at Jude. "I can catch a ride home. If you want to leave."

"I'll stay. Unless you want me to go."

"Stay." The word slipped out too quickly, but he didn't seem to notice.

They fell in behind Bryce as he pushed through double doors into a long, cream-colored hallway. The scent of antiseptic and cleaning agents swirled around her, a familiar mixture. Ahead, nurses in light-blue scrubs circled an information desk like bees to a hive.

"Room 349." Bryce nodded to a door.

Through the open door, Andi saw her mother standing at the foot of a bed on the far side of the double room, her back to the hallway as she talked with a doctor. Relief flooded through Andi when she saw Logan looking on, alert.

Still, she hesitated.

It should be easier to walk into the sterilized room, considering how much time her family had spent in hospitals lately. And yet it felt just as terrible now as it had when it was Bryce and, before that, her father.

"Hey, Mom." Andi waited.

Elizabeth Crawford's perceptive gaze flew to the door. Her expression softened immediately, and she held out her arms to them. "Oh, you're here. Good. Come in."

Logan was covered by a thin sheet and blanket, bandages wrapped around his head like a poorly done bandanna that left tufts of his dark-brown hair sticking up in places. An IV snaked into the back of his hand, and a monitor beeped every few seconds.

Andi took a moment to look over the readouts, but everything looked good. Normal. She let out a breath and opted for humor. "What did you do this time, Logan?"

"Andi." Her mother's reprimand was sharp. "Someone ran him off the road."

Andi's eyes darted to her mother's. "*Ran him off the road?*"

"Mom." Logan's tone was a warning. "It was probably an accident."

"Hey, Mom." Bryce stepped past the exiting doctor and came in.

"Come here, sweetie, there's a seat you can have. Paul, move over, honey." Elizabeth spoke gently to her husband. She rested a calming hand on his arm to guide him away from the chair so Bryce could sit.

"Hey, Dad." Andi greeted her father as usual, trying for a sense of normalcy amidst the confusion. Who could have run Logan off the road? Or was it an accident like he said?

Her dad turned toward her, but his gaze went past and over her shoulder. "Hey, Jude."

Every eye turned as Jude stepped into the lighted portion of the room. He looked sheepish, but she caught the half smile at her father's familiar words. The greeting had turned into a ritual during those long summers ages ago. Her father would always greet him with the lyrics and a smile. The familiarity of it twisted something deep in Andi.

"Jude, what a surprise. It's nice to see you again," Elizabeth said.

Andi could see the weariness on her mother's features, but also the question. What was Jude doing here?

"I—I'm sorry for in—" Jude swallowed. "For intruding."

"Nonsense." Elizabeth pulled her shoulders back. Andi recognized the move of forced strength and wondered how her mother was doing with yet another accident. "You've always been like family."

Jude's response was a smile, and Andi took it as her opportunity to get back to her questions. "What really happened, Logan?"

"It's not a big deal." Logan shrugged, but winced. "I was just driving and—"

"I heard Andi from the hall. Were you really run off the road?" Jude slipped into interrogation mode.

"Sounds like I came just in time." A voice spoke from behind, and everyone turned to see a young Black man in a police officer's uniform.

"Anthony, my man." Logan grinned and moved to hold up a hand before dropping it back to the bed with a groan.

"Forget the handshake, bro. I just need a statement."

"Everyone, this is Officer Anthony Thomas. He's one heck of a basketball player and a cop—but don't hold it against him." Logan winked at the man.

"I'm sorry you have to put up with my brother." Andi stepped forward and extended a hand. "I'm Andi." The guy looked familiar, and she wondered if she'd seen him at one of the twins' pickup basketball games.

"Nice to meet you all." He looked around the room and held up a small notepad. "Mind if I borrow him for a few minutes? The doc said it was okay."

"Of course. Come on, everyone. Let's give the officer some space to work." Elizabeth ushered them to the empty side of the room, though Jude looked like he wanted to stay.

Bryce switched on the lights for them before easing into a vacant chair. Andi helped guide her father away from Logan and the officer, sad to realize that any clarity Paul had found at seeing Jude had disappeared as quickly as it had come.

"It's just one thing after another." Elizabeth shook her head and leaned against the empty hospital bed.

"I'm sorry, Mom." Bryce reached out to take her hand.

"Did he say what happened?" Andi wanted to listen in on his statement but thought better of it.

"Not much." Her mother's gaze shifted back to Logan before coming to rest on her. "Said he was driving home like always when an SUV came up next to him. He said it felt like they were taunting him, but when they pulled back, he was sure he'd just imagined it. Kids out for a joyride or something. But then they revved their engines and slammed into him, forcing him off the road."

"That doesn't sound like an accident." Bryce's brow furrowed.

Elizabeth held back tears, and Andi reached out to take her hand. "He's going to be okay, Mom."

"Did he say anything else? Anything about th-the vehicle?" Jude spoke up from across the awkward circle. His intense focus didn't shift when all of their gazes landed on him.

"No—" Elizabeth paused. "Well, yes. He mentioned seeing a blur of red, maybe? Perhaps it was a red SUV that forced Logan off the road?"

Sudden motion made Andi flinch until she realized it was her father. His hands fluttered at his side and agitation radiated off of him. Sometimes it was hard to tell what her father was aware of. Was he reacting to Logan's accident?

"Dad, it's okay. We're here." Andi moved to his side, careful not to touch him. Not yet. This wasn't her father, not in these frantic moments. She took a steadying breath and continued to speak to him in calming tones. "It's okay, Dad. We're here."

"No!" He shuffled to one side, then the other. "Danger. Too fast—bad."

Andi looked over at her mother and mouthed, *What do we do?*

Elizabeth had turned into a statue, frozen in place.

"Mom?" Andi spoke out loud this time.

"Bad. Danger. Too fast."

Officer Thomas turned to see what was going on, and Bryce pushed himself up to shuffle across the linoleum toward their father.

"Is everything okay?" The officer looked between Andi and Bryce.

"No fast. Bad." Paul had both hands against his head now, twisting back and forth.

"Uh, yeah. Sometimes he has episodes." Bryce looked over his shoulder. "What should we do, Mom?"

"I—I don't know."

Andi gaped. Her mother *always* knew what to do.

"I just need...a moment." Elizabeth turned and walked out of the room.

"Bad." Paul's frantic movements slowed as he grew tired. "Bad, bad, bad!"

"It's all right, Dad. Logan's okay." Bryce turned to Logan. "Finish up your statement. We'll keep an eye on Dad."

Logan nodded, but Andi took a few steps toward the open door, still shocked her mother had left.

"Are you okay?" Jude's softly spoken words jolted Andi from her thoughts.

"Mom's a criminal defense lawyer. I've never seen her turn away from anything. Ever."

"Your dad seemed really agitated." Jude snuck a covert glance at Bryce, but she still noticed.

"It's hard seeing him like that." Andi let the memories wash over her. "I mean, he was a military surgeon and was always so gentle and kind. Bedside manner was his mantra. But the accident changed him. The first day he came home from the hospital was the worst. An item got misplaced—I don't even remember what—and he lost it. Mom was picking up his medicine and nothing could calm him down. I thought..." She shook her head. "I thought a hug would help."

"I'm guessing it didn't." Jude searched her eyes, her own pain reflected in his expression.

"It set him off even worse. I've never seen him angry like that. He swung his arms around and ended up knocking me down. He didn't mean to." She cast a glance toward her father. "He just didn't understand. That's why it's so hard for me to see my mom leave."

"What do you mean?"

"She was the only one who could calm him down." Andi wrapped her arms around her middle, fighting off the chill of the sterilized air.

"Why don't I go check on her?"

Andi opened her mouth to turn him down but closed it. She really shouldn't leave Dad to Bryce alone. He still needed his cane to stand, and she knew there was still a chance their father could turn physically violent. "Actually, would you mind?"

"Not at all."

She met his gaze, those warm brown eyes of his pooling with understanding. The sense of relief confused her. She hadn't seen Jude in over ten years, and yet he felt like coming home.

But why was he there?

5

J ude escaped the tension of Logan's room into the hustle of the busy hospital hallway. He saw a figure moving through an open doorway. The sign above it read Sitting Room, and he assumed that was where Elizabeth had gone.

He'd caught the look of shock on her face when Paul's episode began. Her features, already pale, had faded to an unnatural shade of gray.

Jude rubbed a hand along the back of his neck. He wanted to make sure Elizabeth was all right—he'd promised Andi that much—but there was more going on. Having a gut feeling wasn't something to act definitively on, but it was worth considering. With instincts honed from years of experience with the ATF, he knew to pay attention to the fact they were humming now.

Elizabeth Crawford had looked scared.

That's what nagged at him. A fear that surpassed having a son in the hospital for the second time in several months. Did this have something to do with Sosa and the pictures?

With purposeful strides, Jude reached the door. He'd been

right. Elizabeth paced back and forth in the sitting room, arms wrapped around her slight frame. He hung back near the vending machines and observed.

Her styled salt-and-pepper hair hung to her shoulders, and she wore high-waisted jeans with a cream knit top tucked in at the front. He didn't know much—or really care—about fashion, but she looked effortlessly stylish, even in jeans.

The expression on her narrow features captured his attention. Lines of worry creased her forehead, and she repeatedly bit her lip and then released it. That, coupled with her pacing, screamed something was amiss.

"Elizabeth?"

She spun around to face him.

"Sorry I scared you." He leaned against the doorframe to appear casual. "Is everything all right?"

"You're so kind. I'm fine, sweetie." She forced a smile and pushed a lock of hair from her forehead. "It's just...we've been in this hospital so much lately. I think I became overwhelmed, is all."

His eyes narrowed. *When a woman says she's fine...*

There was a kernel of truth to her words, he could see that, but he caught the cues that indicated she was holding something back. The way her gaze drifted to the left. The light touch of her nose. Classic signs of deception.

"I'm not sure if you're aware, but I work for the ATF." Her gaze shot to his. "My work has put me in a lot of situations where things are overwhelming or seem that way. I know how important it is to talk it out with someone."

In his mind he heard one of his former instructors reminding him to salt his words with personal experience if he hoped to get a suspect to open up. He didn't exactly consider Elizabeth a suspect, but he had found pictures of her and her family at the gated villa of a drug lord, so there was clearly some connection. Whether it had anything to do with Logan's accident, Jude couldn't say, but he needed to make sure Elizabeth knew she could trust him. *Should* trust him.

"In fact"—Jude paused to look at the top of his black boots—"I just lost someone on my team recently and have found the need to process it all pretty overwhelming."

"I'm sorry to hear that, Jude."

"It's been a tough couple of days. No doubt you understand that better than most right now. But I'm here and—"

"Why *are* you here?" The abruptness of Elizabeth's question took him by surprise. More lawyer, less concerned parent.

Perhaps a more direct approach was in order.

"I'm here because of you, Mrs. Crawford."

Her shock was palpable. "Me? Why?" Her eyes drifted toward Logan's room.

Jude weighed his words. He didn't want to say too much, not yet. The images had been in Sosa's possession, but they knew little beyond that. Jude had hashed this out with his team before he'd left because, try as they might, there was no direct correlation to the head of the cartel and the Crawford family. At least, no trail they could find.

There was the obvious, if unlikely, option that the Crawfords were involved with a drug cartel, or a more chilling one: Sosa was handling a hit or some other nefarious act against the Crawfords. Running hits were not his usual lane— at least, not anymore—but if the act resulted in money, Jude had a feeling Sosa might be desperate enough to go down that route.

He needed to learn from Elizabeth who might have a motive against them. And he needed to figure it out quickly, knowing that one of them could be in danger—

Logan. He was injured in the hospital, but not dead. That wasn't the typical act of a hit man, but it could be used as a scare tactic. Was it coincidence or did his accident have something to do with all of this?

Words flooded back into Jude's mind. The recounting of how Logan had been run off the road. He'd said the car came up level with him before backing off and then ramming his car. The only reason for that would be to ensure that the person in the car was the intended target.

"Is there any reason that your family might be the target of someone? Logan in particular?"

"Target?" Elizabeth looked confused for a moment before realization dawned. She covered her mouth with her hand in horror. "You think someone meant to run Logan off the road?"

"I don't know what to think yet." It was mostly the truth.

"But you're here in an official capacity."

"I'm following up on a few things." His boss had been clear. Jude needed to use every advantage to gain information, but he also couldn't treat the Crawfords like the friends they'd been. Not until he had a better handle on the situation. "I had no idea Andi was staying in my grandfather's old house, so it was only by coincidence that I was there when she got the call about Logan. I came to help—I'm here to help—but I need to know what you aren't telling me, Mrs. Crawford."

"There's...nothing." She sank into a chair, head bent. "I mean, yes, it's not out of the realm of possibility. I'm a criminal defense attorney. I've got enemies."

When her blue eyes, similar in color to Andi's, met his, he saw the grit and determination that had seen the woman through case after case.

"Anyone in particular?" He held Sosa's name back, curious to see if she would confirm a connection.

"Do you want a list?" She laughed. "I sound glib, but trust me, I'm not taking this lightly. Many could feel harmed by my work, despite the fact it's the law for everyone to have equal representation. But to target me—my family?" Her gaze dropped to her hands. "There's no one I can think of."

Something in her tone drew Jude's scrutiny. Perhaps grief.

Or was she still withholding something? His stomach twisted for suspecting a woman who'd been like a second mother to him.

He was tired. He'd had a long day. Maybe he was reading into it, or not.

"I'll take a list then. Run it against our database and see what might pop. You never know."

"Jude, what is this really about?"

He considered telling her more but stopped himself. This would go by the book. Stray from that and he risked more of his team *and* the lives of people he'd considered his second family during his teen years.

"I'm serious about a list, Elizabeth. I need to look into anyone that might have a grudge against you."

"There are a few. One case in particular that's going on right now. I doubt they'd have the resources to come after me—or my family—but you never know, do you?"

"You don't."

She sat in silence for another minute before she stood and straightened her top. Her fingers wrapped around his hand, cold and trembling.

"I understand you have a job to do. I really do. But...if it's at all possible, can we keep this between us?"

Jude cocked his head.

"Logan and Bryce." She gave a humorless laugh. "Or Andi, really. They're all too headstrong for their own good, though they come by it naturally. I fear that if any of them even think there is the possibility of danger—for any of us—they'll take matters into their own hands. No matter the reality that both of my boys still need recovery time."

Jude knew where she was heading with this. He didn't want to involve anyone else yet either. He knew enough of Logan and Bryce to agree with their mother. The less they knew, the better. Andi was intuitive and would ask more questions about why he was here. He hadn't come up with what else to tell her yet, but he'd think of something that stayed true to his boss's wishes.

"I hear you, Elizabeth. I'll keep this to myself for now. Please do your best to get me that list soon, though." He handed over his business card. "I'm afraid time is short."

"I will." She took the card and grasped his hand with both of hers. "Where are you staying in town?"

Her question surprised him. "Not sure, really. I'd thought to stay at my grandpa's place, but that's...occupied."

"What about the airstream?"

He frowned. "The trailer?"

"Your mother let Paul and me use it last summer. We went to the lake for a week. It should be fine for this June weather, but I can share some extra blankets if needed." She winked.

"I'll talk to Andi. See if she'd mind."

"I have a feeling she won't." Elizabeth stepped toward the door. "Thank you, Jude."

"Just doing my job."

"I know you'll do your best." Her soft smile said she trusted him.

He watched Elizabeth disappear back into the hall in a beeline toward the nurses' station. She was a good mother. A kind woman who only wanted what was best for her family. It was possible she'd gotten mixed up in something she shouldn't have, but it was more likely someone held a grudge against her for doing her job. Someone that had gone to great lengths to hire Sosa's cartel to scare her by threatening her family.

If that was the case, Jude was confident Elizabeth would get some type of message about their demands. If that happened, his work was done. He'd turn it over to the Last Chance County police and be on his way, looking for another route to get Sosa.

Still...he wasn't convinced it was that simple.

Jude reached into his pocket for his phone. He pulled up his secure email and sent off a message to his boss. It was crucial he keep everyone in the loop, assuring them everything was going smoothly. He knew his hometown, and there was no way a contingent of ATF agents flooding into Last Chance County would go unnoticed, or ignored, by the locals. They needed to keep a low profile or risk Sosa or his men getting spooked and heading back underground.

Would Sosa come here to hide, or had he sent his men to hurt this family?

When Jude stepped back into the hall, he nearly ran into Andi leaning against the vending machines. The same spot he'd used to shield himself from Elizabeth's view.

His stomach clenched at her expression. How long had she been standing there? "Andi. I—"

"You're going to tell me everything, or I'm telling Bryce and Logan."

6

Andi reached out and latched on to Jude's arm. She barely managed to cover her surprise at the corded muscle lying hidden beneath the dark leather jacket he wore. At first, he resisted her, but with one raised eyebrow, he followed her to an unused room left in darkness.

When neither Jude nor her mother had come back, she'd worried and gone in search of them. That's when she'd stumbled on their secret meeting instead.

She hadn't caught the whole conversation, but she'd definitely heard enough to know that Jude was in Last Chance County on ATF business and that he was completely fine keeping her and her brothers in the dark about something. That was the part she'd missed when her friend Charlotte found her lurking by the vending machines.

To be fair, Charlotte was a nurse and had heard about Logan's accident. Unaware of Andi's eavesdropping, she'd wanted to check in, but Andi had managed to plan a quick chat with her after her shift ended. She'd left in time for Andi to catch Jude in the act.

"What is going on?"

Jude's expression remained neutral. Stoic even.

"Fine, I'll go ask my mother. Maybe we can have a whole family meeting about it." She cringed inwardly at her tone, made sharp by her frustration.

"Hold on." Jude moved in front of her, effectively blocking the door.

The scent of his musky cologne flooded her senses and acted as a reminder that he was no longer the teen boy she'd had a crush on. He was a man, and the way his broad shoulders filled the space awakened something in her.

"I just..." She faltered. "I want answers. First, there was Dad's accident nearly ten years ago, then Bryce got hurt in that fire, and now Logan. I don't like being kept in the dark—especially when it's about my family."

Andi's thoughts flew to Logan. She couldn't be sure, but she thought she'd overheard Jude mention something about her brother's wreck—that it was part of whatever was going on. If someone was trying to harm her family, she wouldn't sit by and watch. She was going to protect them.

"Look, I'm not sure what you thought you overheard in there, but everything is fine."

"I'm not a teen anymore." The undercurrent of her words was clear. "I don't want you to coddle me."

His jaw flexed. "I'm in town looking into some leads our office received and, since I'm from here, I took the job."

"What does it have to do with my mom or her practice?" His eyes widened slightly, and she knew she'd surprised him with the extent of what she'd heard.

"Your m-mom..." He paused, taking a deep breath. "Sh-she...sh-sh-she..."

The sight of his hesitation drew up memories from the past. Jude had struggled with a stutter since childhood. By the time she'd met him, it'd rarely affected his normal speech, but the damage had been done. He'd hardly talked.

"Deep breath."

His eyes flew to hers, and she tried to untangle what she saw there. Breathing exercises were one of several ways he'd learned to control the stutter in more stressful situations. The fact she knew that—knew him—seemed to put him at ease.

He took a deep breath. "Your mother has represented some bad guys in the past. I-I'm sure that's no surprise to you, but that falls in line with my work for the ATF. I'm just l-looking into things, that's all."

It was a simple answer that left her with more questions than actual reassurance.

"But you mentioned Logan." Andi took a step forward. "What is going on, Jude? I promise I won't say anything to Logan or Bryce, but if something is wrong...I don't want to be left out of this."

"Andi." Jude offered a half smile and rested his hands on her shoulders. "You're not being left out of anything. Really. There's nothing to be left out of."

"But you were talking with my mom and—"

"And you have nothing to worry about."

They stood there, unmoving. Jude's hands warmed the chill from the hospital's air conditioning, but her memory tripped her up. He'd left once without a word, and he was keeping things from her now.

She took a step back. When his hands fell away, she weirdly missed the touch, though she knew she shouldn't.

Maybe it was just because Jude was a good, standup guy— or at least he had been when she'd known him before. That didn't mean he was perfect, though. He'd lied for her once. She wasn't sure if he would do it again if he thought he was protecting her.

"I don't know if I believe you."

"Trust me, Dee. It's going to be fine."

The familiar nickname sent warmth to her core, and she

suppressed a smile. Maybe she was making more of this than was necessary. Their past was rocky, but that didn't have to define their future.

"I think I've missed you, Jude Brooks."

A shadow passed behind his eyes and he looked away. "It's been a long time."

He shifted from one foot to the other. Was he thinking of that summer? Wondering what could have been had things turned out differently?

"I'm going to stay in the airstream in the driveway—i-if it's okay with you? It was your mom's idea." His tone said he was back to business.

"I'll allow it on one condition." She gauged his response, but he only narrowed his eyes.

"Which is?"

"Work on my fix-it list, Mr. Landlord, and you can stay." She tapped his chest once.

His lips shifted into a half smile. "Deal."

Caught up in the moment, Andi drifted closer again. The dim lighting and the familiarity between them clouded her thinking, and for a second, she wanted to reach out and smooth the lapel of his jacket like they were high schoolers again.

"I have missed you." She wanted to hear him say he'd missed her too. Proof that they could move past their shared history into a new stage of friendship.

He pressed his lips together and pulled back. "I've got to make a few calls. You think your mom can take you home?"

"Yeah. Sure. Of course." Heat flooded her cheeks as he stepped back into the hallway.

What had she been thinking?

Taking a moment to compose herself, Andi mentally walked through their conversation. She'd gotten little to no answers despite her demands, and she'd discovered that her teenage crush was still alive and well. There were many reasons she should push Jude to the back of her mind, but she'd always had a weakness when it came to him.

He was the anchor to her impulsivity. The calm to her storm. Jude made her stop and think when she'd rather just do—but that hadn't always worked.

She caught the sound of his voice in the hall. After she smoothed her hair down and made sure her cheeks had returned to a normal heat level, Andi stepped out of the darkened room.

Jude trotted down the hallway after Officer Thomas. She saw the man slow and offer a smile to Jude. They were too far away for her to hear, but she caught the moment Jude flashed his credentials.

Andi was so engrossed in watching them that she didn't notice her mother until her cool hand alighted on Andi's arm.

"Mom!" She covered her heart with her hand.

"I know he's handsome, but can you tear yourself away from gazing at Agent Brooks for a few minutes to help Bryce with your father? I have a question to ask Logan's doctor."

"Mom." Andi's blush resurfaced. "I—I was just heading back into Logan's room."

Her mother's smile said she didn't believe her but wouldn't press the issue.

"Andi!" Both women turned.

"Mom, you remember Charlotte Duncan, right?"

"Nice to see you again. Excuse me."

Her mother turned toward the nurses' station as Charlotte threw her arms around Andi. "How are you doing?"

"You should be asking Logan that."

"I already did. He said I needed to check on you and Brooks. Who's that?"

Flames engulfed Andi's cheeks again. "I'm going to kill him."

"Please don't," Charlotte said on a laugh. "He's just looking out for his sis. But really, who is this mysterious guy?"

"He used to visit his grandfather, the house to the north of my parents, in the summers."

"No way!" Charlotte's enthusiasm brightened her tan cheeks. "So, you totally had a crush on him, didn't you?"

Andi wrinkled her nose. "He actually ignored me at first. He was two years older than me, and I assumed he was like my brothers—you know, not wanting me around. But I was wrong."

"And?" Charlotte nudged Andi with her elbow.

"He became my best friend." The memories conjured nostalgia from those sunbaked summers. "I can still remember nights on my parents' back porch. He'd play John Denver songs on his guitar and we'd stargaze."

"Sounds dreamy."

"It was. Until it wasn't." Andi checked the door to Logan's room as Bryce came out with their father to walk up and down the hall. She needed to get back.

"What happened?" Charlotte's gentle touch grounded Andi, and the truth slipped out.

"Things happened—some of it stupid teenager stuff—and then the next thing I knew he was gone. Left without a word, and this is the first I've seen him in years."

"No way."

Andi nodded. "It's just...a lot."

"I get it, girl." Charlotte hugged her again, the scent of antiseptic soap and strong laundry detergent wrapping around Andi. "I'm here for you—if you or your family need anything, let us know. Okay?"

"Thanks." Andi forced the tears back. She knew Charlotte was getting off a long shift and had stayed just to talk with her, but it was exactly the support she needed. "Go on. Get home to Kaleb and the kids. You look like you could sleep for a day."

Charlotte laughed. "I think I could, but I'll probably end up doing laundry first. The glamorous life of a working mom. But seriously—call me if you need anything."

Andi nodded and turned back toward Logan's room, pushing thoughts of Jude and their shared past away.

She had to keep her head clear. The last thing she needed was a distraction when she was already fighting the hardest battle of her life.

Proving that she deserved to be on Truck 14.

"How are you feeling?" Andi perched on the bed next to her brother, careful of his injuries.

"I'll live." He grinned at her. "So, Jude's back, huh?"

Not this again. "Yeah, I guess."

"Is he staying long?"

"Not sure." She knew her brother was fishing for information, but she wouldn't play that game. Not like she even knew the answer to his question. She'd wondered the same herself.

"See, he's doing fine, Dad." Bryce led their father back into the room. He looked much calmer than before, which caused her shoulders to relax a bit.

"Lo."

Andi smiled at her father's nickname for Logan.

"Yeah, Dad, I'm okay." Logan forced a bright smile.

"I think it's time we headed home." Elizabeth slipped into the room next to her husband. "Come on, Paul. Time to go home."

"Watch my show," he said.

"Yes, honey. You can watch your show." Elizabeth turned to Andi. "Do you need a ride back?"

"Yeah, that would be good." Andi tried to ignore Logan's penetrating stare. She knew he wanted to ask why Jude wasn't taking her. "I've got to rest up for my shift tomorrow."

"We'll meet you at the car," her mother said.

"Hey." Logan reached out and grabbed Andi's hand before she could follow. "I've got a tip for your shift tomorrow."

Andi narrowed her gaze, wary. "Yeah?"

"Don't rescue any more cats."

"If you weren't injured, I'd punch you in the arm." She glared at her brother, feigning a punch that wouldn't land, as he laughed.

"Okay, I definitely missed something here." Bryce looked between them.

"You didn't miss a thing." Andi paced toward the door.

Logan began to tell the story of her impulsive rescue to Bryce and, rather than fight it, she kept walking. She loved her brothers, she really did. She also knew the only thing that would come from this—aside from a lot of laughter—was yet another suggestion that she go back to being a paramedic.

Even thinking of it now caused her hands to fist, but she borrowed a leaf from Jude's book and took a few deep breaths of the sterilized hospital air. They meant well; she knew that. But she wanted their support instead of their judgment. She worked hard, more so than most of the guys on Truck, and still they goaded her.

She just needed to clear her probationary period. Only a few more months and she'd be on more of an equal playing field with them. They'd have to stop. At least, she hoped they would.

A cool gust of wind tossed her hair into her eyes as she exited the emergency doors into the darkness of the parking lot, where her mother helped her dad into the car with the tenderness she always showed him.

A twist of emotion closed her throat.

She loved her family so much, but sometimes it felt impossible to keep up with them. Even more impossible to earn their trust when her career failed to line up like it should. Mom as a high-powered lawyer. Bryce as the Lieutenant on Rescue, until his injury. Logan, the LT who ran off to fight wildfires on a hotshot crew in Australia of all places. Maybe not so much her father in the past year, but even his legacy was a monolith. They had all achieved so much and she...hadn't. Yet.

God, help me be strong enough to do my job. Strong enough to protect them.

Her prayer felt as feeble as she did when it came to changing her family's mind about her choices, but it was all she had. They meant the world to her, and she knew at her core she could prove her worth to them. She had their love, but she'd earn their respect.

Hunched against the wind, Andi made her way toward her mother's car. She had to get her head on straight. Keep an eye out for her family. Focus on her job as a firefighter. Let the rest fall away.

But did that include Jude?

7

J ude's skin prickled as he walked inside the airstream trailer. It wasn't that cold out, but he still had to suppress a shiver. He dropped his bags on the dinette bench seat and rubbed his arms. Maybe he'd take Elizabeth up on those extra blankets.

It smelled like stale hotdogs and mold, but staying in the trailer would keep him in proximity to Andi and her family. And it was free. One less expense he'd have to submit. He knew other agents liked to treat trips away as if they were private vacations, expensing fancy hotels and over-the-top meals, but that wasn't Jude.

After an hour at the police station going through old reports, he'd stopped at the small grocery store and decided to stock the trailer's mini fridge with essentials. A place to sleep and some fruit and vegetables. That was all he really needed.

The focus was sorting this out—whatever *this* was—and heading back to Southern California. Just two more months and he'd be up for promotion, right on track.

He'd either nail Sosa on what was happening in Last

Chance County, or he'd leave well enough alone and get him another way.

Jude pulled off his leather jacket and yanked on a hoodie. He took out a premade sandwich that had seen better days along with a bag of kettle chips before opening dual reports on the small Formica table.

Something Andi had said at the hospital struck a chord. Her father's accident, then Bryce, and now Logan. He'd looked into the file about the incident where Bryce had been hurt and couldn't see a connection, but something nagged at him when he caught sight of the preliminary report on Logan's accident.

He studied the skid marks again and then flipped to pages from the older file on Paul Crawford's car accident years ago. His file was considerably thinner, but that made sense seeing as it was just a reported accident on a dangerous stretch of road.

There. The skid marks. He twisted the page to the right, then back again. They looked identical to those in Logan's report.

Jude wiped his mouth with the back of his hand and took a swig of water. Since Paul had suffered a TBI and spent months in the hospital, the report was shockingly vague about what had happened.

It had been late, and roads were wet with recent rain. Paul had been headed home after a surgical consultation at the hospital, and it was assumed he'd lost control of his car. It'd skidded off the embankment on a stretch of road Jude knew well from his teen years in Last Chance. It was a nasty area if you weren't familiar with it, and even worse at night, which had earned it the moniker of Dead Man's Curve. Add in slick roads, and an accident wasn't a far cry.

The skid marks jumped out at him again. Testing. Teasing.

Jude stood and paced the length of the trailer's interior to the end facing the street. It took him all of five steps. Then he made two more trips. There'd been one moment when he'd questioned Elizabeth's honesty. A moment he'd assumed was due to exhaustion, but what if he'd read into it correctly?

He paced back to where the table sat flanked by three tinted windows farthest from the street. Bending forward, he caught sight of lights on in the Crawford's house next door. To the left, his grandfather's house sat dark, and he knew Andi must have turned in for the night. It was nearing ten o'clock, and every manner his mother had instilled cautioned him it was too late, but the lights told a different story.

Jude reached for the files but stalled the motion. Showing a mother evidence of her son's recent trauma probably wasn't the best idea. It wouldn't stop him from having a conversation, though.

He stepped outside. The cool night air sought every exposed plane of skin, making Jude shiver. He needed blankets anyway, and he wasn't above using a ploy to open up a more candid conversation with Elizabeth. Maybe being at home would lower her defenses.

He cut across the grass and took the steps at a jog. His knock was quiet but distinct in the evening's stillness and he soon caught the sound of footsteps coming to the door.

"Jude?" Elizabeth opened the door with a curious expression. "Is something wrong?"

"I was wondering about those blankets you mentioned?"

"Come on in. I'll grab some for you." She smiled and opened the door.

The house smelled the same as it always had, as if a fresh batch of cookies had just come from the oven. It was warm and inviting and sent his thoughts racing back to the past.

Him and Andi stargazing in the backyard with his guitar close by. Barbecued hamburgers and corn on the back porch while Logan and Bryce tossed a football. They always tried to get Andi and Jude to play a game with them, but Jude played by the rules and couldn't stand it when they cheated—as they always did.

He'd missed this. Missed the Crawfords. A big part of him had wondered how they would accept him after his actions that last summer, but it seemed memories had faded with time and age for them, even if they were still fresh for him.

"In here." Elizabeth's voice broke his focus on the past, and he followed her to the kitchen. He caught the sound of a television show playing from the living room and popped his head in.

Paul Crawford sat in a recliner, watching a fishing show. He gently rocked the chair back and forth, and his hands fumbled with what Jude thought might be a spinner bait lure, though he hadn't fished in years.

"He likes his fishing shows." Elizabeth's eyes went soft for a moment before she turned back to the kitchen. "Would you like a cookie or two?"

So he *had* smelled cookies. "Sure. If you don't mind."

"I've never minded you eating our food, Jude." Her smile was wistful, and he knew she was reliving the past as much as he was.

He slid onto a bar stool at the island and took a warm cookie from a cooling rack. It tasted like cinnamon and chocolate.

"Oatmeal chocolate chip?"

"Yep. Logan's favorite." She dropped her gaze. "I couldn't imagine going to bed yet, so I baked. Paul needs time to wind down as well, so it worked out."

"I'm sorry you're going through this, Mrs. Crawford."

"It's Elizabeth," she reminded him. Her eyes ran over his features. "You're so grown-up now. You and Andi both. For me, it feels like those summers were hardly more than a few years past, but time is fickle that way."

Jude weighed his next words carefully. "Back at the hospital, when I asked you if you knew someone who might target your family, I think you lied to me."

Her eyes snapped to his.

"I'm not trying to bully you, I promise. But if there is someone you're thinking of—someone in particular—I need to know."

She took a moment to wipe a sponge across the counter as if cleaning it could erase the conversation. He knew she would give him an answer, even if it was a calculated one. He'd learned long ago that the best response to almost any difficult situation was usually silence. It gave a person time to think and allowed him space to hear—both what was being said and what wasn't.

"I have represented many people, as you know, and when confronted with a question like that, a person is going to feel overwhelmed. I did promise to get you a list and to let you know if I think of anything."

She'd said a lot without answering his question, and he was about to point that out when he heard a thudding sound from the living room.

"It's Paul," Elizabeth rushed to say. "That recliner makes a terrible sound when he gets up. Let me check on him." She disappeared into the living room. "Paul, honey, what's wrong?"

Her tone drew Jude into the living room. Paul stood at the window that looked out over the backyard. The man still held the lure and turned it over and over, making the bright colors flash in his hand.

"Is he okay?" Jude asked.

"He gets restless sometimes. I'm sure it's a combination of our trip to the hospital and being out of his usual nighttime routine. Paul, let's go to bed. It's late." She placed a gentle hand on his arm.

The touch seemed to set him off, and he shook his head violently. "Here. He's here. Out there."

The words were an icy whisper against Jude's spine. He reached for his gun only to remember he'd stowed it in his car—like an idiot. He hadn't expected to need it, but Paul's words sounded like a warning. An omen.

"There's no one out there, honey." Elizabeth tried and failed to infuse her voice with confidence. She turned to Jude. "It's the TBI. It changed him. Sometimes he sees things."

"There. He's there. There there there!" Paul's voice crescendoed.

"Okay, Paul. Okay. We hear you."

"There. He's there. Make him go. No no no." Paul raised a hand to his head and rubbed at his ear.

"I'm going to check out the backyard, just to be safe."

"You don't have to." Elizabeth's protest was feeble.

"I'll be right back. Lock the door after me." He caught the flicker of fear his words caused and mentally chided himself, but better he say it than assume she knew what to do.

"Be careful."

Jude nodded. "Always."

He slipped into the night amid the darkness of the back porch and let his eyes adjust. He heard the lock click and relaxed a fraction. They were safe inside and, knowing Andi, she was locked in as well.

The image of her with the baseball bat brought a smile to his lips. She'd be fine.

Jude took the steps down to the backyard and checked the waist-high bushes lining the porch. Nothing. He moved toward the north edge of the property and cleared the areas that were covered by the darkest shadows.

When he'd finished a circuit of the yard and felt sufficiently confident that no one was there, he pulled out his phone and used the flashlight app. He retraced his steps, light in hand this time, and took careful note of the damp soil in front of the porch. His heart thudded, and blood pounded in his ears.

There were footprints.

He told himself to calm down, that there was no evidence they were from a peeping tom—or worse—but they were out of place. The prints nearly matched his own boot size. At six-two, he wore a size thirteen, and these were close to that. So, likely a man.

The rest of his search turned up nothing until he got to the back of the yard, where a path led into the woods behind the house. Jude was familiar with the area but didn't know if the path remained cleared for use. It appeared as if the nighttime visitor had both arrived and left from that direction.

A sinking feeling hit his gut, and he swiped off the light, remaining still. Crickets slowly began their chirping again as they adjusted to his presence, but no sound of movement reached him. Whoever had been here was gone.

Jude let out a breath and thought of the facts.

Elizabeth had a list of potential enemies. Paul's and Logan's accidents looked dangerously similar on paper, though he'd have to wait for confirmation when the final report came in about Logan's accident. Diego Ruiz Sosa had surveillance images of the whole Crawford family in his office. Photos taken recently, if the length of Andi's hair was any indication.

Her hair. She looked good with longer hair.

He roughed a hand over his face. That was the very last thing he needed to be thinking about.

If the visitor tonight was part of this, they were too close for comfort. Jude didn't have enough to connect the dots, but he might have enough to call in a favor.

He swiped open his phone. The brilliant glow momentarily blinded him before he could turn the brightness down and navigate to his contacts.

He tapped the call button and rang the friend he'd relied on so many times over the years.

"Hello?"

"Penny?"

"Jude Brooks. No way. I was just thinking of you the other day."

He chuckled. "Yeah, right."

"No, really. I got a flashback to that time you locked yourself out of your room during test week at ATF training and you were only wearing—"

"Pen, I need a favor."

"Name it." All traces of humor were gone from her tone.

Warmth flooded him at her quick response. They hadn't seen each other in person for several years, but here and there they'd helped each other when needed.

He filled her in on the situation, ending with, "This is not a go yet, but I want you on deck if you've got the time."

"You always like to throw me a bone, don't you?" She laughed, the sound low and dark.

"What's that mean?"

"Ever since I left the ATF, I swear everyone thinks I'm some sort of charity case. I'm living large in the private sector, Book. You know private security is where it's at."

"This is most definitely not a bone. I need your insight on this. Besides, I need it to be below the radar, and if—and I mean *if*—I bring people in, I want it to be minimal and effective."

"Sounds like the job for me. You know, my real name is Penny *Tactful* Mitchell."

"You're about as tactful as a grenade." They shared a laugh. "But just as effective. So, what do you say? Be on standby?"

"You know it." She paused. "This your hometown?"

Out of all the people he'd worked with, Penny was one of the few who knew his full story. Her question, though a surprise, wasn't out of the blue.

"More like a home away from home." *A haven.*

"Good. I'd like to see where Little Jude came from."

He rolled his eyes in the dark. "Watch for my call."

"You got it, Boss."

8

"This is Ambo 21 acknowledging. Show us responding." Andi shifted in her seat.

"Copy, Ambo 21."

Izan Collins flipped on the lights and siren and maneuvered a turn onto the major thoroughfare. Cars slowed and pulled over before them like Moses parting the Red Sea. Or almost as smoothly. He had to slow down for an SUV, and Izan muttered something in Spanish as he braked.

"Come *on!*" Andi pounded the dash of the ambulance. She hated when cars didn't obey the traffic laws and move over. One extra minute could mean life or death for someone.

"Don't worry. We'll get there." Izan's voice was calm, measured.

"Just drive." Andi's words were sharp, and she caught the look Izan sent her.

He maneuvered expertly around the car, and soon they were speeding on.

"You know I drive better than Trace," he finally said. She could tell he was trying to break the tension she'd caused.

"Don't let him hear you say that." She tried for humor, but it fell flat.

She was bitter. It was stupid, but it was true.

Trace had called in earlier that day, and Macon had wasted no time tossing her back to Ambo. She had a feeling it was part of her punishment for the "stunt" with the cat, as Macon had called it, but it just felt like a never-ending cycle. She had worked herself raw to make it to Truck, and now the smallest thing sent her reeling back with no hope of catching up again.

"You okay?" Izan asked.

"Peachy."

"Is it really that bad being here with me?"

She heard the underlying hurt beneath his words and sighed. It wasn't his fault she was here. In fact, if anyone was to blame, it was her.

"It's not you."

"It's being a paramedic." He said it matter-of-factly. "I get it."

They rode on in silence, though she'd hardly call it silence as the siren blared above them. She knew Izan understood. He and a few other guys had been vying for the coveted spot on Truck, and she'd made it over them.

While she knew many of them thought it was because of Bryce pulling strings, she'd demanded that he not interfere. She'd earned her spot, and she was doing everything she could to keep it. Making mistakes like she had the other day didn't help her probationary status. She had to prove to Chief that she was not only capable, but that she deserved to be on Truck.

They drew near to the location of the 911 call and she felt it. Like she always did. The tingle in the pit of her stomach knowing someone was in need and she was going to help them.

"Hey, if you see any cats here, don't rescue them—okay?"

She shot Izan a withering look he avoided by focusing on parking.

Thoughts of the poorly timed joke were a thing of the past as they rushed up to the house with their bags.

Izan banged on the door. "Paramedics!"

The door opened and a rail-thin woman in her early twenties stood there, bleary-eyed.

"Ma'am, we're with Eastside Rescue. Can you tell me what's wrong?"

She looked between them, and one hand went to the inside of her elbow, scratching.

"Ma'am, we're paramedics. You called 9-1-1. Where is the emergency?" Andi's foot tapped the concrete stoop.

"It's Johnny. You've gotta help him." The woman's eyes stayed out of focus. She was high on some type of drug.

"Are you injured?" Andi asked.

"Johnny. He's back there." The woman pointed behind them, then fixed her eyes on Izan. "You look...familiar."

Andi turned toward Izan, but he ducked his head and rushed to where the woman had pointed.

"Hey. Do I know you?" the woman yelled after Izan.

He ignored her and knelt down next to the man on the floor. "Sir? Can you hear me?"

Andi shook off the strange interaction and knelt next to Izan, assessing the man's status. He lay on his side with his back facing them. Before turning him over, they needed to figure out what had occurred before they were called.

"Ma'am, can you tell us what happened?"

"Johnny. He's hurt. Hurt real bad."

"Did you see how he was hurt?" Andi waited as Izan took the man's pulse.

"Hit his head. It's bad." She backed up and scratched more intently at her arm before her gaze went back to Izan. Her focus unsettled Andi.

"Andi." The note of panic in Izan's voice drew Andi's attention to the man.

Izan had pulled him onto his back—before he should have—but that's when she saw the blood.

"Head wound. Get me the gauze." She lifted the man's eyelids and shone a penlight on his eyes, assessing the likelihood of a concussion. The pinpoint pupils alerted her to something far more dangerous. An overdose.

When she turned back for the gauze, Izan was looking up at the woman. She stared back at him.

"Izan?" Andi said.

"I—I, uh..." He swallowed and looked like he'd forgotten where he was.

"Gauze," Andi said. "Now. We've got to stop this bleeding and—"

"Here." He handed her the entire package instead of taking several sheets out. She yanked it free with a look at him to snap out of it, then turned back to the man.

"Ma'am, I need you to tell me what happened here." The patient was catatonic, and she had no way of knowing what had caused his overdose.

"Johnny's hurt." It was all she'd say.

"Izan. Hold this." Andi's tone jerked the young man out of his stupor, and he pressed the gauze against the man's head.

Andi went to the woman, standing between her and Izan. This strange fixation was distracting her. "Ma'am—hey, what's your name?"

"Sheila." She fidgeted and bit her lip with yellowed teeth.

"Sheila, I want to help Johnny, but I need to know what happened. What drugs did he take?"

Sheila looked down. Her fidgeting intensifying.

"We're not the police." At the word, the woman's eyes snapped up. "We just want to know what happened here, that's all. We want to help Johnny."

Sheila weighed Andi's words and finally nodded. "Yeah, he took some drugs. He knows." She nodded toward where Johnny lay with Izan bending over him.

Andi wasn't exactly sure what the woman meant, but she pressed for more and finally got the details of Johnny's drug use. After a dose of Naloxone, they rushed the man to the ambulance.

Andi rode in back with him as Izan pushed the limits of the vehicle to get them to the hospital.

"He's stable," she called from the back. They had a few minutes before they'd hit the emergency room, but she couldn't shake off the tightness in her shoulders. That had been too close. "What happened back there?"

"I, uh, I don't know. I froze." He squeezed the wheel with both hands. "I mean, I've been on the job for almost two years and you'd think I'd be fine, but somehow that head wound really got to me."

She checked the patient, satisfied to see that he was still stable, and peered through the talk-through window at Izan.

"You don't roll someone over without checking them. And you don't forget how to use gauze. You were rattled, and I want to know why." Her tone demanded answers. "People's lives are on the line, and if you can't keep it together, you need to find a new line of work."

"Knock it off, Andi," he called back. "I get it. I messed up and I'm sorry. I'm not bionic like Amelia. And I'm definitely not perfect. "

He made it sound impossible, but she found that practice really made perfect. Especially when it came to medicine or firefighting—you had to be at the top of your game. Had to do everything right. Andi almost laughed, thinking how Jude would love that statement.

Her mind conjured an image of him from the hospital. She wondered when she might see him next, but she shifted her focus back to their patient as they pulled up to the emergency room.

It was go time. No more space for thoughts of Jude.

Izan tried to open the driver-side door. "What's going on?"

"It's stuck." Didn't he know it did that sometimes? She rolled her eyes. "Pull the handle up and push it forward. Then give it a really hard shove."

She heard a grunt, and the door popped open.

He came to the back and opened the double doors.

"See? Easy."

He groaned. "Come on, superwoman. Let's get this guy inside."

They rushed into the emergency room in a windstorm of information that keyed the ER nurses in to the man's vital statistics and the care they'd already given him.

When the nurses took over, Andi and Izan relaxed. They'd have paperwork to fill out, but she'd helped to save another life. She couldn't deny liking the sense of accomplishment she felt at having helped someone.

"Hey, Andi." Izan turned to her, looking exhausted. "Thanks."

Her brow furrowed. "For...?"

"Saving me back there." He ran a hand across the back of his neck. "I'm usually not so useless—honestly."

She warred with herself. Letting him off the hook for what could have potentially been a really dangerous situation seemed too lenient, but all the times she'd ridden ambulance with him, she'd never seen him freeze up like that.

"Just don't let it happen again." She softened her words with a smile.

"Yes, ma'am." He saluted her.

"Hey, did you know that lady back there?"

"Huh?" He paused from where he'd turned toward the nurses' station.

"That lady. Uh, Sheila? It looked like she knew you."

"No way. She was as high as a kite." His words had a forced lightness to them.

Maybe she was reading into it. "Right. Okay."

Izan shifted. "You know you're a great paramedic, right?"

"What?" His words jolted her like a paddle shock.

"I know you're a firefighter now, and I respect that." He hesitated. "But you're, like, crazy good as a paramedic. You go into this whole other plane of existence when you're on the job. It's kind of awesome to watch."

She knew he was complimenting her, but it was salt on raw wounds. His voice joined the chorus of her brothers and mother and even Chief James when he'd asked her twice if she was sure she wanted to be a firefighter.

There would come a day when everyone would see her worth as a firefighter and this would stop—she would make sure of it.

Rather than argue the point in the middle of the ER, she nodded. "Thanks."

"Just call them like I see them." He shrugged, then flashed her a grin. "And I'm not just saying that because you took *my* spot on Truck."

"Whatever." The attitude reminded her of Logan— "Hey, Iz?"

"Yeah?" He looked up from the clipboard of paperwork.

"You got this? I want to go see Logan really quick. He's still here."

"Sure thing. And congratulations, you can head home early after we get the ambo back to the firehouse."

She paused. "Home?"

"Trace just called." He held up his phone. "Left a message saying he'd take over the rest of the shift. His appointment finished early, and he's already at the firehouse."

"Sounds good. I'll be back in a sec." She waved her thanks

and headed to Logan's room. The door was open when she got there, and the TV blared a baseball game.

"Hey, big bro." Andi slumped into a chair by his bed.

"Andi Bear." He grinned at her soiled uniform. "Fun callout?"

"I'm off now. Heading back to the firehouse for a shower and a change of clothes but wanted to see how you were doing first."

"I'm good." When she gave him a pointed look, he laughed. "No, really. The doctor says I won't have to be in here much longer. X-rays came back, and my ribs just need time to heal. Bruised, not broken. I'm hoping it's not too long before I can get back to work."

"You and Bryce—you'd think getting hit with a building and a car would be enough to convince you guys to take it easy for a little while."

Logan laughed. "You know that's not the Crawford way."

She flinched. That was one way of putting it, though she was certain he meant the Crawford *brothers'* way. She looked up and met his gaze.

"You're staring at me."

"My sis." He shook his head. "Out there, saving lives like a boss."

She rolled her eyes. "Give it up, Logan."

"What?"

"You're doing it again." She waved a hand at him. "Trying to convince me to give up being a firefighter."

"I am not."

"Are too." She held his gaze.

"Okay, maybe a little, but it's not that I want you to give it up. I just think you aren't seeing yourself clearly."

She pushed to her feet. "I came to see if you were all right. I'm not here for a lecture."

"It's not a lecture if I care about you, Andi. You're an amazing paramedic, and you jus—"

"If you say I threw it away, then you have no respect for what *you* do, let alone what I'm doing now. I can't believe that. It just means you have a double standard."

"I don't." His tone was even, measured. It drove her nuts. "I care about you."

"But clearly you don't care enough to listen to my words over what you think is best."

Andi was so tired of this argument. So tired of trying to prove herself to her family time and time again.

"I've got to go." She moved toward the door. "Rest up and listen to the doctor. I'll be back later."

She left before he could say anything else. He'd try to persuade her to give up the one thing in her life that would finally help her prove she was, in fact, worthy of belonging in the Crawford family filled with heroes.

9

The sound of ringing pulled Jude from sleep.

"Hel—?" His voice cracked, and he cleared his throat to try again. "Hello?"

"Did I wake you? Isn't it almost nine there?"

Jude tried to place the voice. "Mick?"

He sat up, running a hand over his face. After reassuring Elizabeth about their safety, he'd gone back over the case files late into the night. He'd filled his notebook with thoughts and theories on how Sosa might be connected to anything going on in Last Chance County, but when the secure VPN failed to connect on his laptop, his online reach had been limited. He'd need to contact support today for that fix.

"Yeah. We've got some updates for you that couldn't wait."

Jude stifled a yawn and moved to the counter to start a pot of coffee in the travel-sized coffee maker.

"Sorry, man," Mick Perry said. "I thought you'd want to hear this sooner rather than later." Perry was newer to Jude's unit in San Diego, but he'd more than proven himself on several occasions by discovering information through a series of creative searches. Basically hacking.

"Hey, Boss." A deep bass voice filled the line. "I'm here too."

"Hey, Jackson." Jude could imagine his teammates crowded around the phone. Perry with his fiery red hair and freckles juxtaposed with Keith Jackson towering over him with ebony skin and an easy smile. "Read me in."

"As you know, I sent out a bulletin to our other offices to be on the lookout for Sosa. I think Jackson sent over the report from the Coast Guard, but bottom line is they lost him not long after we did. I don't know if there was no transponder on that boat or what, but Sosa disappeared like donuts around Parker," Perry said.

They all shared a laugh at the reference to the scrawny intern with a penchant for devouring leftover office snacks.

"They are keeping an eye out for the boat you described, but it's probably useless." Jackson took over. "We assume he ditched it not long after the escape and is in Mexico or hiding out in a state bordering the water—my best guess."

"Then what's this intel you're talking about?" Jude stood and stretched.

He flipped on the space heater to get some warmth into the trailer. He could imagine the ribbing his grandfather would have given him, calling him a sissy for needing the heat, but his body had adjusted to the climate—and the sun—in Southern California.

"I got a call from Ben at the Denver office."

Jude picked up on the excitement in Mick's voice.

"He has an informant who swears they saw The Brothers in a biker bar on the west side. In Golden, a small town outside of Denver."

"The Brothers? Really?" Jude pictured the grainy black-and-white images on the office cork board. The two men were known associates of Diego Ruiz Sosa. Whether they were truly brothers, no one knew. But they were bad news with extensive rap sheets. Robbery. Drug-related charges. Murder. And like thunder following lightning, wherever Sosa was, they weren't usually far behind.

"Yeah. We thought it was doubly odd, seeing as you're out that way—ish—following up on that lead about the family. And now they show up?" The sound of tapping keys followed Perry's statement.

Jude poured a cup of coffee. "Do you need me to check it out?"

"I'm in contact with a few guys at the Denver office right now. They're already on it," Jackson said. "We just wanted to fill you in."

"Do you want us out there?" Perry asked.

Jude still didn't want to create havoc by bringing in his team. At least, not yet. He'd called Penny last night to initiate her arrival, but there were also local resources he could tap into.

"I'm still not sure this isn't something that locals should handle. It's unclear if Sosa is working small-time gigs like intimidation or threats, or if this is part of a bigger plan." Jude didn't want to admit that he still couldn't find a connection between the Crawfords and the drug lord, but it was obvious by what he wasn't saying.

"We can keep things up on our end if you're sure you don't need us out there." Perry, always the optimist, had no trouble following Jude's orders. "We've got the Dillon file and the Whittaker Farms surveillance keeping us busy."

"I think we should come out." Jackson was more pragmatic but also more willing to run headlong into danger. "Dillon and Whittaker Farms can easily be handed over to Walker's team."

Jude's gaze ran over the reports on the tabletop as a plan solidified in his mind. "Focus on what you're doing, and I'll keep you guys in the loop. Jackson, work on confirming the report on The Brothers. Perry, I want to know about any online chatter about or including Sosa. He can't go completely underground—he doesn't have the finances for it."

"Got it," they said in unison.

Jude hung up and leaned over the table to look at his grandfather's house. Andi's car was gone, and he remembered her saying she had a shift that day. Doing what he should have done when he first came into town, he put a call into the local police chief, Conroy Barnes.

It was time for a meeting.

Jude made the call, but when he failed to reach the police chief *and* the fire chief, he got an idea. An official meeting at the police station—or even the firehouse—was out of the question at this stage. It would draw too much attention.

Instead, he connected with the liaison to the fire department, Allen Frees, and hatched a new plan.

When Jude sat down in the living room of his grandfather's house that afternoon, he felt like he was trespassing. While he'd texted Andi for the Wi-Fi code to make sure he could get into the house, and she'd reminded him about her fix-it list, he hadn't exactly planned on using the house for this meeting, but there was no way they could meet in the trailer.

A knock drew his focus to the door. He opened it to find a tall man in his thirties with dark, short hair and a strong build standing next to a man in a wheelchair who had light-brown hair and wore an intense but open look.

He extended a hand to them both, and the man in the wheelchair introduced them. "Allen Frees, Fire Department Community Liaison, and this is Fire Chief Macon James."

"Jude Brooks, ATF. Thanks for coming." Jude stepped back so they could enter.

"When Allen calls, we answer," Macon said with a chuckle.

"I hope I didn't pull you away from anything too important." Jude saw an unmarked police car pull into the driveway and left the door ajar for the police chief.

"I've got a good staff," Macon said. "My LT, Amelia Patterson, will handle things while I'm out, but"—he pointed to a walkie talkie strapped to his belt—"if they need me, they'll reach me."

"We'll make it quick, I promise."

"Hello?" A brown-haired man in a crisp suit stuck his head through the door.

"Come on in, Conroy," Allen said.

He joined the group and sat in the vacant recliner. "Nice place."

Jude grimaced. "I'd like to make this quick since this is *technically* Andi's place and I'm *technically* supposed to be fixing something while I'm in here."

Macon checked his watch. "She's on shift for a while longer, covering for Trace on Ambo. Plenty of time for you to get to work."

"Still." Jude shifted in his seat. "The reason I've invited you all here is a sensitive matter that's not yet public knowledge."

He sensed the men's interest and knew he had their full attention. He needed to explain so they could work together as covertly as possible in order to keep the residents of Last Chance County safe.

"I work with the ATF out of San Diego, and I've been on the trail of drug lord Diego Ruiz Sosa. He's a big-time criminal who seems to have fallen on hard times. But as you all know, desperation can cause recklessness. It seems he is getting into previously unexplored territory by targeting someone here in Last Chance."

"How?" Conroy frowned.

"More like 'Who?'" Macon added.

Jude explained how he'd found surveillance images of the Crawford family at Sosa's villa. Then he brought up Logan's accident.

"Officer Thomas seems to think it was a local hit-and-run."

Conroy's brow furrowed in concentration. "You don't think that's true?"

"The reports I looked at were preliminary, but"—Jude pulled out the identical skid patterns and showed them to the men—"I see a connection between Paul's accident years ago and Logan's yesterday."

Allen shook his head. "That's not good."

"I don't like that they're targeting one of my guys." Macon's eyes narrowed.

"Me either," Jude agreed. "I can't be sure of the specific target yet. I'm still digging into things, but there's been another development." He explained about the as-yet-unofficial sighting of The Brothers outside of Denver. Hours away, but close enough to warrant concern.

When he'd finished, Conroy said, "What exactly are you asking of us?"

"I could bring in a team and make it very obvious that something is going on here, but I'm not sure that's the way to go. At least, not yet. That's why I suggested we meet here. I think keeping the investigation under wraps and doing things subtly might be the best way to approach this."

Jude pulled out the sheet of notes he'd compiled while waiting for this meeting. His gaze traveled the room and saw what he'd hoped for—allies.

"Chief James, Mr. Frees, the firehouse is a safe area for the Crawfords. There are security cameras and no one is ever there alone. I'd like to see if we can convince Bryce to stay there when he's not on duty."

"He's a strong-willed one," Macon said. "But I think that's doable."

Jude nodded. "I'll be staying in the airstream, so I can help monitor Andi and the Crawfords, but I think it would be best to put eyes on them." He directed this to Conroy.

"You want them watched without their knowing?" Conroy asked.

"If at all possible."

The man nodded. "I think we can do that. But what about Logan?"

"I have a friend coming to help me out with this. She's former ATF and works with a private security firm now. She'll be discreet, but she's one of the best."

"And Andi?" Macon asked. "What about her?"

Jude rubbed a hand over his jaw. The main part of his job was going to be investigating what was going on and trying to either nail Sosa or at least point Chief Barnes toward the likely culprit targeting the Crawfords.

Andi's safety mattered to him. She'd spot a tail a mile away, but did he press and have her followed for her own safety, or was there another option?

"While she's here, the officers who are watching the Crawfords can watch this house too. Other than that, I'll talk with her." Macon's gaze burned into him. "She knows more than she should at this point."

Allen laughed. "Sounds like Andi."

"I'll handle it." Jude tried for an assertive tone.

"Seems as if you've covered all angles," Conroy said. "You'll keep us in the loop on this." It was a demand, not a request.

"To the extent I can." Jude knew it was a non-answer, but he also had a feeling the chief of police wouldn't pressure him. "This is a sensitive operation because we don't know much. Sosa could be involved, or maybe it was made to look like he is. My team and I will get to the bottom of everything. We play this by the book and things will work out."

He sounded more confident than he felt, but that was to be expected in this circle of men. Failing just wasn't an option.

"And to be clear, we're keeping this from the Crawfords?" Macon asked.

"As best we can. I want them protected, but I don't know the extent of Mrs. Crawford's involvement, and I can't risk that tainting my investigation. Got it?" Jude made eye contact around the circle, but before he could get a response, the door swung open.

Andi walked in. "What are you all doing in my house?"

10

She left the house for *one shift*—scratch that, not even one full shift—and Jude thought he could step in and make himself at home in *her* home?

"A-Andi." Jude jumped to his feet. "You're b-back."

"Just in time for a party, I see." Her gaze stopped on Chief James, whose eyes were wide with surprise.

"They were j-just leaving." Jude flashed an awkward smile at the men. They stood en masse to go.

"Andi." Chief James dipped his head like he was some Southern gentleman.

"See ya around, Chief," she said. "Frees."

He pushed his wheelchair to the door.

Andi nodded. "Chief Barnes."

They moved past her like kids caught with their hands in the cookie jar. That's when she noticed the pair of dirty sweatpants she'd left in the corner of the room. Her cheeks flamed.

Andi rounded on Jude when the room was clear of unexpected guests. "Hosting a meeting in my living room? And here I thought I'd *finally* have a working shower. Some landlord you are." She drilled into him with a stare.

"Andi." Jude took in a deep breath. "I'm sorry. I-I didn't exactly mean to use your house as a-a meeting space, but the trailer..."

"You know, it's not so much that you're here—in the house I pay rent on—and it's not even the fact that my boss was in here with my dirty laundry on the floor." She pointed to the corner. "It's the fact you didn't ask. No, it's worse than that. You lied to me so you could go behind my back and have this meeting about me and my family."

She watched as he opened his mouth, no doubt to refute her claim, but she beat him to it. "Don't even try to deny it. I heard everything."

His eyes narrowed. "Do you make a habit of eavesdropping?"

She laughed, no humor in it, and tossed her bag to the floor. Her top was messy from their last call, and she wanted a shower and a nap, not to verbally wrestle with Jude.

"You do realize you were meeting in my living room with the door open. You were practically begging for someone to overhear."

"I didn't know you would be home s-so early."

"I can't believe this." Andi clenched her teeth and paced. Her shoes squeaked on the hardwood floor. "You come here to investigate and won't give us—people you've known for years—the benefit of the truth. We're in danger, but you don't want to mess up your operation, so your brilliant plan is to keep it all from us?"

"That's not it at all, Andi." Jude's shoulders slumped.

"Mom told me you were over at the house last night and Dad saw someone outside. I mean, should I be worried? Do I need to sleep with my baseball bat or something?"

"I thought you already did that."

She couldn't help but grin, though she turned away so he wouldn't see. Jude had this uncanny ability to get past her defenses. He'd always made her laugh, which was infuriating when she wanted to be taken seriously.

"Okay, I get it. You're not going to tell me anything more. You're here in some secret capacity, and maybe someone my mom represented could be to blame, and that's how my family is mixed up in this all." She waved a hand as if to encompass the rest of what he'd said.

"I thought you heard it all." He had the nerve to grin at her.

"Brooks." She snapped his name and stepped forward, invading his space. An intimidation tactic she'd learned from her brothers, it had the opposite effect when she caught a whiff of his cologne.

"Yes?"

She searched his soft brown eyes for a moment before stepping back to pace the living room. "I thought you agreed to fill me in on this. It's my family." She stopped near the fireplace and faced him from across the room. "I'm sure you'd do anything for your mom, so you must understand how I'm feeling."

Her words hit their intended mark, and she thought she caught his resolve faltering.

"Come here." He moved toward the couch and tugged her down next to him. "This stays between us, right?"

She nodded.

"There's a dangerous man named Diego Ruiz Sosa—he's a drug lord with ties to some really bad men. My team and I were on his trail in Southern California, and we traced him to a hideout via a tip we got. We raided it, but he escaped."

"Okay, but what does he have to do with my family?"

"That's what I'm trying to find out." Jude turned away from her, and she caught the movement of his jaw flexing. This was hard for him to share, but she didn't understand why. "In the villa where Sosa was staying, we found surveillance photographs. They were of your family."

A chill crept up Andi's spine. "How's that possible?"

"That's what I'm trying to find out. We researched any connection between your family and the cartel, but we've come up blank. That's what I was talking to your mom about yesterday. I thought it might be someone she'd represented."

"You think she's holding something back?"

Jude ran a hand across his jaw. "It's possible."

Andi hated thinking her mom would lie to Jude. Elizabeth Crawford was many things. A biathlete, an amazing mother and wife, a strong woman. But she was not a liar. "What does this mean for my family?"

"You really didn't hear much, did you?"

Her cheeks grew warm. "Not as much as I let on, no."

"I've asked for help from the cops here and your bosses at the firehouse so my team doesn't have to come in. Yet."

"Why?"

"I still don't know what we're dealing with here. If it's Sosa, there's a reason he's involved in something all the way in Last Chance County. If it's not him, then there's someone that's involved with or connected to Sosa's organization, and they're interested in your family. I need to get to the bottom of this, but I don't want to draw undue attention until I'm certain it's warranted."

Andi nodded. It made sense, but was it more dangerous for them that way? Could something happen while Jude was staying under the radar?

As if reading her thoughts, he went on. "Chief Barnes will have someone watching your parents' house and yours. I'll be nearby most of the time, and there'll be other protection for your brothers. Your family will be safe while I continue the investigation."

"And Logan's accident?"

Jude looked at her for so long she wondered if he was ever going to answer her. It gave her a chance to think. To reason through all of this. If her mom was involved in anything, it had to be because of a client. That was the only thing that made sense. If that were the case, then she had to have some clue as to who it could be. It was possible there were so many it was difficult to narrow it down, but if Jude compared the names to an ATF database or something, maybe that would help.

"I'm not sure it was an accident." His words yanked her attention.

"There's more you aren't telling me." She could tell by the way he dropped his gaze. Shifted in his seat. "What is it, Brooks?"

"I don't like to jump to conclusions. Technically, I shouldn't even be sharing this with you at all."

"Forget technicalities—this is my family. This affects them and it affects me. Tell me what it is, Jude."

He pursed his lips for a moment, then said, "I think they targeted your father and Logan in the same way. I think it's a warning or a scare tactic. And I think that it's directed at your mother."

Andi blinked. "Do you think someone connected to Sosa did it? But for what purpose? And why my mom?"

"I don't know." He gave a decisive shake of his head. "I've already told you more than I should have, and even what I've said isn't fact. There's still a lot to uncover, but we have to do it carefully. Without tipping our hand. You can't tell anyone, got it?"

She nodded, but her mind raced. Jude had come here because her family was in danger, and he hadn't planned on telling them. Did he really think that being oblivious was better when danger was a real possibility?

"I can handle whatever this is, Jude. I'm stronger than you think."

"I know that."

"No, I don't think you do. You never have." She bit her lip, stopping herself from fully rehashing their past.

"That's not true. And this isn't about the past. I would *never* let anything happen to your family. It's why I met with the chief of police and your boss. I care about you. A-about all of you." He cleared his throat. "I promise you, I am not putting you or your family in harm's way for career advancement, or whatever it is y-you're thinking."

He looked disgusted, but that wasn't what she'd been suggesting. Not really. Still, she had to sort this out. Had to understand the hard facts about what the danger to her family really was. She didn't need him protecting her from anything.

The touch of his warm hands around hers distracted her. She pulled them free. Not that she didn't like his touch—but she couldn't let it sidetrack her from what was going on right now.

"I—this is too much. I'm in a precarious position at the firehouse right now as a probationary firefighter, and I *am* going to move past that probationary period to full-time. At least, that's the plan." She wouldn't let failure be an option here, but it was getting harder to wrap her head around everything he'd said. "I have to focus if I'm going to make it, but I can't do that if I think my family is in danger. If you're trying to shelter me—"

"I'm not. You don't need that. But I didn't tell you these things so that you'd feel responsible either." His calming tone was like a cool breeze on a hot day. "You don't have to do it all, Andi. That's why I'm here—to help."

Her eyes sought out his. She could take care of herself— she'd always been good at that, despite their shared past—but she couldn't focus on being the best firefighter she could be if her family was in danger.

"Just let me take care of it all and—"

"I know you think you have to protect me. You made that very clear years ago." His placating tone irritated her. She hated using the past as a weapon, but she needed this point to hit home. "But I'm not seventeen anymore. I make my own choices, and I own up to my own mistakes. I can handle myself."

"I never said you couldn't—"

"You didn't have to. I see it in your eyes." That hurt more than she wanted to admit.

"Andi."

"Please don't, Brooks." She silenced him with a finger to his slightly parted lips. Felt the warmth of his breath escape before she dropped her hand. She'd made her point. "I'll be okay. I just...got overwhelmed for a second."

"I know." His tone held comfort, and she wanted to lose herself in it, but that was another type of danger.

"Protect my family, Jude. I'll watch out for myself." She turned toward her bedroom but paused at the door, a smile tugging at her lips. "And stay out of my house unless you're fixing something."

She closed the door to her room and leaned back against it. Why did it have to be Jude on this case? It was a lot to take in. Almost too much. A drug lord after her family—maybe—and her mother involved somehow.

She could handle the truth, but her brothers? If she knew one thing for certain, it was the fact that, despite their injuries, they would go off half-cocked and ruin whatever chance at subtlety Jude had.

No one could tell them.

But her? She'd be just fine as long as she didn't let herself get distracted by Jude. That, more than anything else, was going to be the hardest part.

11

"Forty-seven. Forty-eight." The jazz tune of his ringtone cut off Jude's count. "Fifty."

He did a final pushup and popped to his feet. Allowing for the shifting movement of the airstream, he rushed to where he'd placed his phone on the Formica countertop.

"Brooks."

"Did I catch you running?"

He pulled the phone back to check the caller ID, then smiled. "Hey, Penny, glad you called back. I'm just in the middle of a workout."

"Well, I'm glad *you* called. I'm in town."

Jude thought back to his conversation—interrupted though it had been—with those in charge of the town's safety. They were going to get things covered in the most unobtrusive way possible, and that meant bringing Penny in to cover Logan at the hospital.

"Perfect. You got the information I sent over?"

"Yep. This, uh..."—he heard shifting papers in the background—"Logan Crawford is a cutie."

"Don't get any ideas, Pen." He smiled for the first time since

Andi had come in like a hurricane and blown him out of her house with gale-force winds of anger and independence.

"You know I keep it professional."

"Always. I owe you one."

"Oh, you'll pay. Don't worry about that." Her laugh was easy and free. "I'll be at the hospital if you need me."

He hung up and tossed his phone back on the table. It was time for sit-ups. He lay down on the ratty towel he'd found in a cupboard and began his count.

He'd hoped a good, fast workout would clear some of the frustration from his mind, but the burn from his abs did nothing to erase the image of hurt on Andi's face. He should have held the meeting somewhere else...but where?

His gaze traveled around the trailer, and he laughed, causing an added burn. Yeah, he could just see it now. Four burly men—one in a wheelchair—squished around the tiny lime-green table on cracked tan seats. Not only would it have set the wrong tone, it would have been impossible to maintain any status his ATF creds earned him.

Sweat poured down his neck and back as he neared the first count to one hundred. Two more sets and then he'd run a few miles before cleaning up and going in search of some food. Thai food sounded good.

Someone pounded on the door. The thuds rattled the metal trailer.

Jude pushed to his feet and reached for a towel when the door flew open.

"Jude, I—" Andi stood there, her scrubs replaced by black leggings and an oversized shirt. Her gaze took in his bare chest, and she froze.

"Do you need something?" If Jude had been a stronger man, he wouldn't have noticed—or cared—about the way her face flooded with heat at seeing him shirtless. He also wouldn't have waited an extra few moments before pulling on a shirt either.

But he wasn't strong, and he was enjoying seeing Andi speechless.

"I'm, uh..." She ran a hand over her face, blinking rapidly. "My dad. We can't find him."

Jude yanked the shirt over his head, all sense of pleasure at her flustered state gone. "Where was he last?"

Andi backed down the metal steps. He followed. "He was just at home watching his show. At least, that's what Mom said."

"Hold on." Jude rested a hand on her shoulder. "Let me check with the officer down the street."

Andi nodded, and he jogged over to the young man. The officer sat in an unmarked car, mostly hidden from view of the house but with a clear line of sight. The car had arrived shortly after his meeting with the chiefs had ended and offered some relief to Jude's round-the-clock diligence.

The officer confirmed he'd seen no one enter or exit the house. Jude rushed back to Andi. "He saw nothing from the front. Let's go inside."

She nodded, and they raced up the steps. A warm vanilla scent hit him as they entered the home. Elizabeth came around the corner wringing her hands, a pinched expression on her face. "I was upstairs for less than five minutes. Just five minutes."

"Mom, it's not your fault. You know he wanders." Andi went to her mom while Jude paced around the kitchen. Everything looked the same as the night before.

He turned to Elizabeth "What was he doing when you went upstairs?"

"Watching his show. It's what he always does in the afternoons before we take our walk."

He caught the hint of defense and rushed to assure her. "No one thinks it's your fault, Mrs. C." The name harkened back to his teenage years, and the urgency to fix this caused his pulse to skyrocket. He had to keep his promise to Andi by keeping her family safe.

Was it possible Sosa or an associate of his—The Brothers perhaps?—had taken Paul? The officer parked out front would catch anyone entering the premises but... He thought of the night before. Had someone come in from the back?

Jude rushed to the living room. The TV showed images of a sunlit stream. Paul's lure sat on the table next to the lounger he normally occupied.

His eyes scanned every inch until they came to the back door. While Jude didn't have an eidetic memory, he remembered details. There had been a hat by the back door last night. A fishing hat.

"I'm checking out back." He called over his shoulder but didn't wait for a response.

A rush of cool afternoon air washed over the sweat still covering him, and he suppressed a shiver. No obvious new footprints compared to the photos he'd taken the night before, but most of the yard was covered by grass, which wouldn't show much.

Working on instinct, Jude moved to the trail at the back of the yard. He paused at the entrance where the grass gave way to dirt. Fresh footprints. Going one way. "Mr. C?"

He caught voices behind him and looked back to see Andi and her mother coming out onto the porch.

He called again. "Paul?"

The trees on either side of him showed no signs of disruption, but he spotted footprints in the dirt. He looked left and right, then ran down the path, calling out every few steps.

If his memory served, the path led to a fishing spot in a stream-fed pond not too far away. Was it possible Paul had gone there for real fishing when his shows hadn't proved enough excitement? Jude hoped so.

"Mr. C—" The name halted on his lips as he rounded the

corner to see him standing at the edge of the pond. It looked exactly as Jude remembered it, including Paul Crawford standing at the bank.

"There you are." He let out the breath he'd been holding. "We didn't know where you'd gotten to."

Paul didn't move. Didn't even turn around. "Gone fishing."

"Elizabeth and Andi were wondering where you went." Jude approached the man slowly, making sure not to touch him, although the brush around the pond was dense. "Are you ready to head back home, Paul?"

At the sound of his name, the man turned to Jude. There was no recognition there, but he also didn't look angry.

"Are you the police?"

Jude's eyes narrowed. "I work for the ATF. They are kind of like police." He wasn't sure what the man was getting at.

"The yellow snakes." Paul's hand latched around Jude's arm. "Twisting snakes. Bad. Yellow. Snakes! Don't you see?"

"I'm not sure what you're telling me."

"Police. And those yellow snakes." Paul shook his head, tears coming to his eyes. "Twisting yellow snakes."

Jude took advantage of the man's grip and moved toward the house just as Andi broke into the clearing.

"Dad!"

"Dee girl."

Jude saw the instant her father's words hit her. Tears glistened in her eyes, and she nodded, obviously trying to keep it together. "Yeah, Dad. It's Andi. Let's get you back inside. You can watch your show."

"Okay. Show time." It seemed the mania over the snakes, whatever that had been about, was over now.

Paul followed Andi down the path toward the house, and Jude fell into step behind them, scratching the back of his neck.

The minute they stepped into the Crawfords' back yard,

Elizabeth rushed down the steps toward them, holding back her own tears. She mouthed the words *thank you* to Jude and helped Paul up the steps.

Andi stayed behind, seeming to need a minute to take in all that had happened.

"He's safe, Dee." He held back the part about Paul's fixation with the police.

She rounded on him. "Yeah, but what if something *had* happened? I mean, you're one guy and there's the rent-a-cop out there. My parents need protection. I thought you were on this."

Her anger seared him, and he held up his hands, palms facing out. "Whoa, calm down, tiger." He could tell the minute the words slipped from his lips that they were the wrong ones.

"You do *not* get to tell me to calm down."

"You're right, I don't." He cut her off. "I'm sorry. I just mean that it looks like your dad just...wandered off." He didn't add that if it had been the men he was searching for who'd lured him from the house, they wouldn't have left Paul to wander. His fate would have been much worse.

Andi took in a breath and then another, her fisted hands finally releasing at her sides. "You're probably right."

"I'm sorry. I don't think I caught that." He leaned forward as if hard of hearing.

She pushed him back, her palm flat on his T-shirt. He saw her gaze dart to his chest and the heat that inflamed her cheeks right after. "Sorry I interrupted your workout." Her gaze lifted to his.

"This is what I'm here for."

"Finding my dad when he wanders off?" Her smile distracted him for a moment.

"Keeping an eye on th-things." Her lips pressed together as he watched. *Deep breaths, man.* "Just doing my job."

"Then make sure you do." Her hard tone surprised him. "I

go into work tomorrow, and I need to count on the fact that you're watching them. That someone is."

This wasn't the teen girl he'd had a crush on so many years ago. She was a young woman who cared deeply for her family and expected him to do the same. He respected her for that. "I will, Andi. I promise. But can you do something for me?"

Her eyes narrowed.

"Stay at the firehouse unless you're on call. No errands, or breaks outside, or anything like that. Got it?"

Her hands fisted again, this time finding their way to her hips. "You can't tell me what to do, Jude Brooks."

There was a fine line between defiance and flirtation, and he wasn't sure which way she was leaning. Her gaze flickered over his chest before it snapped back to his eyes.

From his experience, nothing good came of having divided intentions. He was here as a friend, or he was here as an ATF special agent focused on her safety. He knew what the book would say—keep it professional. And that's what he'd do.

"True, I can't tell you what to do," he conceded. "But it's not just me. It's your boss too. We all need you to stay safe. That means you stay at the firehouse."

If her eyes had been flames, she would have made him combust right there, but it was better this way. He couldn't let old feelings distract him. Or new ones.

Instead, he offered a polite smile—the same kind he gave older ladies at the grocery store—and headed back to his trailer.

12

A ndi rested her feet on the worn coffee table in the firehouse common room, a book in her hands. The beginning of her twelve-hour shift had started by feeding the endlessly hungry and annoyingly loud Ashes, followed by meetings, training exercises, and a quick callout to the north side of town for a kitchen fire that had almost gotten out of hand.

Since then, nothing had happened.

On the one hand, Andi was glad. No calls meant no one was in danger. On the other, it also meant she wasn't able to prove herself to Amelia or the chief. She could only do so many workouts. Only so many training exercises. Nothing tested her abilities like real-life experiences.

"What ya reading, Probie?" Charlie flopped onto the couch next to her, sending up a puff of dust.

"The Handbook." She brushed at her pant leg. "Ick. Doesn't anyone clean around here?"

"Isn't that what probies are for?" Zack turned around at the table to give her a wink.

"I'd have thought being one month into your status as firefighter would have made you sympathetic to me, Stephens."

He laughed. "Can't be taking it easy on you. They sure didn't on me."

Andi buried her nose in the book, but her thoughts were anywhere but on the manual. She didn't want them going easy on her. She wanted to work for her spot on Truck. To show she was not only ready but an asset.

Yet she'd failed so spectacularly when she'd rushed into that house the other day to save *a cat.*

Every day, someone teased her about that. Every. Day. Sometimes it seemed like her skills would never be enough. Her coworkers, her family...Jude, would never see her as an equal.

The words blurred on the page as her mind went back to her conversation with him the day before. He doubted her. Thought he had to protect her. *Stay where it's safe.* Her teeth clenched. He'd better be at her parents' house now, keeping an eye on them. Her mom had taken an extra day off work—a shock to Andi, since her mom *never* took time off work—but that didn't mean her family was safe.

She picked up her phone and opened a message to Jude.

The alarm went off, followed by, "All call. Truck 14. Rescue 5. Ambo 21. Reported apartment fire."

Andi bolted to her feet. A rush of adrenaline shot through her. It was go time.

Charlie grinned, perhaps at her haste, but he joined her in a light jog toward the gear room. They needed to suit up and be ready to go within minutes, especially with an apartment fire. Andi knew from her training that the potential for the fire to spread from apartment to apartment was great if the building was older, and that spelled trouble.

"Ready, Probie?" Ridge stood at the truck, gear on and

flashing a smile. He had enough confidence in his abilities to fuel the truck.

"You know it." She climbed in past him.

The truck left moments later, sirens blaring. The radio chatter clued her in to the apartment complex in question, and she thought she knew it by the location. If so, it was an older one.

Her mind filled in the blanks about procedure and what to do on arrival, but the moment the truck pulled up, everything fled in the face of the yellow-orange flames devouring the top floors of the complex.

"We've got reports of civilians on the floor below the blaze. A young girl and her grandmother. They are top priority." Chief James's expression was grim. "We're shorthanded today with Logan out. So Stephens, Crawford, I want you going in with Benning. Take his lead." He turned and barked out more orders to the rest of the crew.

"You two. With me." Charlie pulled on his face mask and headed toward the building.

Andi tasted the staleness of the mixed air from her tank as she followed Charlie inside the burning building. It felt as if every moment had prepared her for this one. Her first real rescue—no cats involved.

They barged into the stairwell and attacked the steps toward the fourth floor.

"Shoulda done more cardio."

She caught Zack's muttered words and smiled to herself. She was made for this.

Charlie slowed at the landing on the fourth floor marked by a red 4 painted on the wall next to the door. He held up a hand and motioned them back.

Andi knew he was intentionally making space for a blowback of fire should it have already reached this floor. According to the chief, they were a go, but Charlie was always cautious. Still, her foot tapped. They had to get to the victims. Now.

The door swung open with no sign of flames, and the three headed in.

"Stephens, check the doors on the left. Crawford, take the doors to the right."

"Copy." She and Zack spoke at the same time.

Andi was making her way toward the first door when she noticed cracks in the drywall above them. Smoke seeped out but she saw no flames—yet. The fire was bearing down, and they were running out of time.

The first door she opened led into a sparse apartment. "Eastside Fire Department, call out!" Her shout disappeared into the darkness, but no one came.

She moved to the next door. Then the next.

By the third door, a wave of dizziness hit her. She blinked, trying and failing to get a deep breath. The reading on her pressure gauge said she had plenty of air left, but something felt off.

She was about to radio in when the floor-to-ceiling window at the end of the hallway shattered, scattering thoughts of her equipment. They needed to find the girl and her grandmother and get out of there. Nothing could get in the way of that.

Andi saw Zack at a door ahead of her, and she rushed to the next one. There were only two doors left, and she hoped they were getting close.

This time, when the door flew inward, she caught sight of movement inside. Despite an ever-thickening layer of smoke in the room, Andi spotted two figures huddled in the corner.

"Eastside Fire department. I'm here to help!" Andi took a step inside and swayed. Her vision blurred for a moment, but cleared.

"Come on. We're going to get you out."

The relief on the grandmother's face was all the motivation

Andi needed. She held out her hand, and the young girl, probably seven or eight, rushed toward Andi. The grandmother took longer, but Andi used the time to call in to Charlie and Zack.

They appeared in the door, and Zack helped the grandmother along as Charlie led the way.

"Back through the stairwell," he instructed.

Andi held the young girl to her side, but it was becoming impossible for her to take a full breath. She again checked her O2 meter, but nothing had changed. She tapped it. No change.

They reached the stairwell and took the flights at a fast pace. Zack was all but carrying the grandmother, and the young girl was as eager as they were to escape the blaze. The number 1 on the bottom floor door was a welcome sign of relief, but when Andi went to open the door, she found she could barely use her hand.

"I—I'm just not..." she gasped.

Charlie helped the girl and then Zack with the grandmother through the door. Andi tripped and nearly fell, but regained her footing long enough to stumble outside. Falling to the ground on all fours, she yanked off her mask.

Andi drew in lungfuls of air despite the reek of smoke. Coughed. Drew in more air.

"What's going on, Probie? Can't handle the stairs?" Lieutenant Amelia Patterson's boots filled Andi's vision.

"I—I'm—" Another bout of coughing halted her response. She rolled to her back on the grass. "It was my O2."

"What are you talking about?" Amelia bent down, concern creasing her features.

"I'm pretty sure my tank was empty. Or there's something wrong with my SCBA."

Amelia yanked at the meter. "Readout says it's fine."

Andi ground her teeth, finally able to sit back now that her vision had stopped fading. "My lack of oxygen would say differently." She flinched at the tone she'd just taken with her LT.

"What's going on?" Chief James's imposing shadow fell over Andi.

Her stomach clenched even though he'd directed the question to her LT.

"Says something's wrong with her SCBA. O2 not working."

"As in you had no air up there?" His gaze collided with Andi's.

"Only for part of it. The meter said it was good. I tried to call in, but things went sideways and I knew we needed to get them out."

"That was dangerous."

Andi caught Macon's concern despite his quick attempt to cover it. Was he thinking about the meeting he'd had with Jude?

"It doesn't mean anything. Just equipment malfunction." She pushed to her feet but swayed. Amelia gripped her upper arm, and Andi caught the barest hint of worry. Likely all she'd see from the hard woman.

"Keep your SCBA gear out. I want Ridge to check it when we get back to the house."

She nodded.

"Good work, Crawford." Macon spun on his heel and made his way back to the truck. His praise, an anomaly, was overshadowed as Amelia leaned in.

"Next time, don't be a hero. Call it in." The LT let go of Andi, making sure she could stand, and then strode off toward the truck.

Andi looked down at her face mask. The SCBA, or self-contained breathing apparatus, meant the difference between life and death. It's why they were checked so regularly. Was it possible someone had tampered with it? No, Andi didn't want to go there. The firehouse was safe. Besides, she'd told Jude she could take care of herself, and she *could*.

She *had*.

This was nothing more than a faulty part. Or so she hoped. They would find out soon enough.

Andi checked in on the young girl and her grandmother, happy to hear they would suffer no lingering effects from the smoke, and joined in the clean-up with the rest of the crew.

Washing away the grime hours later, Andi had to admit she'd cut it too close. Her head hurt, and she still got dizzy if she bent down too fast. Thankfully, the steamy shower eased the ache from her lungs and helped relax the knots from her shoulders.

She'd done good today, as her father would have said. Helped with a rescue that she hadn't screwed up. That had to count for something.

Dressed in jeans and an Eastside Firehouse T-shirt, Andi grabbed her bag and continued to towel dry her hair as she left the showers. Her stomach grumbled at the scent of whatever Eddie was making, and she was debating detouring to the kitchen when she caught the sound of a familiar voice.

She rounded the corner and got a clear view into the chief's office where Macon, Frees, and Jude huddled in a semicircle.

"We're not sure it was a targeted attack on her," Frees was saying. His voice carried through the partially open door and into the hall. Andi moved closer while heat flamed up her neck. They were talking about her.

"It doesn't matter," Jude said. "Andi doesn't know when to stop, and—"

"And Andi can speak for herself." All eyes turned to her. "I'm *fine*. My O2 meter probably just malfunctioned. That's all. There's no grand conspiracy about this."

"It's not a conspiracy." Jude's gaze was ice cold.

"You could have died in that fire." Macon gave her his *disappointed chief* stare.

She ground her teeth. "Yeah, well, the people we rescued could have died too."

"That's not the point." A muscle pulsed in Jude's cheek.

Macon scratched his jaw. "Maybe you should take some time off—"

"No way." The chief had barely gotten the words out when she cut him off, but his look told her he didn't appreciate her tone. "I mean, no thank you, *sir*."

"Andi." Jude took a step toward her.

"This is my job, Jude." She lowered her voice and forced herself to meet his hard gaze, ignoring the fact they'd ambushed her. "You're not going to take that away from me." Stepping back, she met Macon's gaze. "I'll be back for my next shift, Chief."

No one responded.

Andi spun around and made a beeline for the parking lot. She wasn't some helpless girl who needed protection. She was fine on her own, and she would show them that.

Even if she wasn't sure today had been simple equipment malfunction.

13

"Andi, wait up." Jude jogged through the parking lot, but her steps didn't slow. "Hey, wait a second."

His fingers closed around her bare arm, and she jerked away, hair flying as she spun toward him. The scent of strawberries and cream swirled in the air between them, and he caught the flush that tinted her cheeks.

"Let me explain."

"You don't get it." She shook her head. "I don't need this." Her hand motioned toward him, waving back and forth.

"What? Me?"

Her blush deepened. "No. I mean the whole 'gotta protect her' thing. I can protect myself, and I do *not* appreciate you going behind my back to talk to the chief like I don't exist. I mean, don't I get a say in how my life is handled?"

"Hold on." Jude lifted his hands. Her safety was part of his job, but he didn't want to undermine her confidence. "This isn't about you being capable or not."

"Isn't it?" She leaned in, and the sweet scent intensified. Damp hair slipped over her shoulder. "One thing goes wrong— something we can't even tie to what's happening—and suddenly I'm supposed to take a vacation? The last few months of my probationary period are crucial, and I won't have my career ruined by whatever it is you've got going on."

She took a breath, and Jude did the only thing he knew to quiet her. He took her hand. The torrent of words she was set to release seemed to evaporate.

"Just...h-hear me out." The soft warmth of her fingers distracted him, but this wasn't about that. "I didn't come in; the chief called me. He told me that your equipment had malfunctioned, and he and Frees thought it best we talk through strategy."

She opened her mouth to challenge him, and he gently squeezed her fingers.

"I realize now how it must have felt to walk in on that." He should have thought of that before they stood there talking about Andi's life as if she didn't have a say in it. "I'm sorry."

He released her hand, realizing it could signal what he wasn't able to offer her, and shoved both hands into his pockets.

"I'm tired of everyone trying to protect me like I'm some kind of fragile flower." She pursed her lips and dropped her gaze to the asphalt between them.

Andi was one of the strongest women he knew. Jude could see that her show of anger spoke more to what she faced daily—even at home—than to the current situation. It had to be exhausting, always trying to prove something, but procedure constrained him. Best practices and the handbook said she—or anyone involved in the case—was off-limits.

"Dee, I have a job to do and part of that job is making sure you're safe." Her eyes met his. "And that your family is safe."

"I get it."

"Do you?"

She shot him a defiant look that was so like her teenage self he laughed. "Okay, you get it."

Silence descended around them, and he realized that, now that they were done arguing over her protection, he wanted to talk more with her. About anything that wasn't this case.

"Hey, you h-hungry?" A tinge of nerves made his stutter appear, but he brushed it off. It was a meal, nothing more.

"Always," she said with a smirk.

"I skipped lunch. Let's grab some dinner at Backdraft and catch up. No work, just life. It's been too long." With the added bonus he'd be on protection detail tonight personally. He'd make sure she didn't have another close call.

Her eyes narrowed, but then she shrugged. "As long as you're paying, I'm in."

"Fine." He laughed and motioned for her to lead the way.

By the time they sat down at a roof-top booth, Jude was having second thoughts. Was it a good idea for him to take her to dinner like this? It wasn't a date—even if he paid. Definitely not.

But did *she* think it was?

He took a seat facing the door and pressed his elbows on the table. Using the menu as a shield, he thought through the scenario. They were old friends catching up. Friends with history, but that had faded with time. He was digging into a case that might involve her family. It was just food.

All of those things added up to this being decidedly not a date. He was fairly confident Andi would feel the same way, but he'd have to watch it. No accidental flirting and definitely no more hand holding. He couldn't risk such a personal touch again.

"What's good here?" He peered at her over his menu.

"Pretty much everything," she said.

"That's unhelpful."

"I usually do a burger or a salad, but they have some great chicken dishes too. Logan loves their ribs, while Bryce prefers the tri-tip sandwich."

He smiled. That sounded like the twins. Similar but always needing to be different.

"I think tonight is a burger type of night." She set down her menu with a sigh. Exhaustion hunched her shoulders.

Mentally marking his choice, he set his menu down as well. "You okay?"

"What, do I not look okay?" Her half smile was teasing.

"I know you're fine," he prefaced, "but you also had a scare today. Being short on oxygen is no joke."

"It was pretty frightening." The admission came from a place of truth—he could see it in her eyes. "All I could think was that we needed to get the girl and her grandma to safety, but I was also dizzy and close to blacking out. I don't want to repeat that."

His gut churned at the thought of Andi blacking out in a burning building. It made him want to punch something. And hug her. He suppressed both urges.

"Okay, let's put today's events aside. Catch me up on the last few years. What's been going on in your life?"

Andi laughed. "Not much."

"Come on. You used to tell me everything."

"I did." The reminder from the past seemed to loosen her tongue. "I mean, I thought I wanted to be a doctor. I went pre-med and—"

"You were pre-med?"

She dropped her gaze, biting her bottom lip.

The waiter appeared to take their order. When he'd gone, Jude pressed in. "Why the switch to EMT then firefighter?"

"Pre-med became nursing after the first year. I figured it was less schooling to get to a point where I would actually be doing something." She pulled the wrapper off her straw and sucked down a gulp of water. "A friend from class told me about being a paramedic. She worked ambo at the Westside Firehouse while pursuing her nursing degree and told me to look into it. I did, and I decided to go for it."

"Let me guess. So you could work the job even faster?"

A smile curved her lips. "Then firefighter was the next step. You know I don't do well sitting around."

"Andi? Sit around and wait? Never."

She rolled her eyes. "Yeah, I guess not much has changed since high school."

"I wouldn't say that." The words slipped out as his gaze traced the refined lines of her face. "I mean, we're both...older." *Good one, Jude.*

"Yeah, I guess we are. No more summers spent doing nothing but swimming and fishing, right? Gosh, I miss that." She fumbled with the straw wrapper.

"I can't imagine having nothing to do for a full summer. I can hardly go a week without my planner."

"You're still the same, huh, Brooks?"

"What's that supposed to mean?"

Andi held her words, assessing him. "I remember those summers. I'd get these great ideas and tell you, but before you'd say yes to anything, you'd ask for every detail up front. When? Where? How would we get there? How long would it take?" She shook her head, grinning now. "It drove me insane."

"I like to be prepared."

"Then and now, I bet." Her teasing felt like an old pair of sweats. Comfortable and well-worn. Like they belonged.

"Maybe. But I also kept us from some pretty terrible adventures." The moment the words slipped out, he thought of the one adventure he *hadn't* kept them from. The one he regretted the most.

Their eyes met over the table, and the weight of that last summer rose between them like an impossible barrier. One founded by his hasty exit from Last Chance County and built up with years of silence. It was on the tip of his tongue to explain when their food arrived.

Andi hesitated. "Mind if I bless it?"

He nodded and bowed his head. For a moment, Jude felt like they were kids again. Teasing, joking, planning their next trip. Praying over barbecue in the backyard.

Then her prayer shifted to everyone's safety, which brought him back to reality with a cold jolt. This wasn't the past, and he was definitely not a teen anymore. The fate of those he protected, and those he'd failed, weighed like a ton of bricks on his chest.

"I guess you saved us from a few terrible decisions." Andi's light tone brought him back. "Like that hiking trip Hank led."

Her smile helped dislodge the ugly memories from the present, replacing them with happier ones from the past. "You mean the one where every single kid got poison oak?"

She pinched a fry between two fingers. "Didn't everyone call them The Flamingos because of all the calamine lotion they had to use?"

"You're right, they did." Jude's laughter joined hers.

When she spoke again, her humor dissipated. "I missed you when you didn't come back. Especially after everything..."

Regret streaked through him like lightening, sharp and sizzling. He'd thought they'd avoided it, but he couldn't keep it away forever. His decision to never come back to Last Chance County had been a hard choice, but the right choice.

"I was young and—"

"You don't have to explain. I understand. I didn't then, but I think I do now." Her gaze drifted, and he saw the weight they both still carried.

Shared tragedy. It had a way of upending things and reorganizing them. His summers with Grandpa had been some of the best of his life. They hadn't felt real after everything that had happened. He'd forced himself to face up to the reality that life wasn't easy. It was full of disappointment and heartbreak. The only way around it was to be diligent in following the rules.

The last year he'd been here in town had been the summer his faith had shifted too. He hadn't stopped believing, just saw God differently. He had given them a rule book for a reason, and when they strayed from it, people got hurt.

Andi lowered her glass. "I know I said it before, but I'm glad you came back...even if the reason you're here is less than ideal." She dropped her focus to the half-eaten hamburger. "It's nice having you around again."

Worry rippled through Jude at how her words resonated in him. It *was* good to be back, but this wasn't where his life was. He was an ATF agent in San Diego. He was good at his job, and that was why he was here. His job.

Thoughts of Andi as anything more than a woman he was protecting were dangerous. He'd seen firsthand what personal involvement did to people. It led them to make irrational decisions and often meant they went outside of the law. No good came from ignoring the rules and doing whatever he wanted.

Jude took another bite of his steak salad, the flavors he'd enjoyed at the onset now coming off bland as his attention shifted. His goal was nailing Sosa and getting a dangerous drug lord off the street along with his lackeys.

He needed to check in with his team and their progress with the list Elizabeth had given them. Then he needed to—

"Jude?"

He looked up.

"I just asked if it was good." She pointed to the salad.

"Oh, yeah. Really good."

She nodded, and he caught the smear of ketchup that marred her cheek. Everything in him wanted to reach up and wipe it away. If it had been his younger self eating with her, he would have done it in a heartbeat, but they were older now. He was supposed to be smarter now too.

"You've, uh, got some ketchup."

She blushed and wiped at her mouth with a napkin. "Thanks."

His internal awkwardness was bleeding out. He needed to bring it all back around to why they were here, together, and working in close proximity.

"Andi." He tossed his napkin down. "Maybe you should take a few days off."

Her jaw dropped. "Are you kidding? I just told you—"

"I know. I'm not saying you should take a month off, maybe just a week. Give us time to investigate the O2 situation."

"No." She answered without a trace of hesitation. "I get that you're doing your job, but no. It's a crucial time for me at work, and I can't just decide to take a vacation."

He'd expected as much, but the agent in him had to try. "I get that. I'm just concerned for your safety."

"I've got a few days off before my next shift. Won't that work?" Her eyes darted away.

He held back a smile. Why hadn't she said that to start off with? "A few days?"

"Yeah."

"I guess that's better than nothing. But, Andi." He waited for her to meet his gaze. "Be careful when you go back."

The hard line of her lips widened into a breathtaking smile. "I always am."

14

The scent of barbecue and wood fires permeated the evening air as Andi exited her car at home. The burger and fries had satisfied her earlier hunger but left her heart empty.

Dinner with Jude had left her wondering what his real thoughts were. The ones he kept under wraps as he did his ATF agent-thing. She saw the war he fought with himself—asking her to take time off at a crucial juncture, but also knowing that she wouldn't. Relying on their history to guide his thoughts of her.

She did the same with him. But when she'd said she knew him, the words had felt like a lie. He was the same—cautious and by the book—but he was also different. More handsome, for one thing. With a commanding presence educated by keen insight. He noticed things that most men overlooked. And he was kind.

Grown-up Jude Brooks was everything a girl dreamed of in the man she wanted to marry.

Andi blushed as she stood alone in the driveway. It was a ridiculous thought, but it was true. She'd been in love with him at one point. Then again, when a seventeen-year-old paid a fifteen-year-old girl any kind of attention, what else was bound to happen?

Andi flopped against her car, face to the sky. She let out a breath and moved her head from side to side to alleviate tension in her neck and shoulders. She'd be lying to herself if she ignored the way old feelings resurfaced. How the sight of him caused her stomach to clench and her heart to pound. But the timing was off.

Not only was her family in danger but this was also a critical moment in her career as a firefighter. Distractions wouldn't help.

God, I need some direction here.

It felt petty to consider her career alongside her family's safety, but she couldn't live in fear. Bryce and Logan wouldn't if they knew the full extent of what was going on. And her mom seemed content to go about her life as normally as she could.

While Jude meant well by asking Andi to take time off, he didn't know the uphill battle she'd fought to get where she was. A vacation—or a desk position—right now would be a death warrant for her career. It would be interpreted as weakness, and someone else—maybe even Izan—was bound to take the opportunity. Then where would she be? Back on the ambulance. All her hard work down the drain.

No. No threat or fear would get in the way of her job on Truck. This was her chance, and she was taking it.

Her gaze shifted to her parents' house, where lights shone into the ever-growing darkness. She caught sight of the unmarked car, and some of her earlier tension eased knowing they were watched. Protected. Her mother's car was absent from the house, and she assumed her father and his nurse were the only ones there.

Andi changed directions and headed for the front walk.

The steps felt familiar under her tennis shoes, and she unlocked the door with her key like she had for so many years.

"Hello? Becca? It's Andi."

"In the kitchen."

Andi followed the scent of garlic and onions and found Becca at the stove making spaghetti. She was in her early fifties and had worked as an in-home nurse for the last ten years, most of them spent with her father.

"Hey." Andi eyed the thick slices of garlic bread. "That looks good."

"Are you hungry? This should be done in about ten minutes."

"No." Her gaze flickered to the bread. "Well, maybe a piece of bread. I already ate, but it looks so good."

Becca beamed with pleasure. "Why don't you go talk with your father? I'll save you a few slices."

"Thanks. I think I will."

Andi wandered into the living room, where a show played on the television. Her father only watched fishing shows these days, but fishing had always been one of his passions. It came in fourth place after his devotion to God, family, and his job as a surgeon.

A familiar ache took up residence in her chest as she watched her dad from the doorway. He had a lure in one hand, turning it over and over as he rocked slowly in his chair, eyes on the screen.

He was a shadow of the man she'd known growing up, the one who got up at five to run with her mom. Who never missed one of her softball games and always insisted on pizza and ice cream on Friday nights.

"Hey, Dad." Andi took the chair next to him. "How are you doing?"

"Fishing." His eyes never left the television.

"I thought we could talk for a little bit." She watched to see if anything registered on his features, but his eyes remained fixed to the screen. "I'll talk and you can watch your show."

She did this sometimes, coming to speak with her father when things were cloudy for her. He didn't respond often, but the unburdening of her heart was usually what helped the most.

"So, Jude's back in town. You saw him at the hospital." The reminder was superfluous, but she gave it anyway. "I—it's hard to see him. Good, but hard. I mean, we're both grown-ups now, and he's this important ATF agent and I'm just a probationary firefighter."

She sighed, leaning back in the chair.

"He's kind of the same, though. In some ways. Still kind and still...handsome." There was that blush again. Her father's gaze stayed unmoved. "I think I still like him, but I can't afford the distraction right now. I *have* to pass my probationary period. How else am I supposed to compete with everyone? You know Mom's practice has grown, and your career was filled with so many commendations and achievements I can't keep track. Then there's Logan and Bryce—they had no trouble stepping into the roles they wanted on Rescue and Truck, and I'm just... floundering. Kind of like that fish."

She pointed to the screen, where a man wrestled to haul in a decent-sized bass. It flopped back and forth, vacillating between fighting the line and giving in. If she gave in and accepted the safe route, she'd lose something important. Perhaps the respect of her family.

Tears threatened to fall as she considered her situation. She knew her feelings went deeper than the job. So deep, in fact, she wasn't sure anything could span the divide she felt between herself and the rest of her family.

"Dee girl." Her father's warm hand rested on hers.

"Dad?"

"Don't cry, my girl." His eyes looked clear, and he reached

up to wipe the solitary tear that had fallen. "Don't cry, my beautiful girl."

Her heart broke at this rare moment of clarity from her father. She wanted to know so many things. What he thought about the situation she was in. What he thought about Jude. What he wanted her to do. But as quickly as the fog had cleared, it rushed in again.

"Fishing at the log. The log..."

More tears threatened, but she fought them back. They might upset her father, who was now focused on his show again. He'd mentioned their favorite fishing spot from when she was a child, but she was certain he didn't know what he was saying anymore.

"Dinner's about ready." Becca popped her head into the living room, looking between Andi and her father. "Want me to make you a plate?"

"No, thanks." Andi turned her back on the woman and wiped her tears. "I'm going to head to bed early. Thanks, though."

"Here's that bread, just in case you get hungry."

Andi accepted the foil-wrapped package from the woman with a forced smile and left the house in a whirl of Italian scents and sadness. She hated seeing her father disappear like that. She wanted his opinion now more than ever.

Soft strains of music floated through the night as she descended the steps of her childhood home.

"Jude?" His name slipped out as she caught sight of him sitting at a round metal table for two outside the airstream. He held a guitar, fingerpicking a complex melody.

"It's a nice night."

She came closer, the emotions of moments before still clouding her judgment. "I guess it is. You still play?"

His eyes didn't quite meet hers as his fingers plucked at the strings. "It relaxes me."

"Yeah." It was all she could manage.

"You okay?" Jude's fingers stopped moving. He shifted to place the guitar in a case at his feet and gave her his full attention.

"I'm..." Her thoughts trailed back to the confession to her father. About Jude. About her family. Things she wasn't willing to admit to the man in front of her. "I'm fine."

Her gaze snagged on a car a few blocks down the street. A dark-red four-door, driving slowly their way. She didn't recognize it.

"That's the most *not fine* statement I've ever heard, Dee."

Her attention shifted back to him. "I'm fine. I just..." She wrapped her arms around herself, the bread sending up tantalizing scents of garlic and butter. "I miss talking to my dad—the real him—whenever I want. You know what I mean?"

His shoulders stiffened, and she instantly regretted her hasty words. She remembered him sharing a little about his father when they were kids. Enough to know they hadn't had a good relationship.

"Sorry. I didn't mean—" The car approached their block. It was driving so slowly. Despite the fact this was a residential area and kids often played in the streets, it was *too* slow.

"It's okay," Jude said, oblivious to her internal thoughts. "You probably remember that my dad is not my favorite subject, but that doesn't mean I don't understand how you feel."

She half listened. This car was giving her the creeps. "Jude, I think—"

"It's okay to miss the person he was. I remember this one time your dad..."

She fully stopped listening as the car passed the unmarked police cruiser and slowed even further as it reached the front of her parents' house. The windows were tinted to an impenetrable black, and everything about it felt wrong.

"Jude." Andi took a step back from the road as the window slid down. "Jude, I—"

Silver glinted in the moonlight as a gun appeared out of the dark interior. Andi froze.

A shot shattered the stillness of the night.

Her thoughts moved in slow motion. A gun. A shot.

Her father inside.

Jude collided with her, yanking her back to reality. They fell behind a row of bushes as another shot spat dirt into the air where she'd been standing. So close. Her heart hammered in her chest.

Jude's muscular arms pulled her close, protecting her. Shielding her body with his. Her hands gripped his arms and breath caught in her throat.

He was going to get shot protecting her!

Screeching tires replaced the stillness after the shots.

She heard tires squeal again, and a sense of urgency took over. She had to stop them before they hurt anyone else. Purpose supplanted her rational thinking.

Andi took a breath, then pushed out of Jude's grip. She jumped from their hiding spot and ran into the middle of the road. The darkness was nearly complete, but she focused on the license plate.

"What are you doing?" Jude yelled as he rushed toward her.

The car was so far away. She was going to track these people down and—

Jude's body collided with hers for the second time as another shot tore into the night.

Her head hit the ground, and the scent of garlic mingled with Jude's cologne filled her nose.

Everything went dark.

15

"Andi? Are you all right? Dee! Dee?"

Her eyes fluttered open, and Jude gasped in a breath. He hadn't meant to tackle her so ferociously, but the glint of a gun out the passenger-side window had made their intent clear. She was a target.

"Oh, man. My head." Her hand went to rest against her temple.

"I'm sorry." Jude reached up and brushed a few strands of hair off her forehead. "Are you all right?"

"I think so."

He shifted back. "Here, let me help you—"

"What's going on? Did I hear shots fired?"

Jude turned to see the undercover police officer emerge from a trail.

"Where were you?" Jude's words held more accusation than he had a right to. He wasn't this man's commanding officer, yet the officer was supposed to be on the job.

"I, uh..." He shifted uncomfortably. "Bathroom break."

"Call Chief Barnes. We need backup here, and I need a partial plate run." He closed his eyes for a second.

"XLU," Andi supplied.

At his look of surprise, she stood up, her hand again going to her head. "I was trying to get the whole plate."

And I was trying to protect you. He bit back the words.

"It was a four-door sedan, burgundy color, and I think it was a Cadillac AT. Will you have them run it?"

"Yeah. Sorry." The man looked at Andi. "You need me to call EMS?"

She shook her head but winced. "I'm a—I was a paramedic. I'll be fine with some ice."

"Got it." The officer looked between them one more time, then rushed to the car to radio in the plate and the incident. Hopefully, backup would be there soon. The shooter could still be in the neighborhood.

"Come and sit. You don't look so good."

Andi glared but let him lead her to a wooden bench at the entrance to the airstream.

"Jude?" A voice called from the porch of the Crawfords' house.

"Just...hold on." He made sure Andi was sitting, then rushed to Paul's nurse. "Hey, Becca, everything okay? You heard the shots?"

She nodded. "Is Andi hurt?"

"Just a minor bump on the head. She's going to be fine. Can you stay in the house with Paul? We're getting more officers on the scene, but he should be inside."

She nodded, her worry clear.

"It's going to be okay." He squeezed her hand.

With a final, worried look, she turned back inside. Jude hurried back to Andi.

"You know Becca?"

"Met her earlier. Now, let me have a look at your head."

"It's fine," she begged off.

"Is it really wise to diagnose yourself?"

"Paramedic training. Remember?"

"Andi."

With a sigh, she shifted to face the light. He gently pulled her hair aside, thankful there was no blood.

"Looks like you're just going to have a big goose egg."

"Thanks, Dr. Brooks." She moved back to face him.

"At least your sense of humor wasn't injured." He lightly gripped her shoulders and felt her subtle trembling. "Are you really okay?"

Her features were hard to see in the dim light from the porch lanterns, but when he leaned close, he could tell the color had drained from her face. She was scared.

"I will be."

"Hold on." He rushed into the airstream and came out with a pack of frozen peas.

"You just have these on hand?" She smirked but quickly applied them to the side of her head. He could see the relief the cold brought.

"I like peas. What can I say?"

She made a face. "Gross."

Silence fell between them, and Jude resisted the urge to pull her close. He'd felt the heat from that last shot as he'd tackled Andi. Way too close for comfort. He wasn't sure what he'd have done had she gotten hurt on his watch.

"Can you repeat the make and model of the car?"

Her request came out of nowhere, but he complied and saw the resulting frown deepen the lines on her brow.

"What is it?"

"I'm not positive, but I think that's the same type of car that hit Logan. The AT part is what I heard him tell Officer Thomas at the hospital."

Jude was an idiot. No wonder he'd been able to recognize the car—it was because he'd been looking up different models of Cadillacs the night before.

"You're right. I think it is."

"Was it the same person?"

"We can't know for sure, but I don't like the odds. I didn't get a good look, but as soon as the officers get here, I'll make sure they know the possible connection."

She dipped her head, but the motion brought her obvious pain.

The adrenaline that had flooded his veins minutes before now dissipated, leaving him weak. His mind replayed images of Andi standing in the road. The shock at seeing the gun appear at the window. Worry he wouldn't be fast enough to reach her. He'd hit her with too much force, but a possible concussion was better than a bullet wound. Every time.

An image flooded his vision. Vanessa lying on the ground. A pool of blood spread out beneath her. Vacant eyes.

Jude dropped his head into his hands. He took a deep, shuddering breath and tried to push the image away. The guilt. Andi wasn't Vanessa. Andi wasn't hurt—at least, not badly. He'd done everything right.

"Jude? What's wrong?" Her hand rested on his back, and the warmth of her touch seeped into his core. The scent of ripe berries clouded his thoughts. He welcomed the distraction.

"Jude?"

"I was just thinking. Remembering." He weighed whether he wanted to tell her about Vanessa. He worried it could change the way she viewed him.

He didn't want to admit he was the kind of leader who let his people get killed. That his subordinates had so little respect for him they went off and did their own thing. Where had he gone wrong that Vanessa paid the price with her life?

They were questions he'd asked himself every day since her death, but he didn't want Andi asking them too.

"You can tell me, Jude." Her hand remained on his back. "Pretend we're kids again."

The corner of his lips tilted up at that. When they were kids, he'd never once wondered how what he told her would shape her view of him. He'd trusted her then. Did he trust her now? "I-it was the last mission I was a part of. A t-team leader."

"This was in San Diego?" Her soft question opened up a way for him to share without being forceful.

"Y-yeah. We w-were..." He paused. Took a breath. Waited. "We were infiltrating this high-security villa, and one of my t-team members—" The words stopped. He didn't want to relive this.

"You don't have to tell me if it's too much."

But he wanted to. Something inside of him wanted her to know. Needed to see how she'd react.

He relaxed his guard, and the words came to him this time. "She was a newer recruit. We all called her Wiley because she was as sneaky as Wiley Coyote—you know, the cartoon?"

She nodded.

"She was a good agent, b-but..." He trailed off. This was harder than he'd expected.

"Was?" She'd picked up on the heart of it.

"Killed in the line of duty. On that mission. She was my responsibility, and I let her get killed."

The words hung between them. One breath. Two.

"She didn't have to die, Andi." His mouth went dry, but he needed the freedom speaking the truth would bring. "She didn't know how to follow rules. I know everyone says I'm a stickler about them, but they save lives. I gave a direct order. I wanted her on our six because I knew she'd protect us. All she saw was a chance at catching a bad guy. She went for him on her own and got herself killed."

"Oh, Jude." Andi's words held no censure. Only shared pain.

"I keep wondering if I messed up and God let me take the fall for it."

"That's not how He works."

Jude shook his head. "Sometimes it feels that way."

Silence dropped between them. He marveled at her faith, so strong despite everything life had thrown at her. He wished he could see God like she did.

"Jude, that's not who God is." She dipped her head to meet his eyes. "Her death is not your fault. It's not your weight to carry."

This conversation was going too deep. He had to shift gears. "Andi, seeing you out there in the middle of the street...it was h-hard."

"I'm sorry. For the loss of your teammate, but I'm also sorry for putting myself in harm's way." Andi dropped her hand from his back to her lap, the other still holding the peas to her head. "All I could think of was getting the license plate. I thought if we had it, we could go after the guys targeting my family. We could end this."

Jude reached out and took her hand. Their fingers laced, and the familiar stab of attraction he'd always held for her made his pulse spike. She'd been pretty at fifteen, but she was beautiful at twenty-eight, and that beauty clouded his judgment.

But it felt right to be close to her and to share one of many heavy burdens he carried. If only for a little while.

"You were doing a brave thing—looking for that plate number. Just don't put yourself in the line of fire again, okay? I don't think my heart can take it." He meant it as a joke, but the subtle widening of her eyes said she had heard it differently.

"I won't do it again. I promise." Her fingers slipped from his hold, and she moved to wrap her arms around him.

The hug took him by surprise, but a part of him welcomed it. It brought back late nights of stargazing, the scent of bonfires, and the taste of sticky-sweet marshmallows. It filled a longing to feel real connection again. Like he had as a teen here in Last Chance County.

Like he'd had with Andi.

Her grip loosened, and he pulled back, but her arms didn't release him. Her face was inches from his. Her eyes wide, lips slightly parted. Just as the hug recalled for him their teen years, being this close reminded him of the one time they'd crossed the line between friends and something more.

The night he'd kissed her and then told her he was leaving.

Jude's heart thudded in his chest at the feeling of her warmth and sweet scent so close. Close enough to bridge the distance and feel her lips under his again.

Warning bells set off the alarm in his head. Kissing her was an action he couldn't come back from. Not as an adult. He pulled back.

"You-you—you'd better get some r-rest." The night air rushed in between them with a needed wake-up call.

He hadn't come back to his summer haven to reignite a teenage fling. He'd come to find Sosa and any connection the Crawfords had to him. So far he'd struck out completely on that front, and now guns were involved. If anything, he was going *backward*.

And Andi was hurt because of him.

His stomach churned. He could have prevented her injury. If he'd secured her in the airstream before going out to see the car's license plate, like procedure dictated, none of this would have happened. Then again, she never would have stood for that. Not that it eased any of the guilt of his reckless behavior or the fact Andi was a major distraction. He had to stop this— whatever this was.

"I guess I probably should go." She stood.

"Good night, Andi." He stayed seated.

He needed to connect with the officers who were arriving, but he also didn't trust himself with her. Only his mind seemed to know that she should leave. If his body had its way, he'd pull her close and kiss her senseless. There would be no coming back from that.

"Good night, Jude. And thanks for saving me."

He nodded once and watched her walk toward her house, though only to make sure she didn't fall.

Saving her? More like he'd endangered her by his lack of focus. It had to stop here and now.

If he truly cared for her, he needed to put the case in front of any attachments he felt. Dig harder into what Elizabeth was keeping from him. It also meant he needed to keep an emotional distance while being in proximity to Andi.

That was proving to be more challenging than he'd expected, but he was a professional. He'd run this by the book, and no one would get hurt.

Especially not Andi.

16

Andi stretched her arms over her head and let out a yawn. Her muscles were sore from the extra hard workout she'd put herself through the day before, and her temple still felt tender where it had connected with the road. With her scheduled time off work coming right after the shooting outside her parents' house, she'd needed an outlet to let the fear and frustration escape. Even after three days she found that no amount of boxing was enough to erase memories.

Today she was going back to work and, while she was glad, her mind kept replaying the appearance of a gun in the car window.

A chill raised the hairs on her arms despite the sweatshirt she wore, but she suppressed the urge to curl up under a blanket. To hide from it all. Instead, she stood up from the couch. This was ridiculous. This fear had to go.

On her way to the kitchen, she paused at the front window to pull the curtains aside. Two marked police cars were parked on the street in place of the one. It felt like their sleepy neighborhood had transformed to ground zero. The day after the shooting, forensics teams had taken what evidence they could, covering every inch of ground between the airstream and the street. Even Chief Barnes had stopped by to see her mother.

While the chaos had calmed, the police presence in front of their homes was still prominent.

She should feel completely confident. And she did...mostly. But it had crossed her mind that if someone were bold enough to take a shot at her, perhaps they had sabotaged her air tank too.

One glance at the clock told her she'd be late if she didn't leave now. Picking up her lunch and purse, Andi headed to her car. Her gaze traveled up and down the street. All clear.

The drive to the firehouse took less time than normal, and Andi arrived fifteen minutes before her shift was scheduled to start.

"Hey ya, Crawford." Jayson gave her a heads-up gesture. "Had to feed your cat the other day." He shook his head as if to remind her of why that was *her* problem.

"You saw the extra cat food?"

"Yeah. Izan pointed it out."

"Then what's the problem?"

He rolled his eyes and walked off toward the kitchen. He'd meant to remind her of her failure, but it lacked the same sting. She'd taken care of the mangy thing, and maybe, just maybe, Ashes the cat was growing on her.

"Andi, can I have a word?"

Andi hadn't even seen the chief come into the hall, but she nodded, her heart pounding. Was he going to put her on leave after the shooting?

"Have a seat." Macon motioned to the chair across from his desk.

She sat, hands clenching in her lap.

"I wanted to update you about your SCBA."

"Oh?" Her stomach twisted.

"You were right for us to withhold judgment. Benning looked at it and he found a faulty part. While I won't say I'm *glad* we have faulty equipment, I can say it's good to know that no one tampered with your gear."

"I agree, sir." She relaxed.

"But, Andi." His look darkened. "I heard about what happened at your folks' house."

Maybe she'd relaxed prematurely. "We're all fine. Mom wasn't even home." She mentally kicked herself. How was that good news when it could mean *she'd* been the target?

"I know. Chief Barnes has apprised me of the situation. Is this a distraction for you? You have my full support if you'd like to take time off." He held up a hand. "And before you turn me down, let me say it will not affect your placement on Truck."

Her eyes narrowed a fraction. Was it possible Jude had told him this was part of her concern? Heat flooded into her at the thought.

"I know you're a dedicated firefighter, which is why I will reiterate the fact that this is not a punishment. It's an option."

Maybe Jude hadn't said anything.

He continued, "I appreciate your enthusiasm. However, your family is facing a lot right now."

"I heard Frees gave Logan and Bryce admin work." She held his gaze. "If they can be here, so can I. After all, it's safer here with all this protection."

He nodded. "If that's your choice, then you're free to go."

"Thanks, Chief." She rushed out of his office and stowed her gear in her locker, turning to rest against it when she was done.

She knew from her mother that Logan and Bryce still didn't know the extent of what was going on. They'd heard about the shooting but thought it was a random attack. How her mother could lie to them, she wasn't sure. But they were both so focused on healing and getting back to the firehouse that they weren't seeing what was right in front of them.

Emerging from the locker room, Andi made her way to the common room in time to see everyone gathered.

"What's going on?" she asked Charlie.

"Look what the cat dragged in." Ridge waved at the entrance.

"Did someone say cat?" Zack grinned.

She ignored him as everyone started clapping. That's when she saw Bryce and Logan hobbling in.

"Let's leave the cats to Andi." Logan's grin was directed at her.

She rolled her eyes and went to greet them. "Glad you guys are here. And healthy." She hugged them.

"We hear *you're* the one dodging bullets." Concern registered on Bryce's face.

"We'll talk later." Andi stepped back to let everyone greet her brothers.

Izan walked in amidst the hugs, but when his gaze collided with Andi's, he flinched. It was an odd reaction she'd never seen from him. As she was about to ask him about it, Jude walked in with a woman at his side.

Andi's stomach clenched at the sight. She wasn't sure why.

No, she knew why. Memories from the night of the shooting flooded Andi's mind. The masculine scent of Jude's cologne— or was that just him? The strength of his arms around her, settling her fears despite the pounding of her heart. The story he'd shared, baring his heart to her.

Then that almost-kiss.

He *had* almost kissed her. Or she'd thought so.

But then he'd been so busy working with the police and running down leads on the car that she hadn't talked to him since. Had she imagined the look of longing in his eyes?

Now he stood next to a woman who looked like a model on

her day off. Gorgeous, but not trying too hard, with long blonde hair and a dazzling smile.

Jude caught Andi staring and looked as surprised as she was.

"Jude, man, good to see you." Bryce slapped Jude on the back and did a double take. A real life, totally embarrassing double take of the woman next to him. "And...friend."

Andi didn't want to admit it, but she wanted Jude to confirm that's exactly who this woman was. A friend. Nothing more.

Logan approached. "Hey, Jude. Good to see you, but why are you here?"

Jude looked back at Andi before he shifted his attention to her brothers. "This is my friend, Penny Mitchell. Penny, Bryce and Logan Crawford."

"Hello, boys." Confidence oozed from every pore.

Andi was going to be sick. Beautiful *and* confident. And was she carrying a gun? Andi's attention narrowed in at the slight bulge at the back of her loose-fitting T-shirt as she propped a hand on her hip.

"Andi?"

The sound of her name distracted her from studying the woman.

"Hey." She joined the group, and Bryce pulled her against him.

"This is our little sis, Andi."

It took one look to see the hearts swimming in Bryce's eyes, but Andi pushed away from his overbearing embrace.

"Hi. Andi Crawford. Nice you meet you..." She looked to Jude, then back. "Penny?"

They shook hands. "Penny Mitchell. Nice to finally meet you. Jude's told me a lot about you."

"He has?" Andi caught the tail end of Jude's sharp look at the woman, but he recovered quickly.

"Andi's an old friend. I mean, a friend from the past. She's n-not old." He swallowed and then shifted his attention to Bryce. "Penny works for a private security firm, and she's working with me on something here."

"I, uh..." Bryce ran a hand across his jaw. "You look really familiar."

"Please tell me you aren't using a line on her," Andi said under her breath.

Bryce's quick jab to her ribs caused Andi to burst into giggles.

"I just mean..." Bryce swallowed. "Were you at the hospital?"

"I've been here a few days." Penny offered a cryptic smile.

"Andi, can I get a word with you?" Jude moved to the side. A light touch of his fingers on her arm sent tingles along her skin.

She followed him outside, and the warmth of the sun wrapped around her shoulders like a comforting blanket. It was a calm morning. She hoped, for the sake of the town, it stayed that way.

"I got some info on the shooter's car."

Her attention snapped to his. "Who was it registered to?"

"It was a rental." He grimaced. "They paid in cash and somehow avoided leaving a credit card on file."

"So there's no way to trace them."

"Not exactly." He pulled out a small notebook. "Chief Barnes had his tech guys look into it and, based on the GPS info the rental company gave them, they can connect the car to several locations. It was at the location where Logan was hit as well as some fast-food places. My team's looking at their surveillance now."

"That's it?"

"Not exactly." She saw the slightest curve of his lip and was momentarily distracted. He said, "Aside from known locations, there was one address in the Grassland Heights community that is unaccounted for. Everything else seems purposeful, but the car went back there multiple times."

"What do you think is there?"

"We don't know. That's why Penny and I stopped by. We're on our way there, but I wanted to check in with you and see if you knew anyone out there. Or...if your mom does?"

She frowned. "I don't. Did you ask her?"

"I did." He worked a muscle in his jaw. "She denied it and left me in the lurch, saying she had to get to a client meeting."

"She's still stonewalling you?"

"Yes. I get it. She's protecting her clients and has a right to—unless I get a warrant—but the list she gave me turned up nothing. No one on there is in the area or is likely to hire a hit—" He cut the words off.

"You think someone was hired to kill me?"

He turned to look back into the firehouse, and Andi followed his gaze. Penny stood in a sea of firefighters, laughing.

"She fits right in, doesn't she?" Andi muttered.

"She's always been like that."

"How do you know her?" She tried for nonchalance, but there was an urgency to her tone. Had he noticed it?

"We went through training together—for ATF. She outdid me on the obstacle course once, and I'll never live it down." He turned back to her. "She's good people. You can trust her, Andi. She's here to keep an eye on your brothers, besides helping me with the investigation."

It was starting to make sense. He'd called in help—but not his team? She was about to ask, but he seemed to make up his mind about something.

"I think someone is trying to scare your mom, and I think she knows who."

Jude's words fell like an anvil between them.

"Do you really think she'd put our safety at risk by not telling you everything?" Andi couldn't comprehend that.

"I'm not sure she thinks she has a choice."

Andi took a deep breath. "I can talk with her—"

"No. Sorry. I wasn't saying this to put you in a difficult position with your mom. I just wanted to keep you informed. Per our agreement." Jude smiled then, and heat pooled in her stomach. "I've got to pull Penny away from the guys." He grinned. "I'll let you know what we find at the address."

He moved to step around her, but she grabbed his arm. "Be careful."

The connection snapped electric between them. Contact it seemed like she needed but knew was dangerous. Her feelings for Jude were growing, but she didn't know how he felt. Could he see her as more than the teen girl he'd known so many years ago? Or was his only focus the job at hand and nothing more?

"I always am. Promise." His words echoed her own, and he grinned, pulling away.

She watched him go, praying he'd hold to that promise, but also praying for direction.

For her and for Jude.

17

"So that was Andi." The teasing was clear in Penny's tone.

Jude kept his gaze on the road. "That was Andi."

"About that—"

"Let me stop you right there. There's no need for..." He searched for the word. "Whatever this is."

"This, my friend, is called you giving me details. You've known her for a long time, right?"

"Yeah." He hesitated, wondering where she was going with this.

"And she's obviously beautiful. Plus she's a firefighter—so cool."

"Are you starting an Andi fan club now?"

"I'd be the second member, because you *clearly* have a thing for her, Book."

"I do not." *That was a lie.*

"You do, and you know it." Penny poked his arm with a pointed finger. "You just need to admit it to yourself. And maybe to her. I see the way you two look at each other. She's clearly interested in you." She said it like a foregone conclusion.

He couldn't help it. He looked over to see if Penny was teasing him.

"What? It's obvious. Her eyes shot daggers at me when we walked in together. I think she might be a little jealous."

"Not with the way you were flirting with her brothers."

"Hey, they're nice guys. And that means something. I work with men all day, so I know what jerks they can be." She laughed. "But Bryce is...nice."

"Bryce, huh?"

"Logan too. Both are very nice. Now, back to Andi."

Jude groaned.

"You like her. Admit it."

"We're on a job, if you hadn't noticed. Going to a house where a suspect might have stayed. We're on the trail of a drug lord. Don't you think that is more important than a crush?"

"Come on, Book. This is not the time to do things 'the right way' or whatever it is you say."

"It's exactly the time." His thoughts supplied the memory of Vanessa lying on Sosa's deck followed closely by an image of Andi, knocked out on the road after getting shot at. If he had a prayer of protecting her, he had to put everything aside to do that. Feelings and thoughts. Desires and longings. It didn't matter when lives were on the line.

"You are zero fun, you know that, right?"

"Just because I won't gush to you like I'm one of your girlfriends does not mean I'm no fun. I just see the value of working the job like I'm trained to. By the book saves lives, Pen. It's a fact."

Penny was silent for a long time as he turned into the Grassland Heights community. They were almost at the house, and he needed them on speaking terms. He didn't think he'd offended her—she had thick skin—but he wasn't sure what she was thinking.

"I get it." Her reply came softer than he'd expected. "I know you haven't exactly had it easy, Jude, but that doesn't mean everything in the ATF handbook is gospel for your life."

He'd called her about Vanessa days after the shooting, and she'd been the exact sounding board he'd needed, but now it felt like his trust was being thrown back at him.

"I'm not saying it is."

"I know." Her voice softened even more, as if she'd caught the undercurrent in his tone. "Okay, we're on the job, so let's be on the job."

He looked over, and she flashed her typical confident grin. Back to the same old Penny he'd known in training.

"Okay," he agreed.

"Let me update you on what my contacts sent in." She shifted back to work easily while Jude still pushed away stray thoughts. "I got a call last night from a guy one of our agents teamed up with last year. He operates out of Denver and confirmed your intel about The Brothers." Penny almost bounced in her seat. "He mentioned another name. Does Fausto mean anything to you?"

"This is turning into a repeat of Sosa's early days."

"I don't know much about the guy, but seems he's in bed with some nasty friends. What's his history?"

"Diego Ruiz Sosa. Once a sniper and hitman in Mexico, he set his sights higher. Wanted to run his own drug cartel." Jude knew the man's background inside and out. "As the story goes, he grew tired of being used as everyone else's weapon, so he staged his own revolution. Used his sniper skills and took out the original leader of the Ruiz cartel."

"Wow."

"Yeah, he's ruthless. He basically stepped into the gap

created by the execution and found himself at the top. With a lot of guys to support him."

"And this Fausto guy?"

"He did jobs for Sosa before he was *Ruiz* Sosa. I can't believe he's in the country though—security is tight, and facial recognition should have caught him crossing the border."

"He didn't cross then," Penny said. "He probably got smuggled in, and someone paid off Mexican authorities to look the other way."

Jude sighed. "You're probably right." He consulted the GPS and made one last turn.

"Do you think this Fausto guy is here for this?" There was an edge of worry to Penny's words.

"If by 'this' you mean the targeting of Andi's family, I don't know. It's the first I've heard of him with Sosa again. He's been out on his own for years, and if they are teaming up it speaks of desperation—but for which one?"

"Or is it both?"

Jude shrugged in reply, though he considered Penny's words. Fausto was a notorious gun for hire—or, more accurately, an explosives expert for hire. Purely mercenary. The Brothers were more loyal to Sosa. The combination of all of them together spoke to something bigger going on.

"What about the mom? Has she spoken up about why they are being targeted?" Penny said.

"No." The house they were looking for would be on the right. Jude slowed. "I think she's protecting someone—but I don't know who. I've requested a full list of her clients, not just the people she's willing to show me, but she's refused. It's like she wants to help but..."

"You think this is about her family? That she's protecting them?" Penny spoke his thoughts.

"Perhaps. With Logan's accident and then the shooter targeting Andi, it's the only thing that makes sense. I need her to open up to me—but a mother protecting her children is a force to be reckoned with."

"Isn't that the truth?" Penny's gaze followed the line of overgrown trees. "This area looks rough."

It didn't take much to see that this section of the community had been long since neglected. Houses were few, but those they saw looked vacant. He took extra care to check for movement in the darkened windows and on neighboring rooftops as they drove past.

"Why does it look like this place is deserted?" Penny asked.

"I have no idea, but what better place for criminals to hole up?"

He caught Penny's nod in his peripheral vision and slowed to park as the house came into view. It was one story, with chunks of siding missing and vines growing through most of the screens in the front windows.

"Charming." Penny pulled out her gun and checked it. "We splitting up or—?"

"No, let's go in together." He didn't like the thought of them being separated without a team to back them up. There was no telling who could still be in the house, though Jude guessed their shooter was long gone.

"Got it, Boss."

They exited the car, and Jude pulled out his firearm. Making sure a round was chambered even though he kept the safety on, he nodded Penny forward.

The news Penny had given him about three of Sosa's men in Denver had Jude rattled. He tried not to let it distract him as they approached the cockeyed front door, but his mind leapt all over the place. First to where Sosa might be holed up, then back to Andi. Then to Elizabeth and his own frustration at why she wasn't willing to tell him more. Then back to Andi.

At Penny's nod, he opened the door. He stepped swiftly inside and panned to the left. Clear. She cleared to the right.

Their movements were second nature, honed through hours of training, and the familiarity of it calmed his nerves.

"Clear." Penny moved through the house.

"Clear." He scanned the area for trip wires before moving down the narrow hallway until it opened up to a living room. He cleared that, then turned back to her. "I don't think anyone is here."

"Agreed." Penny opened a door that led into complete darkness. She shivered. "You want to check the basement, and I'll clear the rest of the rooms up here?"

"How thoughtful of you."

She grinned. "You know I hate spiders. And basements."

He rolled his eyes and turned to the basement stairwell. "Okay, call out when you're done—or if you need help."

He pulled out his flashlight and held it under his gun hand. The steps creaked as he descended. While his mind stayed on the task at hand, a part of him whispered Penny's words back to him.

She's clearly interested in you.

Was Penny right? The thought of Andi being interested sent a shiver up his spine, but he mentally pushed it off so he could scope out the basement as it slowly came into view.

It was one big room with HVAC set up in the middle. Dust covered every surface, which helped him see footprints at the base of the staircase before he'd even gotten there. Someone had been down here.

Jude heard the rhythm of his heart in his ears. No one was here now. Logically, it wouldn't make sense. The Brothers and Fausto would never stick around long in a house they could be traced to.

He trailed his light over the immediate surroundings. The footprints wound around the HVAC and led out of sight. Hookup spaces for laundry were to the right, but not much else. It looked like he had to go around the unit in the middle.

Upstairs, the floors creaked. Penny was still clearing the space. There were closets and rooms she'd have to look in and, with any luck, they'd find something left behind that could definitively tie the men in question to the car and the shooting.

Jude took one step around the heating and air conditioning unit and froze. Booted feet came into view on the ground in front of him. He took another step and legs appeared, then a torso. The body lay face down, arms by the side.

Jude pulled out his phone and typed in Chief Barnes's number. He was about to press Call when footsteps thudded down the stairs.

"Jude! Jude!"

"Over here. I found a body." Jude knelt down near the man's head. He pulled out a napkin and was about to reach into the man's pocket when Penny's shout stopped him.

"Don't touch it!"

"What?" Jude turned to her and saw the alarm on her face through the dim light of his flashlight.

"Jude, we have to get out of here. Now."

"There aren't that many spiders—"

"This isn't about spiders. The whole place is rigged to blow!"

It took a moment for Jude to register what she was saying, but the urgency in her movement kicked his mind into gear.

"Come on!"

The house was rigged to explode. He looked down at it now and saw two small wires leading away from the body. He wouldn't have seen them if he wasn't looking. Then what? An explosion caused by moving the body? "Hold on, Penny."

She huffed. "No holding on. I may not be a bomb expert, but the wiring I saw upstairs is enough of a warning for us to get out of here. Now."

His gut was telling him what she said was right, but he needed to know who this guy was. DNA would do that if he was in the system, but how to get that? Any movement to the man could trigger something.

"Jude, we need to leave. Right now."

He knew she was right. The handbook would have said as much—*with evidence of explosive devices clearly visible, make a hasty exit and call the bomb squad.*

He pulled out his phone and snapped a photo. "Okay, let's go."

Penny raced up the stairs, Jude fast on her heels, but as they rushed toward the front door, Jude slowed. "Do you see that?"

Penny paused at the front door, glancing at where Jude pointed. Piles of crumpled newsprint shifted with the breeze to reveal a small camera blinking red.

The light went out.

"Get out!" Everything slowed. Jude's legs wouldn't move fast enough. He was running through mud to the door.

Penny yanked on the handle and sent it flying back just as he collided with her back, pushing them both out of the door and into the warm afternoon air.

The next second, searing heat followed by a concussive boom pounded his back like a fist. They went flying into the air, chased by a ball of fire. Jude collided with the ground as another explosion erupted behind him, sending flames to devour the surrounding dry brush. It instantly ignited into a dangerous wall of flames.

His last conscious thought was of Andi and if he'd ever see her again.

ndi's heart threatened to pound out of her chest. She gripped the edge of her seat to keep from falling as Ridge pulled the firetruck around another bend toward Grassland Heights.

The same area Jude had said he and Penny were going to.

"Listen up." Lieutenant Patterson sat in the front seat of the firetruck. She received radio communication channel assignments from dispatch and shouted them out. "The admin channel is GREEN4. The command channel is—"

Andi listened to the frequency channels, making the proper adjustments to her radio, but her mind strayed to Jude. The call had reported an explosion and resulting fire.

Had Jude...

She pressed her lips together and tried to swallow past the dryness in her mouth. She wouldn't let herself think it.

Ridge pulled the truck to a stop, and Andi raced down the steps. A decrepit building consumed by flames was ahead of her, bits and pieces of wood scattered everywhere. Lights from Ambo 21 circulated red and blue, diverting her attention from the flames to the forms on the ground where Trace and Izan bent over them.

Jude! His brown leather shoes. His black jacket. Her gaze shifted to Trace and saw blonde hair. Penny.

Andi started toward them, but her radio crackled to life.

"Crawford, Stephens, I want you on hose. We need to douse this thing. Surrounding area is too dry. There's a high probability of spread." Lieutenant Patterson barked orders like a drill sergeant. "Get to it."

But Jude needed her. Izan had completely spaced it during their callout with the man who'd overdosed. Was he really at his best?

Zack hauled the hose out, and his gaze connected with hers through his face mask. Divided didn't begin to describe how she felt.

"Crawford, is your radio broken?" Amelia asked.

"No, Lieutenant."

"Then get moving."

"Copy that." Any argument died on Andi's tongue. She was on Truck—right where she wanted to be—not on Ambo. This was her job now and, no matter how badly she wanted to know if Jude was all right, she needed to trust the paramedics to do their job.

The hose wrestled against her, heavy and unruly, as she stepped in behind Zack, aiming the spray over the flames. Her gaze drifted back to where Jude still lay on his back on the ground. Penny was sitting up, a hand to her head, but Jude was still down. He should be awake now, unless—

"Andi, wrong way." Zack played tug-of-war with the hose, directing the spray toward the heaviest areas of heat.

"Sorry."

Radio chatter indicated the structure was unstable. They needed to back away. If it went down, a gust of extremely hot wind would rush out to flood the area with embers and ignite the dry grass around the house, sending the blaze wide.

"Stephens, Crawford, get the surrounding grass. Stat!"

"On it," Zack said.

"Got it," Andi said.

Andi helped him redirect the spray so it drenched the dry areas, hoping it would be enough. If Izan and Trace didn't get Jude and Penny out of there soon, it could be bad for them as well. They were too close to the danger radius.

"Why aren't they moving?"

"Huh?" Zack asked.

Andi ground her teeth. Somehow she'd left her mic on. "Nothing."

"Crawford, keep your focus on the fire. Got it?" Lieutenant Patterson was suddenly standing next to her. The fire reflected in her eyes was no match for her searing expression.

"Right. Sorry."

"Don't make me think you're not cut out for this job."

The words were like ice despite the heat. "I—I won't. I just thought that they should move Jude and Penny in case of collapse."

"Keep your eyes on the fire. Last warning or I'll send you back to Ambo, where it seems you really want to be."

"Copy, Lieutenant."

Andi shifted her attention back to the fire as the first pieces of the roofline fell away in chunks. It was going down. She resisted checking on Jude, knowing procedure stated Izan's next move was to get him to the hospital. She needed to trust he would do his job. Just as she needed to do hers.

"Let's move—"

"That way?" Andi pointed to the right side of the fire, and Zack smiled.

"Read my mind, Crawford."

They moved as a team, shifting several feet north of the fire to get a better angle, careful not to let the powerful stream of water take away the supporting joists and cause a collapse sooner.

They were beginning to make a difference. Zack's grin said he saw it too.

The small victory pulled her back to reality. She was a firefighter. She'd done everything in her power to move beyond being a paramedic. Would she really let one incident derail that? She couldn't let this one moment define the rest of her life, no matter how much she cared about Jude.

If her LT was serious about putting her back on Ambo, Andi needed to show her that would be a mistake. She needed to give her all to this. To be the best firefighter she could be.

"Nice job, you two," Amelia said over the radio. "It's almost out on that side. Shift southward."

They complied, and Andi smiled to herself at the change in her LT's tone. Good. Amelia needed to see that Andi could do this. Would do this.

HOURS LATER, ANDI DROPPED HER BAG ONTO THE FLOOR BY HER front door and headed for the fridge. As she pulled out a sparkling water, her wet hair fell over her shoulder. Even after washing her hair two times with her favorite strawberry shampoo, she could still smell the smoke.

She reached for a sleeve of chocolate mint cookies in her cupboard next to the sink. The tasty pasta dish Eddie had whipped together from the leftover chicken he'd roasted the day before had filled her up, but she needed something sweet to distract from the challenges of the day.

She'd almost left work to go to the hospital to check on Jude, but the thought had died before it grew roots. She was a firefighter, and that meant her duty was to the firehouse and her shift. Especially during her probationary period.

Instead, she'd settled on a text to Charlotte to settle her anxious thoughts. Andi had wanted to know more than what Charlotte could legally share as a nurse, but her friend alluded to the fact Jude would be released before Andi's shift was over.

When she left the firehouse, a call to the hospital had confirmed Jude's release, so she'd come home only to find his car missing from the driveway.

Headlights flashed across her front window. She sank into the couch, and her stomach bottomed out. Thoughts of the gunman stalking her caused her pulse to spike, but her worry cleared quickly. Police were staked outside. She was safe.

Still, she went to the window and peeked out just as Jude emerged from the car. He moved slowly, like he was in pain. The thought of a snack disappeared as she rushed outside to meet him.

He glanced over and she slowed, suddenly hyperaware of her old sweats and T-shirt. "Hey. How are you?" Her chest tightened as he drew closer.

"I feel like a house fell on me." He shrugged, but the action made him wince. "It's just a mild concussion."

She caught sight of the takeout bag in one hand and his ripped up leather jacket in the other.

"That's seen better days." She pointed to the scorched holes.

"This thing saved my life is what it did." He offered a grin. "Wanna sit?"

"Sure." She followed him to the chairs they'd sat in just a few nights prior. She checked the position of both unmarked police cars to assure herself they were safe to be out here. "Do you need anything? Aspirin? An ice pack? Dessert?"

He chuckled, the sound soft and low. "I'll be fine with this burrito."

She watched as he unwrapped one end and took a bite. Her gaze went back to the jacket. It had saved his life. Her stomach churned with the thought of what could have happened if he hadn't been wearing it.

No. She cared about Jude, but her feelings couldn't go beyond that. At first, she'd thought maybe they could. That maybe he'd come here to rekindle something from the past. It was an overly romantic notion she definitely didn't have time for. She knew that, but it *had* crossed her mind.

Today changed that.

When they'd arrived at the burning house, Andi had found herself caught between the tug of her duty and the pull of her emotions. She'd nearly abandoned her team for Jude, but where would that have gotten her? Izan had done his job—well, according to Trace—and she'd done a good job on the fire with Zack.

"You're quiet." Jude's words broke into her thoughts.

"Today was intense."

"Tell me about it." He wiped his mouth with a napkin and pulled a chip out of the bag. "You guys did a good job putting the blaze out."

"You were unconscious for most of it."

"Logan stopped by to see me at the hospital. Gave me the details."

"He did?" She knew her brother wasn't back on active duty, but she hadn't seen him leave the firehouse either.

"Yeah." Jude dug for more chips. "Said it went well."

"I guess."

The fact her brother had gone to see Jude when she hadn't distracted her. Was there a chance Chief James would have let her visit if she'd asked him? A request like that felt like a sign of weakness—one Lieutenant Patterson would capitalize on.

"There was a body in the basement."

"What?" Her attention snapped back to Jude.

"Dead. I wanted to turn it over, but thankfully Penny caught me first. We think it was rigged to blow the house."

"If you didn't touch it, how did the house explode?"

Jude crunched another guac-laden chip before answering. "I saw a camera as we were leaving. I think someone was watching."

"They weren't trying to kill you, then?"

"I don't know. Maybe it was a game to see if we'd miss the trap. Either way, while it makes little sense, I'm happy they didn't pull the trigger before we got out."

Me too.

Andi held the words on her tongue. She wasn't sure why she didn't speak them. They were true, but something about admitting she cared for him felt far too intimate. Sitting here tonight, while the bistro lights glowed above them and Jude's musky scent reached out to her from where he sat, had her senses on overload.

She shivered.

"Here." He handed over the tattered jacket, and she put it on even though it smelled like a housefire.

She needed to get them refocused on the case. It would sober her up, and maybe she could help him think things through. "Who do you think the dead body was?"

"I honestly don't know." He shook his head, and she saw his gaze travel to her parents' house. "Your mom came by the hospital too."

"She did?" She took his change in subject in stride. "What did she say?"

"Not much. I think she felt bad. Gave me her *complete* client list—the one I've been asking for since I got here."

Andi heard a note of bitterness in his words. Why wasn't her mother fully cooperating with Jude? What did she have to hide?

"I sent it to my team, and they called back within an hour.

While I was still in the hospital. The nurses loved that."

"I'm sure you flashed that badge of yours and charmed them into letting you take the call."

"How did you know?" His lips curled up on one side.

"What did they say?"

He assessed her. His gaze traced over her face, causing her cheeks to heat, before he crumpled up the takeout bag and pulled his chair closer to hers. She wasn't sure why at first, but then he lowered his voice to answer her. "Have you ever heard the name Camilo Rojas?"

"No." She searched her memory, but it didn't sound familiar. "Should I have?"

"I wouldn't expect it, but I had to ask."

"Who is he?"

"He's doing twenty to life in the federal prison, ADX Florence." A muscle in Jude's jaw worked. "Your mother represented him in one of the few cases she's ever lost. She's got an incredible record."

Andi nodded. She was all too aware of her mother's prowess as a defense attorney.

"My tech guy said there was an anomaly in the data of that case. What he means is that something weird happened with the case based on the information we have. And he changed his not guilty plea to guilty one day after your father's car accident."

Andi's breath caught. "Is there a connection to this Sosa guy? Do you think...do you think my mother made him do that?"

"My people are still looking into it, but I can't see the connection." Jude leaned back against the trailer and let out a bone-weary sigh.

"You've always been good at puzzles. You'll untangle this one." She reached over and squeezed his hand to emphasize her next words. "And I'll be here to help you."

19

J ude's gaze lowered to Andi's lips for a moment. Her words of support meant so much to him. As did the fact that she hadn't laughed him off for grasping at straws when it came to her mother's involvement.

"Dee, I'm getting lost in the fog here." He forced himself to be transparent. "I'll need to bring in my team soon, and I don't know what to give them except for a bunch of random pieces to a puzzle. Logan run off the road—and maybe your dad too. Shots fired at you. A dead body. An explosion. What's the connection? What am I missing?"

In the end, that's what it felt like. His mistake. His fault. Some connection he was too blind to see.

He turned to look at her, and words faltered. He'd leaned close during the conversation to keep it private, and now they were almost nose to nose.

The glow from the lights overhead made her light-blue eyes glassy and played across her pink cheeks in a beguiling way. She was beautiful and, looking at her now, he forgot their history. Forgot the girl he'd known as a teen who'd matured into the woman beside him.

Had he also forgotten what it meant to risk for the sake of feelings?

He played things by the book, but it was possible he'd made a wrong call with Andi. He'd mentally pushed her away because he was trying to do his job to the best of his abilities, but that felt like a copout now. Like he'd taken the easy way out instead of fighting for something that could be worth the risk.

The events of the day crashed into Jude like a tidal wave and forced him to relive the moments before the explosion. He'd come close to death today, and that put his life into sharp relief.

"D-Dee." Jude faltered and his hand fisted at the stutter. Deep breath. One, two, three. "Dee, I almost died today."

She blinked in surprise. "But you didn't."

"I didn't." The urge to touch her overwhelmed him. "But I thought of you when that bomb went off." He reached up and brushed a stray lock of hair from her forehead. Her skin was smooth under his fingers. She held his gaze, not moving. Barely breathing. "I think I even saw your face before I passed out. I thought about what would happen if I never told you."

"Told me what?" Her words were light as air.

"That I'd forgotten how empowered you've always made me feel. That I can't get enough of your smile. That you're brave and beautiful and probably everything I've ever wanted in a woman."

With the rush of words and the flow of his emotions too great to ignore, Jude leaned forward and softly pressed his lips to hers. He knew it was wrong. That his boss would be livid despite the fact it was clear Andi was a victim in all of this. He just didn't care.

His fingers slid into the hair at the nape of her neck, and his heart pounded as she leaned into the kiss. The scent of sweet strawberries and vanilla intoxicated his senses, and something broke free inside of him.

He'd chased after one thing with a singular focus: advancing in his career by following the rules to the letter. It was a worthy goal. He helped people through his work with ATF, but he'd neglected a part of himself with such a narrow focus.

The part of his heart that desired companionship. Not just of a friend or a colleague, but of a woman. Like Andi.

Not just like Andi. The woman herself. The one who tasted like sun-warmed honey and promises. Their childhood kiss had nothing on the swell of desire that rose inside of him at the feel of her lips under his.

Their past created a rock solid foundation for a friendship he could see progressing—

Andi placed a hand on his chest and pressed. He instantly moved back, his heart pounding against her touch. Her eyes were wide, cheeks red in the dim light. She looked...stricken.

"I can't."

"I—I'm s-sorry. Should I have n-not done that?" Maybe he'd misread the acceptance in her eyes or the way she'd kissed him back.

"No. Yes. I mean—" She brought a hand to her forehead. "I don't know."

"Andi, t-talk to m-me." He needed to control his breathing. Needed to focus. He was slipping into dangerous territory, becoming flustered by the situation and his stutter. It would only get worse if he didn't give himself time to think before he spoke.

"I'm sorry." She ran her hand down the side of her face without meeting his gaze. "I gave you the wrong impression. I... I can't do this." She motioned between them. "Us."

He took a deep breath. Then another. He could play it off, tell her he hadn't asked for more. But his kiss had. And he didn't want to deceive her.

"I'm sorry," she repeated. "There's a lot on my plate right

now. I have to get past my probationary phase at work, and with everything going on with my parents, it's just too much. I can't seem to focus on my job with all of this...distraction."

Jude flinched at the implication.

Was that what he was to her, a distraction from her job?

Then again, only moments ago he would have said the same of her, at least until his mind cleared enough to remind him of what was important. The job, yes. But people? Even more so.

"I get it, Andi."

"I don't think you do." She stood and paced, her arms wrapping around herself, engulfed by his jacket. "I'm one of two women in the firehouse. Just two. It's such a hard field for women, and I have to prove to myself that I can do this. I have to prove that I won't let anything get in the way of being the best at my job. They need me, Jude. Distractions are dangerous."

Her gaze speared him with the added weight of her words. But he had to wonder. Was she trying to prove herself to *herself*, as she said, or to her brothers? Her family?

He'd known Andi well when they were younger, and he knew the strain she'd always felt at being the youngest Crawford. The youngest *super*, as he'd always called her.

The family was impressive, but spend one day with them and you could see their love for her had nothing to do with how good she was at her job.

"I meant what I said, Jude. I'll help you find this Sosa guy. Whatever it takes to keep my family safe. Because if I don't..." She faltered. "Do you remember me telling you about my grandfather?"

He blinked at her change in topic. "Uh...yeah, I think so."

"I was young. Maybe ten or eleven." Her fingers tightened their grip on her elbows. "He always used to take me to the woods with him. We'd go on adventures—that's what he called them."

Her gaze went soft at the memory.

"But one day we went so far we traveled into hunting territory. I didn't realize it until Gramps stepped on a bear trap." Her hand moved to her neck. "It was...awful. He cried out in pain, and I freaked out. I couldn't help him get it open. I wasn't strong enough, so he sent me back home. Told me to go as fast as I could. So I ran and ran, but I got lost." She wiped tears away. "I finally came across a family on a hike, and they helped me. The paramedics came and took Grandpa to the hospital, but he lost his foot. We never went on adventures again."

"Oh, Dee. I'm sorry." He could see the little girl in her, lost and hurting at such a traumatic event.

"It's just..." She cleared her throat. "I overheard my parents talking one night after Gramps came home from the hospital. I'll never forget when my mother said, 'If only she'd been faster.' I was a kid, but I still wasn't good enough. That haunts me, but it also pushes me to be the best I can. I don't want to be in that situation ever again. Not fast enough. Too distracted. Whatever it is. And you—us—it's a distraction."

"Andi." He stood and came to her. Gently took her hands in his and tugged her back to her seat. "I understand."

"Do you?"

"I do." If she'd asked him if he agreed, it would have been another answer, but he understood.

"Thanks, Jude. I know this was a lot—I'm sorry."

"Stop apologizing, all right?" He forced a smile he definitely did not feel. "Don't make this weird."

The forced levity seemed to do the trick, and she offered a faint smile. "Definitely not."

He didn't miss the way she pressed her lips together. Had she really not wanted the kiss? He needed to put that thought aside. He'd told her not to make it weird, and he needed to follow his own advice.

"So, to, uh, finish the conversation we were having..." He scratched at the back of his neck. It felt wrong to go back into work mode, but maybe that's what they both needed right now. "I think there's a connection between Sosa and Rojas, and I hope once we find it, things will become clearer."

"Do you think he's doing this Rojas guy a favor? Ruining our lives based on some past slight?"

Jude had thought of that angle, but it didn't add up. "I don't think so, but it's not clear yet."

She shifted to look over at her parents' house. "You're going to catch this Sosa guy, Jude, right? I need him out of our lives."

He almost laughed. He wanted this guy in jail as much as— if not more than—Andi did, but he understood the sentiment. "Right."

His gaze traced the way her nose curved down to the softness of lips he'd tasted not moments before. The urge to kiss her again was strong, but he wouldn't give in unless she wanted him to.

"I'm going to head over and check on Dad." Andi stood abruptly. Had she caught him looking? He didn't want to make her uncomfortable.

"Andi, I'm sorry—"

"Stop apologizing." She used his line. "It's okay. I just have to focus on work."

He guessed the line was a weapon to keep him at bay, but he'd accept her reply.

"And Jude?"

"Yeah?" His heart beat faster at her look, almost playful.

"Don't forget to fix my shower. It's getting really old showering at the firehouse or my parents' house."

He laughed. "Does a partial concussion get me a few extra days?"

She pretended to think, hand on her hip and finger tapping her chin, then gave him an exaggerated sigh. "Fine."

"How gracious of you." The banter reminded him of old times, and he thought maybe it would be all right. This wouldn't be so bad. "Tell Paul I say hi."

"He probably won't even remember me, but I will." She looked back at Jude, something close to regret in her eyes—or was he seeing what he wanted to?

"Good night, Dee."

"Night, Jude."

She walked off across the lawn, and he watched her go. His heart sank at how things had turned out.

What was he supposed to do now?

Everything he'd told her was true. His last thoughts as the explosion overtook him and Penny had been about Andi. About how he'd missed his chance. How one foolish move from the past had ruined his future.

Tonight he'd had hope again. The way she'd looked at him—like she was feeling what he was—had convinced him that maybe the past could be forgotten. That the future could be as bright as he hoped.

He'd clearly misread that.

What do You want from me?

He hadn't meant to ask it, but now that his thoughts turned to God, the question hung there. It was raw. Honest.

He'd done everything by the book. He'd even opened his heart for the first time in a long time. And he'd gotten shot down. He'd missed his chance with Andi, and it felt like God was against him at every turn.

Jude took a sip of his soda. His head pounded, but it was nothing compared to the gaping wound in his chest. The one Andi had exacted with her words. He'd heal, he knew that from experience. But he regretted what could've been.

Jude picked up his trash and was about to head inside when a scream rent the air from inside the Crawford house.

He tossed the trash back to the table and paused only long enough to pull his gun out before he raced to the house.

20

The feet were the first thing Andi saw. White rubber shoes leading up to scrub pants. The nurse lay on the floor in a pool of blood. While her paramedic instincts were still there, she'd reacted as a daughter first and screamed.

Her father was missing, and the nurse was likely dead.

She shook off her fear and focused. Rushing to the nurse, she felt for a pulse, but there was none. Next, she ran to the living room. The fishing show her father always watched still played, but the room was empty.

The front door burst open and banged hard against the wall.

"Andi!" Jude called out. "Where are you? Are you all right?"

"Living room." She spun in a slow circle as if she could make her father appear by searching.

The sound of doors opening and closing clued her in to the fact Jude was clearing the house on his way to her. She waited and heard him fumble a chair in the kitchen. He'd seen the body.

"What's—"

"She's de-dead." The words stuck in her throat.

"Are you all right?" Jude rushed into the living room, gun out, and came straight for her. He placed a hand on her shoulder and looked her over as if she were the one who'd been harmed.

"I'm fine. I just came in and saw..." She couldn't bear to say the woman's name out loud. Becca had been such a loyal member of their family for so long it pained her to think of the loss. "Dad's gone. We have to find him."

Jude nodded. "I'll check upstairs. You call it in."

She nodded and reached for her phone. Typed in 9-1-1, but paused. She had to let Logan and Bryce know. They had to help her look for Dad.

The text was short but would bring them to the house quickly. It was an all-hands-on-deck situation. Then she dialed dispatch to call in backup.

Jude came back from upstairs and shook his head. "He might have wandered off again."

"His nurse is dead. Do you think he just took a walk after seeing that?" Her voice broke, and she pressed a fist to her lips. She would not break down. Not right now.

Without responding, Jude paced past her to the back door and opened it.

"It was unlocked?" They'd kept it secured since her dad wandered out the last time.

As she came to his side, he said, "The lock has been forced from outside."

"Someone's taken him, Jude."

"Hey." Jude pulled her close, and she couldn't help but bury her head against his chest. "We'll get the officers outside to check the area, and more will be on their way. We're going to find him."

"But what if we don't?" She'd lost her father once after his accident, but lucid moments were still gifts she longed for.

Those moments when he became himself again reminded her he wasn't gone—at least not completely. Her whole family would be wrecked, his absence devastating.

Slamming car doors drew her back from Jude. "I think that's my brothers."

"You called them?"

"Texted. They needed to know."

"But I can't explain—"

"Can't explain that you're keeping things from us, Brooks? Big things?" Bryce strode in like he'd never been injured.

"Yeah, what is all this about, Jude? I mean—Becca? She's dead." Logan pressed his lips together, and Andi almost lost it.

The tornado twins were here, and nothing was going to stop them.

"Where's Mom?" Bryce asked.

"I don't know." Her mother's car wasn't in the driveway. "She's probably on her way home from work." Her stomach cramped at the thought. Mom didn't need to come home to all of this.

"She's with a protection detail on her way home." A voice spoke behind them. "And I'm going to have to ask you all to step outside."

Andi turned to see Detective Savannah Wilcox in the doorway. Her long blonde hair was pulled back into a ponytail, and she wore an expression that said she was decidedly unhappy they were hanging out in her crime scene.

"Sorry, Detective Wilcox," Bryce said.

She motioned for them to leave, but Jude moved to talk to the detective.

The moment they stepped outside, Logan whirled to face her. "Dee, what in the world is going on?"

Red and blue emergency lights colored the darkness, their flashes casting a nightmarish pallor over the yard.

"Dad's missing. That's what's important right now. We need to—"

"You need to let my deputy take your statement, Andi," Savannah said from the doorway.

"But my father—"

"We've got cruisers out looking for him, and I'll assemble a team to search these woods."

Logan nodded. "We can help with that."

"No, you can't go out there." When Logan began to protest at her words, Andi put her hand on his arm. "The terrain is dangerous, and you're still healing."

"I'll let you all decide on this," Savannah said. "But I've got a crime scene to work. Please remain outside." She went back into the house, and a forensics team followed her. Andi shifted toward the far side of the porch and watched as they filed into her childhood home. Now a crime scene.

"I'm not going to sit here like I'm worthless," Logan said. "Clearly I'm doing fine."

"Hey, why don't we all calm down and talk strategy?" Jude joined them on the porch with a practiced air of someone who often dealt with tragedy. She saw her brothers' immediate reactions and flinched.

"You wanna talk now?" Bryce stepped up to Jude.

"Listen, man," Jude started.

"Don't 'man' me." Bryce squared his shoulders and faced Jude. "I talked with Penny, and she filled us in."

Andi heard Jude's groan, though she was pretty sure it had escaped without him meaning for it to.

"Why didn't you tell us our family is being targeted?" Logan demanded.

"Because of this." Jude gestured between them. "I knew this would happen and—"

"This? You mean us actively protecting our family? That's

our *job*, Brooks. Not yours. Even if you are back to staring at our sister like a lovesick puppy dog."

Jude matched Logan's intensity, though not his tone. "I'm sorry I kept you out of the loop, but I needed this quiet."

Andi could see Logan's teeth grind together in an effort not to say something he'd regret.

"Our sister gets shot at, and now our dad's missing. Are we supposed to just accept that? Not do anything about it?" Bryce scoffed. "That's not happening."

Andi had heard enough. "Stop. Stop it right now." She placed a hand on Logan's chest and one on Bryce's and pushed back. She needed to remind them all of what was most important. "Dad's missing. Let's focus on that and berate Jude later. Okay?"

Logan stared down at her. "Of course you'd side with him."

"I'm not siding with anyone." She'd expected the push back, but it still stung.

"You're not siding with us—with family—that's for sure." Bryce had fire in his eyes. "I bet you knew everything this whole time."

"Don't blame Andi." Jude stepped up beside her.

"I don't need you to fight my battles, Brooks." She shot him a look and saw the words die on his lips. "Sure, he probably should have told you, but this was Mom's doing. She's the one who didn't want you guys involved."

"How do you know about this?" Logan asked.

Andi met his hard stare with one of her own. "I found out on my own and forced Jude to tell me."

"And you kept it from us." Bryce sounded hurt, but she couldn't care about that right now.

Andi sighed. "I get it. We're all mad, but let's keep this in perspective. Mom has been holding out, and I think—"

"I haven't done it without reason."

The three siblings turned at the sound of their mother's

voice. She stood at the base of the porch stairs, wearing a pencil skirt and blazer. Two officers hovered a few feet behind her. It was clear she'd come straight from work, and Andi's cheeks flushed at the hard look on her face.

Becca was dead, Dad was missing, and they were *still* arguing.

Andi said, "Mom, tell Jude what he needs to know."

"I will, honey." Elizabeth came slowly up the steps until she was level with them all. "I was wrong to keep this to myself, but"—her gaze traveled over their faces—"I thought I was doing the right thing."

"Mom, Becca's—" Andi's throat closed.

"They told me. I...I'm devastated. But your father—"

"We're going to find him." Bryce lifted his chin.

"Yeah." Logan stepped next to his twin. "We're joining the search."

For a moment Andi thought her mother might suggest they stay where it was safe, but she caught the moment Elizabeth gave in to the reality that her sons were warriors. They wouldn't be deterred, no matter how dangerous something was. They were firefighters, after all. Running into burning buildings was not only a hazard of the job but something they did regularly.

"Be careful, sons." Elizabeth forced a smile, and the twins headed for the steps.

Logan stopped short, spinning to nail Jude with a sharp look. "If anything happens to our dad, it's on you, Brooks." Logan pointed his finger at Andi. "And don't think you get a free pass in this, Andi."

Her mouth gaped. They were blaming her?

"He's right, Dee. How could you keep this from us?" Bryce shook his head, then turned to race down the steps with Logan. They disappeared into the darkness, leaving Andi feeling like the forgotten sister she was.

"I'm sorry, Jude," Elizabeth said. "I put you in this position, and I'm afraid they're too close to this to see that."

"It's all right, Mrs. C. I don't really care what they think right now. They're angry and worried, I get it."

"How are you, sweetie?" Elizabeth turned to Andi and cupped her face. "You found...the body?"

Andi nodded, fresh tears pooling in her eyes. "We have to find Dad."

"The police or your brothers will. Why don't you go home and—"

"No." Andi stepped back, wiping under her eyes. "I'm going to look for Dad."

"I don't think that's a good idea. Dangerous men are out there and—"

"And what? Logan and Bryce can go out and they'll be fine, but I'm too weak to handle myself?"

"I didn't mean that."

Andi ignored the hurt reflected in her mother's eyes. "I'm going. I probably know Dad better than them, anyway. If he wasn't taken, I might find where he went."

"Andi." Her mother reached out, but she brushed off her hand.

"I'll be fine." She descended the steps and made her way into the middle of the yard. She needed space from her brothers' egos and Jude's calm strategy. Space from her mother's worry.

She was just as capable as Logan or Bryce—when would they see that?

"Andi, you can't go out on your own." Jude spoke from behind her.

"Ugh, not you too. I can handle myself." She kept walking. If she were her father, where would she go if she were afraid?

"You're not bulletproof, Super."

She couldn't help it. Her lips quirked at the use of her old nickname, but the humor was short-lived. Where was Dad? "I'm looking for my dad—not some drug lord. There's a difference."

Jude was silent for so long she turned to face him.

"You're not invincible and neither are your brothers."

She shrugged. "I know I'm not, but I also know where my dad might be. I'm going to find him—with or without you."

Andi took a step and then berated herself, because she paused. She might be able to make grand speeches about how she didn't need anyone, but her heart betrayed her. Maybe she didn't need Jude, but she wanted—

"With," he said.

She frowned. "What?"

"You're going to find him—with me."

Yes, together. "Thanks," was all she could say.

She spun on her heel and raced toward the back of the house, relieved she didn't have to do this alone.

21

J ude ran through the darkness, his head pounding in rhythm to his feet. He pushed the pain back, narrowly avoiding low-hanging tree branches and roots that jutted up from the path.

Ahead of him, Andi had her phone out with the flashlight app illuminating the way, but he was running on snatched bits and pieces of light. It wasn't enough to feel confident in, but it had to do since his phone was low on battery power.

"Just up ahead," she said.

He knew where she was going and realized he should have thought of this first. They were back near the fishing spot where he'd found Paul the first time he'd run away.

He could be nowhere near here and this was a waste of time.

There hadn't been any obvious destruction at the house. While the kitchen showed some signs of a struggle, the living room was clean. Except for the body, it looked as if Paul had simply stepped away for a moment. He hadn't hidden in any of the closets or been found in the immediate vicinity of the house—Jude had heard that much over the radio.

He'd either been taken or he'd run away. *Lord, which is it?*

Andi slowed, and Jude caught himself before he ran straight into her. He lightly gripped her upper arms as he came to a stop behind her. The warmth from her skin sent an electric shock through his palms, and he quickly let go. Her words from earlier reminded him she wasn't interested in anything more than a friend. Touching her, no matter how innocent, felt like a violation of that.

"He's...he's not here." Andi spun in disbelief, shining the light around the full area. "Dad? Are you here? It's Andi."

"This is where I found him the first time."

"I thought..." She spun around again, slower this time. "I mean, if he came here the first time, why not again? Dad?" She called out into the darkness once more, but no response.

Jude circled the area, and she led the way with the light as he went. Nothing. He couldn't hear anything aside from their footsteps entering the clearing.

"Where is he, Jude?" Andi's voice quavered. "Why would someone take him? What could he do for them? He barely knows who his family is."

She sniffed and wiped under her eyes, making the light in her hand jump. Andi didn't cry—or cry often—and seeing her like this broke him. It took everything he had to keep from stepping forward. From pulling her close. He'd have to use his words to comfort her instead.

"A lot of people are out looking for him. Just because he isn't here doesn't mean he's nowhere." He flinched. That sounded like the stupidest thing he'd ever heard. "What I mean, Dee, is we're going to find him and bring him home. I promise you that."

He shouldn't make that promise. Everything in the rules said never to pledge more than he could deliver, but Jude wanted this for her. Wanted to assure her they could do it. *Would* do it.

"Thanks. That—" She stifled a sob. "That means a lot."

He took a step toward her but swayed, the pounding in his head intensifying.

"Jude? Is it your head?"

He ran his fingers over the tender spot at his temple. "I just need a minute to—to catch my breath."

"Of course." Her eyes searched his. "You probably shouldn't even be out here."

"I'll be fine."

After a moment of shared eye contact, Andi nodded and turned off her light, likely to conserve the battery. The stars shone above them through the darkness—just like when they were kids. He'd come over for a bonfire, but they would outlast the flames every time. In the darkness, they'd lie back on blankets to pick out their favorite constellations.

If he thought back hard enough, he could hear the creak of the back door. The soft footsteps followed by a gentle call for Andi to come in for bedtime. Mr. C had always wished him a good night. Had always been kind.

"Your dad was like a father to me, you know? During those summers." Pressure built in his chest. He needed to tell her. She had to understand. "I'd never had a man like that in my life. Someone who showed up when he said he would—like that time your dad took me fishing at dawn. I got up an hour early, and by the time he was supposed to come over, I'd convinced myself he wouldn't show. I'd almost gone back to bed when his knock came on the back door."

That had been the best morning of Jude's summer. At least, the best out of those that hadn't involved Andi.

"Your dad never took you fishing?" Her words were small, tentative. She knew enough about his past to tread lightly, but she had no clue as to the extent.

"My dad was...e-exacting." It was the best word for William Brooks without being crass. "I was in a p-play at school in fourth grade. The k-kind you can't get o-out of." His stutter chained him to the memory. Made him force the words out one at a time as his mind replayed the moments. "I was the state of Maine."

He could remember the bright lights. How they blinded initially. He'd blinked so many times until his vision cleared, and the audience came into focus.

"He came. My mom m-made sure of it, but when it came time for me to—" Jude paused and forced himself to take a deep breath. "It was time to recite my lines. I froze. I've never stuttered s-so hard b-before in public. It was h-humiliating."

"Oh, Jude." Andi came closer, taking his hand in hers.

"I mean, everyone knew I h-had a stutter. I was in speech therapy for it and doing b-better, but the pressure of everyone watching me, and my d-dad...it was too much. Solutions for situations like this from therapy went out the window." He shook his head. "I had to watch as my dad stood up and left the auditorium. Shaking his head. That's when I knew I would never be enough for him. N-never."

Even though he'd tried. Oh, how he'd still tried to please his father. To follow the rules from his therapy, to anticipate his dad's needs, to hope for just one moment that he'd make his father proud.

"Clearly he didn't deserve a son like you." Andi's palm rested against his cheek. "Someone so kind and caring."

Jude saw the sky reflected in the darkness of her eyes. Depths like a galaxy drawing him in. Her words were a balm to his brokenness, but more so her understanding. He'd told no one about seeing his dad leave, but he wasn't afraid to share that with Andi.

He *wanted* to share it with her.

"Thank you," he whispered. His forehead dropped to hers, the throbbing at his temple diminishing as her hand slipped to his neck.

Before he knew what she was doing, Andi's lips pressed to his. He tasted the salt of her tears and pulled her close as if their kiss might erase both of their wounds. Like it might seal up the cracks inside him and cover the loss she felt over her father.

His fingers wove into her hair as they had before, and a heady sensation coursed through him at the softness. The passion with which she kissed him. He was lost to her in that moment when the past faded.

It was all he hoped for then, to forget the hurt and humiliation and look to the future of something with Andi. Her understanding of who he was and her support.

When he pulled back, he took a moment to memorize the way she looked by the glow of the stars. Just as beautiful— maybe more so—but was her kiss genuine? Or was it gifted out of pity?

"I—"

He silenced her with a light touch of his lips to hers. "Don't apologize. Not this time."

"I'm not sorry I kissed you. You're all the things I said and more, but I am sorry about the timing." She pulled back, cool air rushing into the space between them. "We have to find him, Jude."

He mentally shifted gears. Her father. They needed to be looking for him, and this was exactly what she'd feared—a distraction. Both for her and for him.

The lingering fog from their kiss cleared, and he took another step back to give them both room. It was easy to want the release that came from feeling so connected to Andi, but it didn't change the fact that Paul was missing. That Jude had a job to do.

"Yeah. Okay. So, where would your father go that's close? A neighbor he remembers? Would he hide? Maybe try to get to the police station or something?"

"No." Andi paced back and forth. "It's hard to say for sure since he's not the same as he used to be. Some things still matter to him, but it shifts from day to day." She looked over, but went back to pacing. "If this had happened before the accident, I don't think he would have run. I mean, once a Marine, always a Marine. He had training, and he would have fought back."

She was trembling. He could see it despite the dim light as she wrapped her arms around herself. Attraction aside, Jude had to focus on helping her. Had to find Paul. Not just for her, but for himself too. It was selfish; he knew that. But even as a changed man because of his TBI, Paul was the closest thing to a father he'd ever had.

"Maybe he thought of a buddy from back then? I mean, the mind is a strange thing. It can recall things from the past as if they were in the present. At least, I've heard of that in people with dementia."

"Yeah, but his TBI doesn't really work like that. He's usually, I don't know, in his own world?" She paced back to him. "I mean, if he's not watching a show about fishing, he's— wait." Andi reached for his hand.

"What is it?"

She looked up at him. "I think I know where he is."

22

"You remember where it is, right?" Her breath came in gasps as she mentally tried to shove aside any thought that wasn't of her father.

"Past the house. Down that little trail to the north?"

"Yes. To the fallen log." Andi wanted to double her pace but held back.

She wasn't sure why the spot hadn't occurred to her sooner, but if thoughts of Jude were to blame, she'd never forgive herself. No matter how hard she tried to erase their kiss, the feeling of warmth in the pit of her stomach and the soft touch of his caress wouldn't fade from her memory.

She ducked beneath a low-hanging branch, the near miss bringing things into perspective. Her focus needed to be on finding her father. He was what mattered, not some passing fantasy of a life with Jude that would end when he left town... again. Everything she'd told him earlier that night was true—she couldn't afford the distraction he would be to her.

Yet, as she looked back at him doggedly following behind her despite the injuries he'd sustained earlier that day, she sensed a shift in her heart. Where she'd once only focused on her job and family, a space had opened up to her teenage self's best friend. To the possibility of something more with Jude.

It scared her.

The divide appeared up ahead, and she pushed herself forward as fast as she dared in the darkness. Her phone light illuminated the path well enough, but it jounced with every step, casting everything in shifting shadows.

Her heart hammered in her chest as they moved north toward the stream. A branch appeared in the path before her, and she almost didn't stop in time. Tripping to a halt, Jude barreled into her. His arms wrapped around her protectively, and together they stabilized before he released her.

"Sorry," she muttered.

He said nothing, merely reached for her hand to help her over the tangle of limbs. On the other side, she raced off again. She hadn't been to this spot in ages, and it was clear no one else had taken the time to clear the path. She hadn't been fishing in a long time either, come to think of it. Her father seemed content to watch the shows he loved, but she hadn't thought to see if he wanted to go out.

It made sense to her he would go to this spot in a time of distress. She'd seen him do this more than once when she was a child. Especially when Logan and Bryce were acting like willful teenagers. Mom had always faced their disobedience headfirst. The lawyer in her couldn't stand to lose an argument, and the parent in her had the high ground.

Dad had never acted that way. He'd taken time out to think. Perhaps it was the meticulous surgeon in him, but he'd been famous for stepping away from whatever needed fixing— whether that was other people or his own family—to seek the Lord first and think things through. He always came back with a clear head and direction.

Was some part of his brain doing that now? Taking him to a

place where he'd found solace before, hoping the painful reality might fade?

Andi slowed as she came to the clearing. A shape appeared at the edge of the stream. It was hard to see, but the starlight gave off enough illumination to make out that it was a figure. It had to be her father, didn't it?

"Get behind me." Jude had a gun in hand and a look of steel on his features.

"But—"

"Please."

He was the officer. He had the gun. It made sense. But if that was her father...

He knew Jude. It would be okay.

She stepped to the side.

"Wait here."

She nodded, their eyes connected, so she knew he'd seen the gesture. Then he stepped in front of her and approached.

The sounds of night erupted around her, slipping past her noisy thoughts. Bugs chirped. The stream bubbled. In the distance, an owl sang out his nighttime greeting.

"Andi, it's him." The soft call from Jude was all the encouragement she needed to move toward her father.

"Hey, Dad. Are you okay?" She spoke softly.

The question would go unanswered—it always did—but she couldn't pretend it wasn't her father standing there shaking by the stream. The little girl inside longed for him to be all right.

"Dark. Fishing is...fishing." Paul turned blank eyes toward her. "So dark. It's time. They...take. No. No no no. They're coming..."

Andi switched into paramedic mode and visually assessed him, or else she knew she'd risk bursting into tears. With her light held high, she looked him over. When her gaze landed on his arm, she gasped involuntarily. He'd pressed part of his shirt against the wound, but blood seeped out anyway.

"Dad, I—" Her voice caught in her throat. "I need to see your arm."

He looked at her. "Bad men. Bad bad bad. Need to get safe."

"You're safe with us. You remember Jude, right?"

Her father's gaze shifted to Jude, but there was no sign of awareness.

"Come on, Mr. C. Show Andi your arm. That looks like a pretty nasty cut."

"Cut." Paul blinked a few times, then looked at his arm. "Blood."

"Yeah, but it's going to be okay. Just let me see it."

"Stop them. Make them go away. Bad bad bad."

He grew more agitated and, while she knew it could have disastrous ramifications, Andi reached out and touched her father's shoulder. "Dad. It's okay. We're here to help."

He stilled, and she prepared for a storm of anger, but it didn't come.

"Help." He nodded. "Here to help."

"Yeah, Dad. Show me your arm."

He pulled the fabric of his shirt away. Bile rose in her throat. The cut was too deep for her to wrap with a bandage. It would need stitches, and he was likely in a lot of pain.

"That looks like a knife wound," Jude whispered to her.

She nodded. "Okay. Let's keep that wrapped." Andi pulled her oversized T-shirt out from under Jude's jacket, found the seam, and ripped. A section tore from the hem, and she used it to wrap her father's arm. "We need to get him to the hospital, Jude."

"Got it." He stepped away from them, turning his back, and she heard him radio in their location and her father's condition.

Of course—she hadn't even thought to call it in. Her mind

was a jumble of emotions, and all she could think of was getting her dad to safety.

An image of Becca lying in the kitchen blinded her. This night needed to end. She'd walked in on worse scenes as a paramedic, ones that would never be erased from her memory, but this one lingered. Her childhood home defiled by violence. Her father hurt. It was a waking nightmare.

"Come on. They're going to meet us."

She nodded and turned back to her father. "Dad, can you walk with me?"

"Fish...time to go. Show?"

"You can watch your shows after we get your arm fixed up. How about that? Let's go find Mom."

At the mention of Mom, Paul went rigid. "Keep...safe. Bad men. No hurt. No yellow snakes!"

Andi's heart leapt at the sudden emotion in him, but she forced calm. "Jude's going to keep us all safe, Dad. It's okay. Let's go with him."

Her father's cloudy eyes alighted on Jude, and he seemed to understand, though he said nothing else.

The walk back through the path took longer than Andi would have hoped, but her father's gait was unstable. She didn't want to rush him and cause further injury, so she took one side—the injured side—and Jude took the other as they hiked back through the woods.

An influx of people and lights greeted them at the back of the yard.

"Andi, you okay?" Izan rushed up to her.

"It's my dad. Looks like a knife wound, and it's deep."

"Got it." Izan's gaze met hers, and something flickered behind his eyes. Why did it look like regret? "Hey, Mr. Crawford, let's get you to the ambulance."

"I'm coming with." She sent a look to Jude that warned against any argument.

"I'll meet you there." His support was a relief.

"Bring my mom?"

He nodded.

Andi jogged alongside the gurney Trace brought over, her hand holding her father's uninjured arm. She wasn't sure where her mother was, but she needed to be at the hospital. Even if her father didn't always recognize his wife, he always relaxed in her presence.

"It's Andi, right?" A voice spoke at her elbow, and she turned to see the officer who had taken Logan's statement.

"Uh, Officer Thomas, right?"

He offered a muted smile. "Good memory. I hate to intrude. I know you've got to get to the hospital, but has your father said anything? Um, anything of use?"

Her father was muttering now, but it was gibberish. Nothing made sense aside from one thing he'd said. "Bad men."

Officer Thomas's eyebrows rose. "That's it?"

"I know it doesn't seem helpful, but my father has a traumatic brain injury. His thoughts aren't always linear or rational to us, but the fact he knew enough of what was going on to warn me...that's significant." She hadn't realized how much until then.

"Got it. Anything else?"

Her thoughts flashed back to "yellow snakes," but that made no sense. At least, none that could help the officer. "I'm sorry, but I'm afraid not. He's likely in a state of shock from this entire experience."

"Oh yeah, of course. I'm sorry to bother you."

"It's your job. I get it." Andi pulled herself into the ambulance, the move familiar, and took a seat next to her father.

Officer Thomas leaned in. "If you think of anything or he says anything else, please call me." He handed her a card and then closed the door behind them, slapping it twice as a sendoff.

Andi held on to her seat with one hand and her father's arm with the other. He looked dazed, and she assumed the pain was finally registering.

"He's going to be okay, Andi." Trace flashed her a supportive smile, and she nodded. She knew the injury wasn't severe, but it still rattled her. Someone had broken into her family's home, killed her father's nurse, and almost killed her father. Nothing was okay right now.

The ambulance came to a stop at the ER doors, and two nurses in blue scrubs rushed out. Once Trace filled them in on the non-life-threatening injury, they slowed but still worked quickly.

Andi followed behind when they went inside, but kept an eye on the parking lot. She needed to make sure her mother knew where her father was. Where was Jude?

It was like coming out of her own type of shock as she paced the ER area. Though it felt like she'd been there for hours, a glance at the clock showed only fifteen minutes had passed when a hand alighted on her shoulder.

"Andi?"

"Charlotte." Relief surged through Andi at the sight of her friend. "Are you here about my dad?"

"Yeah, he's doing great. They're about to stitch him up. Did you want to go back there?"

"My mom—"

"Andi." She spun to see Jude coming toward her through the sliding doors, her mother behind him. "How is he?"

"I'm not sure if the doctor wants to keep him overnight or discharge him." Charlotte addressed her mom. "He was pretty shaken up, but he's going to be fine."

"I'd like to go see him," she said.

"This way, Mrs. Crawford." Charlotte sent an encouraging

smile at Andi before turning. Her mom followed her friend toward the double doors with purposeful strides, and Andi's stomach unclenched. Her mother was a force to be reckoned with. She would get answers to the questions Andi hadn't thought to ask.

"You okay?" Jude lightly gripped her upper arm.

"Yeah, I—"

Logan and Bryce came through the door, looking like twin storms.

"Where's Dad?" Logan demanded.

"Is he all right?" Bryce looked between Andi and Jude.

"He's going to be okay." Andi let out the breath she'd been holding. She watched the relief those words had brought her reach her brothers. "The knife wound should heal easily enough once it's treated."

"Knife wound?" Logan shifted his gaze to Jude. "My father was knifed?"

23

Jude saw the anger and hurt in Logan's eyes, mirrored by Bryce's. He needed to defuse the situation before it escalated in the lobby of the ER.

"Just take a second—"

"This is all your fault—" Bryce began, his finger poised over Jude's chest.

"Check that anger." The commanding voice came from behind them, and Jude shifted to see Penny. He'd called her on the way to the hospital, and she'd come just in time. She frowned, the action pulling at the butterfly bandage on her forehead. "Don't put this on Jude."

A muscle worked in Bryce's jaw. "If he'd said something, this wouldn't have happened."

"Oh yeah?" Penny stepped into Bryce's personal space, her gaze glinting like steel. "So Jude is able to control others? Or are you saying *you* are? That if you'd known, you could have stopped this?"

Bryce didn't respond.

"I get it. You're angry that he didn't read you in, but that's not just his call. Besides, if I were him, I wouldn't have told you either. Neither of you." Logan and Bryce looked at one another and then back at Penny. "Why? Because you're a pair of hotheads who think they are God's gift to Last Chance County—or at least that's how you're acting."

Logan leaned forward. "That's not—"

"That *is* just it. So calm down and let Jude fill you in."

They turned toward Jude, and his stomach clenched at the pressure Penny had put on him. Still, he was thankful. She'd defused the situation as best she could, though not exactly the way he would have. She got results, and that's what mattered.

"Well?" Bryce demanded.

"I don't think it's his place to tell this story." Elizabeth came from behind the boys and placed her hands on their shoulders. "It's mine. This is all my fault."

Jude's gaze connected with hers. Was she finally ready to tell the truth?

He'd been trying to get her to trust him, but perhaps the danger had come closer than she'd expected, and she was finally ready to bring him into her confidence. Either way, they needed to get to a private room and sort this out.

"First, how's Dad?" Andi sent a pointed look at Logan and Bryce as if to remind them why they were at the hospital in the first place, but neither of them spoke.

Her mom nodded. "They are sedating him now so they can finish the stitches. He was too upset for them to do it while he was conscious."

"Do you need to be in there?" Jude asked.

Elizabeth wore a weary expression but shook her head. "Not until they are done. Besides, this is important." She took time to look between Andi and her brothers. "This confusion and frustration ends now."

"There's a conference room we can use." Penny flashed a smile at the older woman.

Jude turned to her and knew she saw his surprise.

"What? I talked with the staff before I came to keep an eye on Logan. I'm very good at my job."

Jude barely contained a smile at that. She *was* extremely good at her job.

"You were keeping an eye on me?" Logan sounded shocked.

"That's where I saw you before!" Bryce said.

"I don't need anyone to watch out for me!"

"Come on." Penny ignored Logan. "This way."

They followed her, Jude stepping in at the end of the line. His head pounded in time to his steps, but the pain killers he'd downed when they got to the hospital seemed to be kicking in.

He placed a hand on Andi's back, but when she flinched, he removed it. He only wanted to show her support, but perhaps it was too much with her brothers there and the conversation they were going to have with her mother. It had to be difficult knowing Elizabeth had held things back.

"Okay." Jude stepped forward once they'd all taken a seat. "I want to start off by saying that I know you're frustrated." He made eye contact with Bryce and Logan. "But you've got to realize I was only doing my job, following orders. I don't tell you how to fight fires."

"We get it." Logan shook his head. "We don't tell you how to keep our family safe."

Jude wasn't sure if it was a jab or not, but he rolled with it. "In talking with Elizabeth, I was trying my best to find a connection between a drug lord I've been on the trail of and your family." He described the surveillance photos he'd found at the villa and could tell The Brothers weren't happy to learn that Andi had known most of this.

"Don't be angry at Jude," Elizabeth said. "I told him to keep it from you."

"Why, Mom?" Bryce placed his fist on the table as if he'd like to pound it. "Why not bring us in? This is our family too."

"Yes, but honey, there are things you didn't know. Couldn't know." She trailed off. Her gaze moved to where her finger traced a pattern on the tabletop.

Andi spoke into the silence. "Then tell us."

"It was years ago," Elizabeth began. "I was growing in my field as a legal professional and felt somewhat invincible. That's when I was presented with Camilo Rojas's case."

Jude's pulse spiked. He'd known there was something off about that.

"He was accused of killing his wife in a brutal murder in a run-down motel just outside of Denver. I defend all of my clients as if they are innocent, but as I spoke with him, I came to believe one thing. He truly *was* innocent." She shook her head. "But it wasn't that simple. Camilo had worked for a well-known drug lord in Mexico. Diego Ruiz Sosa. He said he'd known the man during his childhood, and when Diego took over the Sosa cartel by force, he brought Camilo in as an accountant."

Jude's heart pounded in anticipation. This was what he needed. The true story—the connection to Sosa. Elizabeth had known it the whole time. He tried not to be frustrated, but it was proving difficult. His hands fisted under the table, and he took a deep breath.

"Camilo said Sosa saw him as a friend. A confidant, though not truly part of the cartel, which gave Camilo access to many things."

"But he pled guilty." Jude blurted the words and flashed Elizabeth a silent apology. He was getting ahead of her.

"It's not that simple. His access included files and finances, but it also included people. Camilo fell in love with Sosa's girlfriend, Renata, while Sosa was away on business in the US, and you can imagine the fallout that would have caused. Even more so when she became pregnant.

"Sosa wanted to marry Renata, mistakenly thinking the

child was his, but Camilo knew he was the father. It took careful planning, but Camilo fled Mexico with the woman carrying his child."

Jude leaned back. There would have been a target the size of Russia on the man's back.

"They ended up in Denver through connections Camilo had, and the child was born. They'd started over, or so he thought. But one night a few years later, when they had relaxed their guard, Sosa and his men found them. He murdered Renata in front of Camilo and made it look like Camilo was the murderer."

"They framed him?" Jude had trouble believing that. Sosa was one to exact revenge through murder, not framing.

"According to Camilo," Elizabeth continued. "He claimed *he* called the police."

"So he was set up after he called for help, and you represented him. But you lost?" Andi frowned.

"I did, but it was on purpose."

The silence of the room echoed around them.

"I don't understand." Bryce looked at Jude and his mother. "What does this have to do with us? The guy went to jail. End of story, right?"

"As I dug into Renata's death with my PI, we discovered evidence that linked Sosa to the killing. Small things, but things I could have used to prove Camilo's innocence beyond a reasonable doubt."

"You could have put Sosa behind bars." Jude couldn't help the bitterness in his tone.

"I was finally moving ahead with it when Paul had his accident." The way Elizabeth said it made it clear she believed it was no accident.

"Sosa found out and threatened you." Andi bit her lip.

"His men did. They made it clear that, should I throw the

case and get Camilo behind bars, they would not come after my family."

"And you gave in?" Logan spoke, but it was clear he hadn't thought before his words tumbled out. "I mean...you know we would have stood by you."

"I know. And I wasn't one to give in to pressure like that, but Camilo insisted."

"He wanted to go to prison?" Jude asked.

"He wanted to keep certain things safe." Elizabeth's words were cryptic, but Jude was gaining a better understanding of this.

"Camilo confided in you?"

"He did. To an extent." Elizabeth turned to look at her sons. "They are dangerous men—clearly. And I knew that if you got wind of this, you wouldn't stop until you either caught him or something terrible happened to you. I couldn't risk my children for this. Sosa is too powerful."

"What does he want?" Andi narrowed in on the same thing Jude had. A piece of the puzzle was still missing.

"It was only more recently that I discovered Camilo had taken something from Sosa when he left."

"What?" Bryce asked.

"Money. A lot of it."

Jude leaned back in his seat. That was the missing link. The reason The Brothers and Fausto would involve themselves with a dying cartel. It also explained the absence of cash flow that had been years in the making. How much had Camilo taken if it had decimated Sosa's operation so badly?

"How do you know this?" Jude asked.

"Camilo sent me a letter." Elizabeth averted her gaze as if there was information she still wanted to keep close to the vest. What was she holding back? And how could he get her to trust him enough to be fully truthful?

"You know where it is?" Andi asked. "Sosa's money?"

Jude's shoulders stiffened. If she said yes, the whole Crawford family was in more danger than he'd imagined.

Elizabeth shifted in her seat. "No."

Jude studied her features. He was certain she was lying, but what he needed was to find Sosa.

Penny's phone rang and, after looking at the caller ID, she flashed Jude a pointed look.

"I should go check on Paul." Elizabeth pushed back her chair and stood.

Jude watched Penny step out and then redirected his focus to Elizabeth. "You can do that, but we need a plan first."

All eyes focused on him. He needed to make sure the family was safe, but he also needed to research what Elizabeth was saying. Camilo was in prison. Sosa had to know that, but ADX Florence wasn't part of his territory. Had Sosa gotten to Camilo? And what else did Elizabeth know?

"I've got a shift to get to." Bryce looked over at Logan. "He's got paperwork at the firehouse."

"I'll go with you," Andi said. "I could use a workout."

"But what about Mom and Dad?" Bryce said.

"I'll stay here at the hospital." Penny came back into the room.

"Who exactly are you?" Bryce looked between Penny and Jude. "Not just a 'friend' of Jude's, right?"

"We trained together as ATF agents, but I decided I was better suited to the private sector. I'm here to help; that's all that matters." She gave Jude a piercing look. They needed to talk.

"Why don't you guys go check on your parents, and then I'll take us all to the firehouse? Okay?" He looked at Bryce, then Logan, and then Andi. Each one nodded and he watched them file out of the conference room, leaving Penny behind.

The minute the door closed behind Andi, Jude said, "What is it?"

"Bomb materials from the house explosion have been

connected to Fausto. And we got the identity of the man found in the basement." She chewed on her lip.

"Well?"

"His name is Esteban. He's a former inmate just released from ADX Florence."

"The same prison Camilo is in."

"Exactly. And you know what else?"

Jude waited.

"Guess who his cellmate was for the last two years."

"Camilo Rojas."

"Bingo."

Jude ran a hand over his face. "Everything is intersecting, but nothing makes sense yet. Camilo stole money from Sosa, but Sosa doesn't have him killed? He wants him in jail?"

Penny tapped her foot. "Maybe he didn't know Camilo took it."

"Until after he was in prison?" Jude nodded slowly to himself. That would make sense. "And by then, Camilo was locked away where Sosa couldn't reach him."

"What do Elizabeth and her family have to do with all of this?"

Jude thought for a moment before answering. "There's a catalyst. Something we don't know that's happened. It brought Elizabeth into the forefront for Sosa and, rather than kill her and her family in revenge, he seems to be endangering them to get to her. She knows something."

"She does," Penny agreed.

"Keep your ears open."

"That Elizabeth's a tough one." Penny tapped her index finger against her arm. "I doubt she'll say anything."

"Listen. That's all I ask." Jude stifled a yawn and rolled his shoulders, wincing at the soreness in his muscles. He needed to get the siblings back to the firehouse, and he needed sleep— but more than that he needed answers. "You stay here. I'll keep an eye on everyone at the firehouse, and we can reconvene in the morning with any new intel."

"Sounds good, Boss." She turned toward the door, but paused. "This is going to get worse before it gets better."

He nodded. "I know. Let's just make sure it goes our way."

ndi woke to morning sunlight streaming straight into her eyes through the window in the women's bunk room. She shifted on the small bed and heard a disgruntled *meow*.

"Ashes?" She shot up in bed only to laugh at the cat occupying the area behind her bent knees. As much as she'd gotten flak from the guys about rescuing the cat, they sure seemed to like Ashes when they thought no one was around.

The events of the night before rushed back as sleep dissipated from Andi's mind. Becca dead. Her father lost then found but slashed with a knife. Angry words between her and her brothers. Jude's kisses. Her mother's confession.

Jude's kisses.

Out of everything from the night before, why was it his kisses that haunted her so? And why, after all that she'd wanted when she first saw him, did she feel like his shift toward her made her want to back away?

Andi rose from the small bed and, after a quick shower, got dressed and ready for her shift. She needed to push thoughts of

Jude out of her mind unless it pertained to the case he was working.

The one that involved her family.

Anything else would only distract her from her job. Now, more than ever, she couldn't afford to be preoccupied.

Eddie glanced over when she came into the kitchen. "Got some griddle sandwiches going."

"I love those. Can I have three?"

He flipped a sausage patty and grinned. "Pancakes for the bread, or the biscuit ones?"

"Two biscuits, one pancake."

"You got it."

Her mouth watered as he assembled his famous griddle breakfast sandwiches. Eggs, hash browns, bacon, sausage, and ketchup on biscuits—though he was adding pancakes to the mix now, and she wasn't mad about it.

Her gruesome workout the night before had left her limbs shaking and her mind dull, which was exactly what she'd needed in order to get to sleep, but now she was starving.

A steaming plate appeared in front of her, and the resounding grumble of her stomach made Eddie laugh. "I'll take that as a thank-you."

She smiled, mouth already full of her first bite.

"That all for *you*?"

Andi's heart leapt, and she nearly choked on her sandwich when Jude took the seat next to her at the island.

"Yes." She eyed him, speaking around her nearly finished first sandwich. "I'm hungry."

He grinned. "I see that."

She made a face and dug into the next sandwich while Jude bit into an apple. He was still here. She should have known that—should have guessed he'd stay in the men's bunk area with the threat of violence heightened after Becca's murder. But somehow she'd thought the firehouse would be her haven. The one place where her mind could be focused on work.

"I talked to Penny this morning." He chewed and swallowed another bite of apple. "She says your parents are doing well. Your dad is resting at home, and Penny convinced your mom to stay home from work. Penny will stay at the house in addition to the officers out front and around back. They're safe."

The last ounce of tension dissolved. Andi had worried about them, but the more she'd considered the heightened security that would no doubt surround them after last night's attack, the more she'd relaxed, knowing they'd be safe.

"What's the endgame here?" She turned to face Jude. "I mean, so they killed Becca, but why? To scare us?" It was senseless, and she wanted to find an answer her mind could settle on.

Jude chewed thoughtfully and then tossed the apple core into the trash in the corner. "It could have been accidental."

"What?" An image of her father's nurse lying on the floor in the kitchen assaulted her. "You don't murder someone by accident."

"Sorry. What I meant was that she probably wasn't the initial target. I think they went in to get your father and, unfortunately, Becca was there."

Andi shivered. "But why kill her? Why not incapacitate her and take Dad? Not that I want that."

"It's possible it was an intimidation tactic."

She lowered her coffee mug. "How so?"

"Your father seems like a logical choice in order to put pressure on your mom. Your brothers have been in highly secured areas, and I've been with you most of the time. There hasn't been a chance for you guys to be kidnapped, but your father is usually at home with his nurse. While the police were out front, the kidnappers knocked out the officer patrolling the back yard. By some miracle they didn't kill him, but it's clear that's how they got in."

"Dad must have fought them to get away."

"And then escaped when they—" He swallowed and rubbed a hand over his jaw as if unable to finish the sentence.

"When they killed Becca."

He nodded. "If they'd been watching your father at all, they might have thought he would stay put while they did what they had to. I bet they didn't expect him to escape into the woods. Becca probably tried to stop them."

Andi nodded in agreement. Her father, though not himself by any means, had gotten away in time. He'd saved himself. She smiled at that.

"So then what's—"

The alarm sounded, visibly startling Jude.

"Truck 14. Rescue 5. Ambulance 21. Car fire. All units respond."

"Duty calls." Andi jumped up and turned toward the gear closet.

"I'm coming." Jude was at her side.

"This is my job. I'll be fine." She tried to keep the panic from her voice.

Jude couldn't come on this call. It was bad enough that she'd gotten distracted at the fire in Grassland Heights, but she'd proved herself there. That couldn't happen again.

"I'm coming. Your chief already knows."

Andi ground her molars. "Then come."

She set off to do what she needed to do and left Jude to find his own way onboard the truck.

When he didn't join them, she thought maybe he'd left her to do her job, but one look at the rescue squad engine as it pulled up next to Truck 14 corrected that.

He'd taken Logan's seat, since Logan was still on desk duty.

Jude wasn't in gear, but he was alert, and his perceptive eyes were taking in the scene in front of them.

A car sat with its front end ablaze in the middle of a busy intersection. Police were already on scene, directing traffic away from the area. The blaze looked contained to the car itself, and the verdant green of the nearby woods signaled it wasn't likely to catch fire.

Andi smelled the scent of burning plastic and—

"Get that hose out. Rescue needs cover for a possible body inside the car." Amelia shouted her orders, and everyone bolted into action.

Andi's gut churned at the thought of someone inside the car. There was no way they could be alive, could they? The heat from the engine alone would be stifling. Then again, she didn't have a full view of the car.

"Copy." Andi voiced her reply to the LT and joined Zack with the hose, dragging it free of the firetruck and preparing for the thick stream of water that would flow once connected to the nearest hydrant.

"Get the hose out there." Amelia's voice was doubly loud as she stood right next to them with her mic keyed on, but it was the motivation Zack needed to pull the last coil out.

She hefted the hose and followed his lead as they jogged toward the car. The powerful stream of water came in the next second, and she attacked the blaze. At first, it only seemed to aggravate the fire, but then she saw some of the oxygen quenched by the heavy stream. The burn slowed and dissipated the flames.

Holding the hose at such an unnatural level caused the muscles in her arms and back to ache, but it was the only way to direct the water into the broken glass of the car window. Still, they were seeing success. She regretted her overly ambitious workout from the night before but wouldn't let that stop her. She had the strength she needed. She'd trained for this.

Crack!

Andi jerked at the concussive sound. What was that? She looked around, still trying to keep her hold on the hose steady, but chaos was erupting around them.

Crack, crack, crack!

"Gunshots!" Lieutenant Patterson's voice came over the mic with an edge of panic to it. "Someone's shooting. Everyone get down!"

Zack dropped the hose, which caused the force of the water to jerk Andi to the right. She lost her balance and toppled to the ground just as more shots went off. Her helmet muffled the sound, so she couldn't tell where they were coming from.

When she raised her head, Jayson was running toward them, crouched over, but then his body jerked like he'd hit an invisible barrier. His leg gave out and he went down. It took a second for her mind to make sense of what she'd just seen.

"Jayson!" Andi screamed into her helmet. The force of her breath created fog but it cleared quickly. *He's been shot.*

Zack was already headed back to the truck for cover. Only then did Andi recognize Amelia shouting at her through the mic. "Get back here, Crawford. The cops are on their way."

Andi ripped off her face mask. It was only getting in her way now that she wasn't near the fire, and she needed to see clearly. She had to help Jayson, no matter what the LT ordered.

Jayson could die if she didn't do something.

She couldn't hear any more shots, but that didn't mean they were safe. This was her chance while there was a lull.

She crawled toward Jayson. He clutched at his leg, blood on his fingers. It covered the ground behind him at an alarming rate. The flow had to be stopped in front and in back. Now.

Andi kept her head down. "Jayson, I'm here."

Another shot went off, and she heard the distinctive *ping* of metal. The bullet had gone into the burning car, only feet away from them.

"I've got you." She kept low and pressed her hands on top of his. "Just your leg?"

"Just?" He coughed a laugh, and the veins in his neck bulged with the effort.

"I'm going to get you back to the truck so we can stop the bleeding, but it's going to hurt like the blazes."

"Do...it." Jayson gasped the words. He was pale, close to passing out from the pain and blood loss.

"On three." She moved behind his shoulders, but a shape materialized next to her.

"Let's do this, Super." Jude crouched, and her irrational fear almost caused her to tackle him to the ground. He couldn't be out here. In the open.

"Jude, what are you doing?"

"I've got a vest. Let's go." He patted the front of his black vest with the word "Police" on it in white letters.

They stayed there, eyes locked, for an eternity of seconds. She wanted to argue, but Jayson was a big, muscled man. She was strong, but was she strong enough to get Jayson back by herself?

There was nothing but a promise in Jude's eyes. He was here to help her, and he wasn't leaving until he'd done just that. She dipped her chin.

"On three."

"That's my line." She grinned and shifted so Jude could get hold of Jayson's other shoulder.

"One. Two. Three."

They hefted the bulky firefighter toward the safety of the firetruck. They were halfway there. Andi could see Izan and Trace waiting to take over. Three-fourths of the way—

Crack! Crack crack crack!

Andi screamed but kept going. The shots, fired in succession, seemed to come from everywhere and nowhere. They hit the asphalt and the trucks behind her with loud *thunks.* Shards of rock shot up like miniature explosions all around her.

But she didn't feel any pain. They'd missed. Turning to the side, she saw they were nearly to the safety of the truck. Hope mingled with adrenaline, giving her the boost she needed. "We're almost there."

Jayson's bodyweight shifted. She strained to compensate in order to keep her hold on him and turned to see what had caused the change.

Her heart stopped.

Jude lay on the ground, motionless.

From across the chaos Bryce yelled, "Andi! Keep moving!"

Jude was down. Jayson was bleeding out. This rescue was on her.

25

S ound faded in and out. Shouts in the distance and the scent of acrid smoke.

Then pain.

Intense, jolting, aching pain. Like an elephant had run across his chest and left everything broken in its wake. He fought for breath, but every movement of his chest pressed shards of glass deeper.

"Jude? Jude, can you hear me?"

Someone was calling his name.

"Andi?" Jude's eyes flickered open, expecting to see her looking down.

Instead, he saw blue sky. Then his eyes focused on Bryce, who said, "He's awake."

Jude frowned.

"I know. I'm not as pretty as my sister." Bryce winked.

Jude tried and failed to sit up. Spasms of pain radiated throughout his chest and arms. He let out a groan, but fear crept past the pain. Was he having a heart attack?

"Hold on. You took two in the vest, man. You've probably got a few broken ribs by the size of the rounds they were shooting."

He'd been shot. In the borrowed police vest. It was a relief to know it wasn't something more serious, but even the thought of sitting up brought more pain.

"What caliber...rounds?"

"I'd guess a .45, but I'm no expert. Probably sniper rifle though. Don't think they were too great of a shot." Bryce looked up and called something out as Jude tried, and failed, to sit up again. "I said take it easy, man."

Bryce didn't understand. He had a job to do. "Where's Andi?"

"Don't worry, she's behind the truck. Helping with Jayson's wound. It's nasty, but they think they have him stable enough to take him—"

Crack! Metal pinged against metal as a bullet struck nearby.

"You've got to be kidding me." Bryce ducked.

"More shots?"

"Yeah. I thought we were far enough back."

"We need to move." Jude took in as deep a breath as he could, clenched his teeth, and sat up. Earth-tilting pain arrested his chest and stole the air he'd just sucked in. His vision faded in and out until he got his breathing under control.

"You okay?" Bryce asked.

Jude nodded. "Let's go."

The seriousness of the situation had sunk in and, without a word of protest, Bryce helped steady Jude as he stood. They rushed around to the back of the firetruck.

And just in time. More shots fired. They pinged the metal above Bryce's head, and Jude yanked him down, his vision going splotchy with the effort. "You need to lie low, man."

Bryce turned back to him, head cocked to the side. "This is about what's going on with Mom, isn't it?"

"It has The Brothers written all over it."

"The who?"

"Brothers. They're assassins. Snipers."

"You sure about that?" He pointed to Jude's chest as if evidence of their poor shooting. It was just the opposite.

"They did exactly what they should have if they thought I wasn't wearing a vest. Plus, I think the shots are coming from the other side of the burning car. In the woods. There's a lot of interference to shoot through."

Bryce nodded. "Now what?"

"You keep your back to this." Jude patted the truck. "And stay here."

Bryce looked like he wanted to argue, but he pressed his lips together with a sharp nod.

Good. At least one Crawford could take orders.

First, Jude needed to make sure Andi was okay. He caught sight of her on the ground, kneeling next to the firefighter who had been shot. She was behind cover, which was good. He wanted to rush to her, but the open space he'd have to cross to reach her, and the pain radiating through his chest, made him hesitate. She was safe, for now.

Next, he needed to deal with whoever was shooting at them.

Jude took a tentative step away from the support of the truck. He pulled out his gun, though the action caused more pain to slice through him. He gasped, his free arm going around his side.

Jude looked out over the crowd of firefighters and police. "Where's backup?" Some officers had come to the cover of the trucks, guns out, but it was clear they didn't know who or where to shoot.

"There's a traffic jam the size of Texas out there, and the cars can't get through." Bryce shrugged.

It figured. The Brothers had done their homework and found a place that would provide them the perfect vantage to pick people off. The fire had only been to lure out the Crawford siblings.

What would they do next?

More gunfire interrupted Jude's thoughts, and he shifted to press his back against the rescue squad's engine. If he could convince Andi to let one of the other paramedics take over, he could get the siblings to safety. But to where? It wasn't just the emergency vehicles that were gridlocked.

Jude should have trusted his gut and driven himself. Then again, it wouldn't matter if the roads weren't clear. Besides, even with reinforcements, they faced danger until The Brothers were neutralized.

He shifted to the edge of the rescue truck and watched the directionality of the shots now that he was standing. Several hit the firetruck. The next ones pinged off the ambulance just north of it. The shooters were on the move.

The angle of the shots changed, and he reassessed the situation. Andi would soon be in their line of sight. She was their target.

"Bryce, stay here. You got that? Stay behind the truck."

"I already told you I would, even though one of my guys is injured."

"Just making sure." Jude held his gaze to show the seriousness of his command and then turned toward Andi.

She was twenty feet away, but fifteen of that was open air. He didn't have a choice, and he still had the vest. He was going to risk it.

Jude pushed himself into the open. More than fearing bullets, he feared movement. Every step he took burned through his abdomen like glass shards pressed into his side. Then he was behind the safety of the other truck. He slowed, but kept his focus on Andi. "We need to get out of here."

She grimaced, sweat on her hairline, as she held pressure on the downed man's leg. "We need to get Jayson into the ambulance."

Jude turned to see where it was parked. Close to the

burned-out car but also in front of the firetrucks. There was no way they could make it.

More shots erupted and glass from the firetruck's window rained down near them. That was when Jude caught sight of Trace, the other paramedic. He was running their way.

The dark-haired man slid to a stop. "You have another gun?"

Jude frowned. "What?"

"Gun. I need a gun."

"He's former police." Andi's explanation shifted Jude's perspective of the man.

"Here's my backup." Jude handed over his Beretta APX Carry from his ankle holster.

Two guns were better than one—especially if it gave them a chance to end this without anyone else getting hurt.

Trace inspected the gun before looking up at Jude. "They're on the move."

"Probably trying to get a better angle back here, but we can't let that happen. We're too exposed if they make it past the burning car," Jude said.

He knew the only way to end this would be to stop the shooters.

Trace nodded. "What's the play?"

Jude pulled him to the edge of the firetruck, suppressing a wince as sharp pain radiated from his side. He pointed discreetly, saying, "You lay down cover fire, and I'll head straight toward the car. If they're distracted enough, I can make it to the tree line. I'll be covered from there."

"Then what?"

"I stalk them while you keep them busy." Jude's answer came a second too late. They both knew there wasn't much else they could do if backup was delayed. "It's the only way."

It was risky. The time Jude would be without sufficient cover was too great, but what other choice did they have?

"I—" More shots cut Trace off.

"We don't have another choice."

"It's a good plan, but you're injured, so I'm heading for the car while you supply cover fire." Trace's look said there was no room for argument.

Jude gave a curt nod and stepped out from the security of the fire engines to lay down cover fire as Trace took off like the friendly shots were the start of a race.

He watched for the shooters to retaliate. When he saw a figure in the trees illuminated by a muzzle flash, he took aim. The man went down.

Tense minutes passed as Trace disappeared into the forest, and soon the returning fire stopped. Was it possible Trace had apprehended them? It took everything in Jude not to rush into the forest to help, but without his cover fire, it would be pointless until Trace called the all-clear or...

Jude didn't want to think about an alternative option. There wasn't one he would accept. Trace would have to be successful.

Trace emerged from the tree line a few minutes later, waving a hand above his head.

Relief coursed through Jude, but the next second he heard Andi barking orders. They needed to get to the hospital stat.

"Bryce." Jude called him over. "You go straight back to the firehouse after this. Got it?"

"I will, but you have to protect her." The man's gaze drifted to his sister. "I saw the shots. The shooters were going after Andi. Do what you have to do to keep her safe."

He nodded to her brother. It wasn't something he agreed to lightly. "Keep your head down."

"You know I will." Bryce grinned.

"I'm coming with you." Jude rushed to Andi's side, shifting aside as Izan, Trace's partner, came over with a gurney.

"I don't care what you do." She kept her focus on the injured firefighter. "I can't release pressure or he'll bleed out."

Jude saw the seriousness of the situation juxtaposed with the utter calm on Andi's face. She knew exactly what she was doing. She was in what he'd call "the zone." He felt it when he was close to solving a case and all the pieces aligned. The same calm someone experienced when they were good at their job. An expert in it.

Andi the paramedic had more confidence than he'd ever seen in her, and it was awe-inspiring.

"All right. Then tell me what to do."

She took a moment to look up at him. Was she surprised that he wanted to help?

"Help strap him in, and let's get him into the ambo."

"You got it."

26

Andi washed her bloodied hands under a stream of cool water. She scrubbed until the water ran clear, then reached for a towel. Her hands were clean, but her turnout gear still showed the signs of the trauma. Reminding her of everything that had happened.

Emerging from the bathroom, she wandered the antiseptic-scented halls of the hospital to get some of her nervous energy out but soon found herself at the vending machine. It taunted her with chocolate and salty chips, and she gave in, feeding dollars in until she had a good-sized hoard of snacks.

"I had the same idea." Penny grinned at her over a handful of dollar bills. "Heard you did some amazing work today."

"The fire was a tough one." Andi unwrapped a candy bar and stuffed half the chocolate-and-nougat-filled treat in her mouth.

"I meant the guy you saved. Heard he's going to be okay." Penny gave her an odd look. "Kind of trumps a car fire, doesn't it?"

"Jayson is okay?" Andi swallowed a mouthful of chocolate.

"Doc came out just a few minutes ago to update everyone."

"That's great news." Andi sagged against the wall. She'd been waiting on an update. Of course the woman would be talking about Jayson—she'd barely done anything with the fire.

"You hear about the guy Jude shot?"

Andi's attention snapped up. "What?"

"He and Trace, I think it is? They went on the offensive, and Jude got one guy. According to my sources, they're pretty sure it's Sosa, actually."

Andi's jaw dropped. She didn't care if there was chocolate around her mouth. "Sosa was there?" She lowered her voice and looked around. "*He* was shooting at us?"

"Looks like it." Penny shoved dollars into the vending machine and started pressing buttons like a professional. "Not sure if you knew this, but Sosa was once a sniper himself. They think he had someone—maybe The Brothers—set up the car fire to lure you and your brothers out. It worked—thankfully not well enough, though."

"Yeah. Thankfully." Andi echoed Penny's word, but her mind raced ahead. Sosa was dead. This nightmare was over. She could get back to focusing on her job.

It also meant Jude would leave soon.

"They caught one of The Brothers, but the bomb guy—Fausto—is in the wind. Either way, the head is cut off the snake, which is the most important part." Penny grinned. "You should look happier."

Andi forced a smile. She *was* happy. She was also overwhelmed. The last few days had been filled with impossible things and so much danger. But now...she wasn't sure she knew how to reconcile the fact it was all just over. "I think I'm still in shock."

"I get it." Penny's voice and expression softened. "It's a lot to take in."

"Do you know where Jude is?" The question slipped out, but Penny didn't seem surprised she'd asked.

"I think they've got him in a room for observation, though I doubt they'll get him to stay overnight."

"I can imagine. Hey, thanks for all your help with this, Penny." Andi held the woman's gaze. "I know you've done a lot to protect my family, and I'm grateful."

"It's my job." She paused. "But it's also my passion. Protecting people."

Andi could understand that. She felt the same way about being a firefighter. Saving people was her calling. "You're good at it."

Penny grinned, and Andi left to find Jude. She made her way down familiar halls, thankful her father was safe, and praying that no one else in her family would need to be admitted to the hospital again anytime soon.

Several doors down from where Penny had pointed, Andi heard male voices and slowed.

Logan laughed—or was it Bryce?—and she couldn't help but smile, thinking that they were finally warming up to Jude. They'd liked him just fine during his visiting summers, but they also hadn't been around much during that time. Sports, girlfriends, and summer parties had taken them away from home most evenings, but she hadn't minded then. It had given her time with her best friend Jude.

She missed the quiet way he'd listened to her. How he'd made her laugh so easily. Even his stutter—maybe especially that—had made him stand out to her. He'd faced a lot in life but hadn't let it change him. She'd always admired that. And she'd always had a crush on him too, if she were honest.

With a decisive smile, she moved forward on a collision course with the open doorway when she heard her name.

"...Andi just doesn't see it." That was Bryce, given the way he laughed after.

"She saved Jayson's life. How can she think being a firefighter is more important than that?" Logan this time.

"She's passionate about both." Jude spoke from a place of thoughtfulness, his voice tender, and her heart softened.

"Maybe, but there comes a time when the cold hard truth has to hit you." Such a typical Logan way of approaching life.

She ground her teeth and almost stepped into the doorway when Jude spoke up again. "Just because she doesn't see it now doesn't mean she won't see it later. Sure, we can all agree she's a much better paramedic than a firefighter, but she has to come to that conclusion on her own. Having her big brothers tell her that won't change anything."

"Maybe not," Bryce said. "But maybe it should. We've been there. Done that. She should trust our judgment when we tell her to go back to being a paramedic."

The words cut deeper than a knife wound. They didn't think she could cut it as a firefighter. No, they thought they *knew* she couldn't. They were convinced, and Jude agreed with them.

All the warm feelings she'd harbored toward Jude evaporated.

She'd almost let herself believe he understood her. That he would stand up for her against her brothers, who always thought they knew better than she did, but here he was agreeing with them.

She needed a man who believed in her. She needed someone who would fight alongside her, not against her. Someone who would support her no matter what.

Her hands fisted. How dare they discuss her like this? She was about to turn away when her brothers appeared.

"Oh. Uh, hey, Andi." Bryce had the good conscience to look ashamed.

"Dee, what are you doing here?" Logan looked from her to

Bryce and back. She could tell they were both wondering how much she'd heard.

"I was coming to see Jude."

Bryce and Logan now both looked like they wanted to explain, but rather than watch them backpedal, she stepped into Jude's room and closed the door. The finality of the click and following silence was a welcome reprieve.

"Andi." Jude sounded as surprised as her brothers but didn't look half as guilty.

He sat on the edge of a hospital bed in torn up slacks and no shirt. A bandage had been wrapped around his bare torso, but she could see the purpling of bruises spreading out beneath it. She forced her gaze to his eyes, not allowing herself to take in his muscular chest and arms. The attraction she felt for him.

Instead, she channeled her anger. "How could you side with them?"

"I wasn't."

"You were." To her horror, tears threatened at the back of her eyes, but she willed them away. "Everyone thinks they know what's best for me. You said it yourself—I'm passionate. Where you got it wrong is in thinking that my passion still rests with being a paramedic. That's not me."

She'd almost admitted again that she'd tried and couldn't save everyone. *That* was the harshest blow of all.

When she worked as a firefighter, she was part of a team, and she was fighting a foe she could understand. Fire took predictable courses. Human bodies did not.

"Dee, I don't know what you th-think you h-heard." He took a breath. Then another. "I kn-know you do your best as a firefighter. This isn't a-about that. It's about the fact you're an amazing paramedic. You could be a doctor someday if you w-wanted."

She rolled her eyes. "It's not what I want. Okay? Everyone thinks they know what's best, but I thought you were different." Her voice broke, and she turned her back on him to compose herself. "Clearly, you and my brothers and everyone else in this world think you know me better than I do. Well, I'm over it. Okay? Done. It's my life and I'm going to do what I think is best."

"Dee, you're not h-hearing m-me."

"I'm hearing you fine. And you know what this is? This is the gorge all over again."

Her mention of their past—of that summer—seemed to leech all the oxygen from the room.

"This isn't that." A shadow passed over the openness she'd seen in his eyes.

"It is. You thought I couldn't handle owning up to my own mistakes, so you took the blame. Did you think I was so weak? I mean, come on, Jude." She shook her head erratically. "I was seventeen, and I definitely knew better. I could take the punishment—but you never let me."

"It wasn't your m-mi-mistakes I was worried about. It was m-mine."

She clenched her teeth. "This is about me and my choices. Just like being a firefighter. All I need is for you and my brothers to leave me alone. Let me do what I think is best. I don't need you to fix me or take the blame for me. I don't even need you to fix my shower. I'll do it myself."

He jerked like she'd slapped him, but she didn't care. She needed him to know she was serious. She couldn't entertain thoughts about a life with Jude if he was just going to undermine her.

Andi spun on her heel, yanked the door open, and stomped down the hallway. She'd check on Jayson and then she'd go home and shower—no. She'd go home and *fix* her shower. That would show him.

The dark storm of her thoughts distracted her, and she

nearly ran into Amelia. "Lieutenant." Andi staggered back in surprise.

"Crawford. I mean, Andi." Amelia flashed what she probably thought was a smile, but it landed like a placating grimace.

"What are you doing here?"

"Came to see Jayson." Her expression softened. "I heard you did a good thing out there today."

"Thanks." The word lodged itself in Andi's throat.

"You know, you're really talented as a paramedic."

"Thank you." She wasn't sure what else to say.

"I hope you've thought through your decision to remain on Truck."

"What are you trying to say, Lieutenant?"

"Hey, I get it. You want to prove yourself, and you're doing a good job as a probie, but you did an *excellent* job as a paramedic today." Amelia let the words sink in. "Make the choice that's best for all, not the one that's best for your ego."

The words were like a bucket of icy water.

"I'm always going to tell it like it is, Crawford. Besides, us ladies have to stick together." She flashed that smile again and turned toward the ICU.

Andi stood frozen for several minutes. Amelia's words were all kinds of confusing. She was looking out for Andi but questioning her? How did that work?

Emotions welled up in her, but rather than face them head on or let them eat away at her, Andi decided on action. She was going for a run. A long one. Then she'd fix her shower, eat a tub of Ben and Jerry's, and sleep until noon.

The sooner the mess Sosa left behind cleared and Jude was gone, the sooner she could get back to her life. To finally prove her worth as a firefighter to everyone who doubted her.

27

J ude pressed his arm against his side as he stepped off the sidewalk into the parking lot, squinting to avoid the late-afternoon sun. The doctor hadn't been happy to release him, but there was no way Jude was staying in there any longer.

Andi's words haunted him. He knew she'd spoken from a place of hurt, but it bothered him he hadn't been able to make her understand where he was coming from. She was incredibly talented, and yes, if she wanted it, she could be an amazing firefighter, but just because she could didn't mean she should.

He winced, unsure if the reaction came from thinking the words he knew she'd hate or the motion to get into his car. He was thankful Bryce had agreed to drop it off when he and Logan came to check on Jayson with the rest of the squad, but he was rethinking the decision to drive himself.

The engine revved to life, but he paused before shifting into gear. Sosa was dead according to officers on scene who had taken over when he left for the hospital with Andi. His team was prepping to come out to help him wrap the case. One

Brother was in custody, the other being tracked. The nightmare was over.

But Andi.

Jude rubbed a hand over his face and groaned. Every movement shot pain through his chest and abdomen, but it was nothing compared to the look of betrayal he'd seen on Andi's face. He'd wanted to encourage her, to remind her she could do amazing things as a paramedic if she'd just see her own talent.

That had backfired.

Something inside of him wouldn't let him give up. She'd said a lot of things in anger in the hospital room, but he couldn't leave Last Chance County again without telling her how he truly felt.

He shoved the gearshift forward and sped out of the parking lot. She wouldn't want to see him, but he didn't care. He'd left once after messing up, and he would never do that again.

He flew past cozy neighborhoods as he made turns by rote. His grandfather had been the one to teach him to drive on these very roads, and he sometimes felt he could have gotten home with his eyes closed.

When his grandfather's house came into view, his spirits dipped. Andi's car wasn't there.

Pulling in, he thought to call her, but an idea struck him. He'd fix her shower. Show her he was serious. Then he'd wait—no matter how long—to talk with her.

Within the hour, he was back on the porch. The repair had taken less time than he'd expected, and now he shifted in his seat, waiting for her. The ache in his ribs made it hard to get comfortable. His gaze traveled up the road, then back down. No Andi. He tried to stretch his arms and sucked in a breath at the spike of pain. He'd need to take another pain pill soon.

Still no Andi.

When a truck turned down the street, he stood, but it was

Logan and Bryce. Probably coming to check on their parents. He ambled down the steps, thinking to ask about Andi, but when Bryce hopped out, he beat him to it.

"You seen Dee?"

A frisson of worry edged past Jude's rational thoughts. Sosa was dead. His motive had died with him. There was no need to worry she was in danger. He blamed the worries on the fact he cared for her, but there was no discounting the danger the Crawford family had all been victims of.

Jude frowned. "I assumed she was at the firehouse."

"We were just there." Logan made a face. "Paperwork."

"She left the hospital before me." It was the only thought Jude had.

"Yeah, Amelia said she ran into her outside of Jayson's room. I thought she'd be home by now."

"Not since I got here." Jude checked his watch. "Been about two hours."

Bryce frowned. "I don't like this. She doesn't go many places." Then, as if hearing how that sounded, he amended. "I mean, work, gym, home. I guess she could be at the gym?"

"I'm sure she's fine." Logan closed the truck door with a bang. "Sometimes she needs space, you know? Maybe running off some steam after overhearing our conversation."

So they knew she'd heard. "Yeah, she wasn't thrilled about that."

"Sorry, man." Logan grimaced. "We kind of left you hanging there."

Jude opened his mouth to reply, but the sound of a car drew their attention. It was Penny in the monstrous black SUV she'd rented. She pulled in behind Logan's truck.

"Sheesh," Bryce said. Jude caught his look that was halfway between awe and intimidation.

"Hey, fellas." Penny hopped down and came toward Jude, focus in every one of her booted steps.

"That's quite a vehicle, Ms. Mitchell," Bryce said.

"I like to be prepared for all situations." Her half smile was a bit on the flirty side.

"I bet you do." Bryce's responding flirty answer got an eye roll from Logan, which made Penny laugh.

"Sorry, guys, but I need to talk shop with *Ms. Mitchell* here." Jude cut to the chase, hoping to avoid a sibling argument.

"Sure thing," Logan said.

"It was, uh, nice to see you, Ms. Mitchell." Bryce all but waggled his eyebrows, and Jude held in a laugh.

"It's Penny. And same to you."

Bryce looked as if he wanted to say something, but Jude directed Penny toward the chairs in front of the airstream.

"He's a flirty one," Penny said once the brothers had gone inside.

"I am not talking about boys with you."

She laughed. "Spoil sport. At least tell me if he's single."

"I have no idea, nor do I care."

She folded her arms with an unamused expression. "Well, fine."

"What's up? Do you have info on the Brother who's on the loose? Do they think he's circling back to town?"

"Locals hope to have an update soon. They say he was headed into wilderness terrain the last time they caught sight of him, but visibility is pretty awful. The helicopters were struggling to see through the dense foliage."

He nodded. "Makes sense."

"I was about to head back to my hotel, but I wanted to see if you needed anything else."

Jude shifted, the metal chair causing his ribs to ache. "I've got my team working on leads at the moment, but they head out here tomorrow afternoon. Mainly, we need to chase down anyone who might step into Sosa's place. I doubt anyone wants to claim that sinking ship, though."

Penny shrugged. "If someone had the money, it wouldn't matter."

"Is his network worth it?"

"Criminals are strange. They could see it as opportunity or clout. It's best to keep an eye on things for a time."

"True." He looked back down the road again, hoping Andi's car would turn toward the house.

"You okay?"

He blinked away from his thoughts. "Uh, yeah." Words jumbled together in his mind. "It's A-Andi."

Penny smirked. "I knew there was something there."

"Maybe. Yeah. I-I don't know."

It bothered him that Andi thought he was against her. That she'd brought up a difficult part of their shared history like it was proof.

"Well? What's the problem?"

Besides the fact he didn't know where she was? "I think I blew it." He filled Penny in on everything that had happened at the hospital, and Penny nodded in understanding.

"I think she'll come around." Penny crossed her jean-clad legs. "She's a strong woman, and it's obvious she's fought for her place at the firehouse—even if you and her brothers can only see her potential as a paramedic. It's hard being a woman in certain professions, and I think the thought of having to fight those she cares about as well as everyone else telling her she won't make it might be too much. You have to be honest with her. You can't go back on what she overheard, but you can explain and let the chips fall where they may."

That didn't sound too hopeful, but he considered what Penny was saying.

"And you might need to play outside of your rules a little." Penny grinned.

"Rules?"

"You know what I mean, *Book*. When the time comes to talk to her, you'll know it."

"That's cryptic."

"All I know, Jude, is that sometimes things work out. We think a certain moment is the right moment for something, then it falls through. Or we plan for something and it never happens. We're creatures of disappointment when what we want gets in the way of what's best for us."

Jude could see where she was coming from. But that didn't make it easy. Give him a plan and he'd follow it to the letter, but leave it up to the heart...that delved into unknowable territory. Too many chances for something to go wrong.

"It'll be okay, Book." Penny lightly rested her hand on his arm. "If it's meant to be, there isn't anything in this world that'll stop it."

She stood and flashed him one last smile before climbing back into the SUV. The engine noise tried to drown out his thoughts, but that was impossible.

If it was meant to be? Andi was the woman for him, no question. Nothing was going to change that.

Jude pulled out his phone and put in a call to Andi. After a ring it went to voicemail. She'd turned it off or put it on Do Not Disturb. Maybe Logan was right, and Andi just needed space. He could give that to her.

His team would arrive, and they would take over a conference room at the police department. He'd already cleared that with Chief Barnes. Then the hard work would begin. Following leads fueled by rumors was never easy, but justice pushed him forward. They'd ripped out Sosa from his cartel like a weed, and it would be his team's job to ensure all traces of his power were erased.

Besides those leads, he had paperwork to fill out and meetings with Chief Barnes as well as the ATF office in Denver before he'd head back to San Diego. It would be busy, but he'd be here for a few days. In Last Chance County. That felt like the right choice for the first time in a long time.

He just needed to do like Penny said—be on the alert for an opportunity and take it when the time came.

Jude pushed to his feet. He'd called his colleagues before he'd left the hospital, so it was too early to get an update from them. Nothing worse than being an overbearing boss. But with Andi gone, he wasn't sure what to do with himself.

Get started on paperwork? Nah, he wasn't feeling it.

Go over and hang out with the Crawfords? It was tempting, but he also wanted to give Logan and Bryce time with their parents without them having to worry about him as a guest. They were facing their own type of grief with the loss of the family nurse and the brush with danger they'd each had. It took time to move past that.

His gaze traveled toward the familiarity of his grandfather's house and the obvious wear. He missed the older man.

Inspiration struck. Hadn't Andi given him a full list of things that needed fixing, not just the shower?

With nothing else to do and a desire to prove his devotion to the woman he was falling for, he'd step into the role of Mr. Fix-It. Anything to prove to Andi he was serious about his devotion to her. Serious enough to play by her rules.

28

A ndi wiped the sweat from her brow against the shoulder of her T-shirt without breaking stride. The muscles in her legs burned along with the ache in her lungs as she struggled to pull in air. It felt good, though. The type of burn that made everything else fade to the background and ensured results. She'd be sore in the morning for the grueling pace, but it also meant she'd sleep well.

She picked up her pace as she rounded the bend of the high-school track. This was the last quarter mile, and she needed to push. To push hard.

She sucked in a breath. Pumped her arms. Tucked her chin. The pace she'd initially set gave way to a full-on sprint. Everything in her propelled her forward, one foot after the other. Faster. Then the finish line, set out in her mind, came into view.

All thoughts faded to black as she laser-focused on the line. Ignoring the warning signals she'd reached the end of her energy reserves, she gave just a little more until her foot crossed the line.

Her pace immediately slowed, and her legs quaked with the

exertion. She wanted to collapse into the grass, but she needed to keep moving in order to let her heart rate slow.

Life flooded back in, and thoughts of Jude took advantage of the lapse.

She was still angry, even after a punishing workout and five-mile run. How did he have this kind of hold over her still? His ability to get under her skin irked her. He'd probably thought encouraging her abilities as a paramedic was helpful, but it was the opposite. Salt on wounds.

And then there were the words she'd thrown at him. Mean, spiteful words. Words he didn't deserve.

Maybe she didn't need him, but did that mean she didn't want him around?

Hands on her knees, Andi drew in lungfuls of air until she felt her heart rate slow. She chugged her water, then switched to the Gatorade she'd gotten from the vending machine at the hospital as she paced up and down the track for a few additional minutes. The sun sat low to the west, and a group of teens entered the field with a frisbee. That was her cue to leave.

Back in her car, she sat with the windows down, unsure of where to go. She'd had a grand plan that involved fixing her shower, but one complex YouTube video had cured her of that notion. The plan for ice cream was still in the back of her mind, but the thought of taking it to her house and eating alone while knowing Jude was in the airstream seemed disappointing.

She could always ask him to join her.

Andi dismissed the thought immediately. She was still mad. At him. At her brothers. Even at Sosa for creating this whole mess.

There was only one place she could go get a shower and sleep in peace.

The firehouse.

On the way there, she stopped by the grocery store and

picked up her favorite mint and fudge brownie ice cream, then pulled in just as the parking lot lights flickered on.

The sweat from her run had dried, and she shivered as she climbed from the car. She reached into the trunk and grabbed the freezer bag of ice cream and her go-bag, thankful she always had one ready.

The sounds of mariachi music came from the kitchen. She dropped her bag on a couch in the entryway and peered around the corner. Izan swayed back and forth, singing in Spanish at the top of his lungs with a bread knife in one hand and a long Italian-style loaf held in front of his mouth like a microphone.

"Sounds pretty good, Izan."

He flinched and turned toward her.

His startled expression made her laugh. "Sorry to scare you."

"I definitely couldn't hear you over the music." He placed the bread and knife on the cutting board and turned the volume down.

"Where is everyone?" Quiet nights were common, but Andi was used to seeing a few firefighters around, studying for a test or watching a show.

"There was a callout for a bonfire that got out of hand, which didn't need Ambo, so Trace is getting some rack time. Apparently, I can't sleep on an empty stomach." He held up a plate, a double-layer sandwich stacked next to a mound of potato chips.

"Looks good."

"Want one?"

She shook her head. "No. It's a Mr. Ben and Mr. Jerry night for me."

"Should I be worried?" He quirked an eyebrow.

"Nah. Just needed some chocolate after today." Not to

mention they were the only men whose company she could stand right now. "How are you doing after all of the craziness?"

She'd seen him working on a few of the other firefighters who'd gotten caught by shrapnel or grazed by bullets, but nothing like what she'd had to handle with Jayson.

Izan set his plate down and let out a deep sigh. "Not great."

"It was pretty terrifying." She could admit that. Her fear had almost gotten the best of her.

Working under the stress of a fire with differing conditions was one thing, but trying to do that while being shot at was a completely different matter.

"It was. But it's more than that." Izan wouldn't meet her gaze, and she grew worried. He was acting strangely, almost as if he were hesitant to tell her something. Or guilty. "I, uh, have something I wanted to run by you."

When he paused, she felt the urge to push him on. "What is it? You know you can talk to me, Iz." She thought back to the day he'd gotten distracted while on the job. Did this have something to do with that?

Her mind raced ahead, jumping to unfounded assumptions. The woman had said Izan looked familiar. Was it possible he was going to confess a drug addiction? If so, why would he tell her? Sure, they'd bonded over both wanting the coveted spot on Truck, but she'd never considered him a confidant.

She tried to reel in her wild conclusions, but his hesitation had lasted so long already she could only go deeper into her own questions.

He finally raised his eyes to meet hers. "It's about—"

Meow! Meow! MEOW.

"Ashes." She uttered the name like a curse.

Izan laughed, some of his tension falling away. "Can't believe that thing stays around." He ran a hand along the back of his neck.

"It's the food she likes." Andi had thought about not feeding her, but she softened at the thought of the cat fending for itself. For as much trouble as Ashes'd gotten Andi into, she'd also started to let Andi pet her. The only one at the firehouse she showed any affection for.

MEOW.

Izan flinched. "She's really persistent."

"You know what they say about cats. We're just here to do their bidding." Andi rolled her eyes. "Let me feed her and then we can talk. Toss this in the freezer for me, will you?" She slid the ice cream toward him and watched for any sign of what he'd been about to say. The only thing that came across was his own uneasiness.

She wanted to put off feeding the cat because of whatever Izan had to say—it was clearly important—but Ashes would only cry louder. They didn't need that distraction.

Grabbing a can of cat food from the pantry where she'd stocked it, Andi pulled the top off and headed out into the night. Her thoughts were a cloud of questions about the young man.

"I'm coming, Ash. Just hold on, you little demanding fiend," Andi muttered to herself as she picked her way through the darkness at the back of the firehouse near the ambo bays. The cat liked to hang out in the tree next to her window and would come scratching to get in, but Andi had taken to letting her in through the back door at night instead.

"Ashes?" She peered through the darkness for any sign of the cat's reflective eyes.

She looked over the back parking lot where several of her co-workers' cars were parked. It was dark with one of the parking lot lights out, and Andi didn't have high hopes of seeing the black cat.

Her eyes skimmed over the first rescue squad member's truck and then moved past the second, and then the third, but something about that one was off. She looked back and, as her eyes adjusted to the light, she saw what she thought was a person slumped against the front bumper.

Her first impulse was to rush back inside for Izan. Not that she was afraid, but she didn't want to put herself in a dangerous situation alone. Transients sometimes came to the firehouse seeking odd jobs or a handout, but usually not at night.

Then she heard a moan. Pulse pounding, she took a few steps toward the person. Were they hurt? If so, that was another matter.

"Hello?" she called out.

Another moan, louder this time, filled the night.

"Hello? Do you need help?"

"Hurt. Bad." She heard the masculine voice over the uptick of wind through the oak trees.

"You're hurt?" She took a few more steps in his direction.

"Yes. Need... help. Please."

Pulse racing, Andi warred between the urge to help someone and caution.

"Please."

One word, but it was the only one she needed. She'd taken an oath when she became a paramedic, and even though she was now a firefighter, she couldn't forget. She had vowed to do everything she could to save lives without doing harm. Harm, in this instance, would be to do nothing.

"Okay, hold on. I'm coming."

"Hurry." His voice was faint, and he sounded on the verge of passing out.

Pushing thoughts of Ashes aside, Andi threw the tin of cat food onto the back porch and rushed toward the vehicle where the man leaned.

"I'm coming, sir. Just hold on." She pulled her phone from her pocket since it appeared the man had little time before he collapsed. She'd call in to the station and have Izan come out to help her.

"Please." The man's voice was a whisper as she reached him. He wore a dark hat, his head bowed.

"Sir? What's the problem? Where does it hurt?"

"Here." He motioned toward his abdomen, where both of his palms pressed against a ragged blanket.

She leaned closer, the dim light making it hard to see. "I can't—"

His head came up, and the emblem of twisting yellow snakes on the front of his hat gave her pause.

Yellow snakes.

Like a lightning strike, his arm wrapped around her neck. He maneuvered her so that her back was against his chest. His arm clenched around her windpipe in a fierce chokehold.

Andi's senses came alive with fear. She couldn't breathe. Couldn't move. The man's arms were like steel, and the one around her neck cut off her airway.

She needed to scream. Needed to alert Izan to the danger. But her voice was cut off with her air supply.

She clawed at the man's arm, but the thick jacket he wore provided protection from her nails. She tried to kick his legs, but his stance left no window of opportunity. Even tried to dip her chin like she'd learned in self-defense class, but his hold was too tight. He was too strong.

She had no air.

No breath.

He was going to kill her.

29

Fire pulsed in Jude's side. He'd knocked Andi's list back from ten items to three. He'd only left the tasks that required a trip to the hardware store, but he was confident he could finish them up in an afternoon.

He stood tall as he stepped out onto her porch. The cool evening air greeted him like an old friend with the scents and sounds of his past.

He heard the muffled chatter of a television show alongside the chirping of night bugs. Smelled the promise of rain come morning. He shivered in his T-shirt as a gust of wind rang the chimes on Andi's front porch.

It had been almost three hours since he'd started Andi's list, and she still wasn't home. She hadn't called him back either and, despite being able to rationalize away a lot of things, he was worried. His last call had been thirty minutes ago, and it had gone straight to voicemail. Again.

He popped the top of a diet soda, and the can hissed. It'd felt odd raiding her fridge, but after the work he'd done, surely she wouldn't mind.

He eased down into a wicker chair on the porch and

surveyed the night. Everything was quiet now that the threat of Sosa was over. It was a blessing, to be sure, but it felt wrong enjoying the peace without Andi.

The sound of footsteps drew his attention to the walkway, and he saw Elizabeth on the pathway, coming toward him with a foil-wrapped plate. His stomach growled in anticipation.

"The boys said you were working on the house over here."

He sat up straight and tried not to wince at the pain that stabbed him in the side every time he moved.

"They also said you took a bullet for my daughter." She placed the plate between them and sat in the other chair. "Jude, what can I say?" She sniffed and wiped under her eye.

"It's all right, Mrs. C." He fought for the words to encourage her. "It's part of my job."

"I think it's more than that." She sniffed again before leveling a look at him. "You still have feelings for my daughter."

Jude's response lodged in his throat.

"Don't look so surprised. I may have been busy back then, during those summers, but I wasn't blind. You both liked each other but did nothing about it. Well, to my knowledge, neither of you did."

Heat crept up his neck. Sitting on the porch of his grandfather's home discussing his feelings for Andi with her mother felt wrong in some ways and right in others. Who better than Elizabeth to know her daughter's heart?

"I never got up the courage t-to ask her out." Not officially, anyway.

They had done plenty of things together as friends, though. Maybe, in retrospect, that was better. He'd been two years older than her and always had to go home at the end of summer. Where could things have gone?

There was that kiss, though.

"I think she knew how you felt. Or at least, hoped."

Elizabeth sounded wistful. "In fact, I think those feelings are still there."

Jude swallowed. Took a deep breath. "I...I might have ruined all of that."

"You mean what you and the boys said? She has always been sensitive about criticism."

"That's just it. I wasn't criticizing her—I think she's an incredible paramedic."

"If it isn't what she's focused on, those words go in one ear and out the other." The woman smiled, tugging at a thread on the sleeve of her white linen shirt. "She gets in her mind that she has to compete. With everyone. Even with herself sometimes. Jude, don't let her bristles push you away forever. Andi is headstrong and focused—sometimes too much. Perhaps she's too much like me. But at her core, she's bold and unrelenting about the right things. How she loves her family, how she attacks her job, how she loves."

Jude knew all of this to be true of her, but none of it mattered if she couldn't forgive him—for the past and in the present.

Elizabeth continued, "I think she needs someone like you in her life. Someone calm who can help her play by the rules now and then. But also someone who's going to give it to her straight when she needs it."

"I'd like to be that someone." The admission felt personal, but Elizabeth didn't react.

"Good."

He shifted in his seat. "Do you know where she is?"

"If she's not here, she's usually at the gym or—"

"At the firehouse."

"Exactly. I'd try there. I know she's been having problems with her shower. Maybe she stayed there for the night."

"Thanks, Mrs. C."

She stood and pointed to the plate. "Just some leftover

enchiladas." A moment of sorrow passed over her features, and she closed her eyes. "Becca made them. They're incredible."

"I'm sorry for your loss, Elizabeth."

She nodded, fingers to her lips. "I hate to think we could have avoided all of this had I simply admitted to knowing where the money was."

Her words sent a spark through Jude. "You know where it is?"

She looked startled at his statement, surprised. "I—I shouldn't have said anything. I promised him I wouldn't."

"Elizabeth, I need to know *all* of what you know. No more half-truths. No more holding things back." He stood, ignoring the sharp pain, and moved to her. "What else do you know?"

"I suppose I should have told you this when I shared at the hospital, but it didn't feel like my place to say. "

Jude nodded, encouraging her to go on.

"I told you about Camilo. He was a good man—"

"Was?"

She nodded, lips pressed tight. "He passed away a few months ago. That's when I got the letter."

Why hadn't this information come out when Penny's contacts had looked into his roommate at ADX? His death seemed like a vital detail.

"I suppose you could say it was like his last will, of sorts. He wanted me to come to the prison because he had things to share with me that no one else could know—not even his roommate, who'd transcribed his other letters for him."

Pieces of the puzzle were falling into place. "It was about the money?"

"Yes, and his son. He told me about what he'd stolen and how to access it. And then instructed me to give it and a letter to his son when the time was right."

Jude stood straighter. "You know who the son is?"

She avoided his question. "As Sosa's accountant, Camilo

had been siphoning money from his accounts into one he could access anywhere, and his intention was always to provide for his son. Camilo was very good with numbers and hiding his tracks.

"When they left for America, Camilo put his plan into place, and the money left with them. He'd set it up so that Sosa wouldn't immediately realize it was gone. The ploy worked to buy them time to disappear."

Jude could imagine the anger over losing a girlfriend to a friend, but it wouldn't hold a candle to the wrath of Camilo stealing money from Sosa.

"When did Sosa find out about the money?"

Elizabeth shook her head. "As far as I understand, he still didn't know when he found Camilo in Denver."

Jude blinked. "How is that possible?"

"I wasn't privy to the specifics. I just know that after Sosa killed Renata, he demanded to know where the child was. He still thought it was his. Camilo told him the baby had died, and by then the police were on their way. Sosa left Camilo to his fate with the authorities."

"Then the threats against your family were to ensure the information linking Sosa to the crime was buried?"

"Yes, and that Camilo would live the rest of his life in prison. We convinced the DA and the judge to put him in ADX Florence, where Sosa had no connections. It was the only way Camilo could protect his son—by being out of Sosa's reach."

"Camilo knew Sosa would find out about the money."

"Exactly. And he did, but by then it was too late. Camilo was off-limits."

Jude shifted to lean against the porch post. If Camilo had allied himself with a rival cartel on the inside, he would have been safe. So would the money. But it would also mean his son would know nothing about the money or his father. The wash of information was impossible, and yet it aligned with what Jude knew.

"What about the child?"

"Somehow, Sosa found out that the child—a son—was still alive. Someone must have told him."

"Esteban, the cellmate. This is making sense."

"Who is Esteban?" Elizabeth's brows furrowed.

"We found his body in the basement of the house that nearly blew us up. He was Camilo's cellmate, but I couldn't figure out what the connection to Sosa was. Didn't you say that Camilo had his cellmate transcribe letters for him?"

"Yes. Camilo got cancer while he was in jail and was on his deathbed. He said his cellmate had offered to write the letters for him since his eyesight was bad."

"Esteban was released months ago, and Sosa must have gotten to him—or he went to Sosa."

The color drained from Elizabeth's face. "You think this Esteban talked to Sosa? Camilo wrote to me in vague terms about the money and thanked me for my help with the boy, but I don't know that he ever said the son was his. I already knew. What if Sosa thought the boy was his heir?"

Jude's stomach churned. It was likely he had, and to a cartel leader, knowledge of an heir would be powerful news. Both a son and money meant Sosa would have thought he had a legacy to protect.

He'd have to come back to the fact that she said she'd *helped* with the boy. "What I don't understand, Elizabeth, is if Sosa knew about the money...why wouldn't he go after you?"

Elizabeth flinched. "Because he knew better."

Her response surprised him. "How so?"

She tucked a strand of hair behind her ear with a shaky hand. Elizabeth was a strong woman, just like Andi, but that didn't mean she was immune to fear.

"I had a meeting with him during Camilo's trial. He knew

we had incriminating evidence against him and tried to intimidate me. I told him he'd never get what he wanted from me if he threatened me."

"So he threatened your family."

"Yes. I...was this all my fault?" She dropped her chin.

He didn't know what to tell her. Now that the danger was gone—Sosa was gone—there was room to breathe. They could sort this out. Still, he found the fact that Fausto had rigged the building Esteban was found in entirely too coincidental.

Fausto and The Brothers had to know about the money. And that knowledge filled his gut with lead. This wasn't over, and Andi was in danger.

"Elizabeth, go back inside. Tell Logan and Bryce to stay with you. In fact, call Chief Barnes and have him send a few men over. I've got to get to the firehouse."

"Sosa's dead. Do you think we're really in danger still?"

"What you've told me changes everything." There was still one Brother out there that knew about the money. "Besides, I'd rather be safe than sorry."

She gripped his hand. "Please, find Andi. Make sure she's okay."

He gave her a nod and rushed to his car. The seatbelt tugged uncomfortably around his chest, but it was an afterthought. His focus was getting to Andi. He couldn't explain it—that gut feeling again—but something Elizabeth had said about heirs nudged at him.

If Sosa knew she had access to the money and also had knowledge of his son, what might he do to gain that information? It would be about more than just money—it would be about blood.

Jude slammed a hand against the steering wheel.

Leverage. It had always been about leverage. It had been Sosa's move from the start. He'd frightened Elizabeth by hiring out Paul's accident, and then he'd hired The Brothers and Fausto to scare them—or, more accurately, scare her.

Sosa had been priming her from the start. Now that he was gone, it was likely the missing Brother knew about the money. It would be hard to pass up a payday like that.

The tires squealed as he took a corner too fast. His phone pinged to life, and Jude saw Penny was calling. He punched the Answer button and silence filled the car.

"Pen?"

"You didn't take out Sosa like we thought." She dropped the words like an anvil over the phone connection.

"I don't...what do you mean?"

"I ran by the morgue just to confirm, but the gunman we thought was Sosa was actually one of The Brothers. I identified him by a fake Russian Bratva tattoo I know they both have but Sosa doesn't."

"How did this happen?"

"Someone looked at a mislabeled photo of one of The Brothers when they identified Sosa. I don't know how it happened—take that up with Barnes."

"Sosa wasn't even there. He's been playing a shell game this whole time." The realization crystalized to sharp points. "The PD is still tracking him, right? And the second brother."

"We don't even think Sosa was at the staged burning car. But there's more."

"Tell me."

"Sosa was recently spotted at a gas station off of Highway 96."

Jude immediately knew the place she meant. It was right down the street from the fire station. "I've got to go. Sosa's going after Andi."

ndi's head pounded with the worst headache she'd ever had, and she couldn't remember where she was. Her hands were tied behind her, and she couldn't see anything. It was so dark.

What had she been doing?

Fighting her memory, she was suddenly thrown forward, and the sound of a horn blasted nearby. She was in a car and she was freezing. The floor was smooth and as cold as a block of ice.

It was dark past the blindfold too. She could see that much when she opened her eyes, but nothing more.

She shivered in her T-shirt and regretted not changing after her run. Hunger ate at her stomach as well. Was that why she had such a headache? Her neck hurt—

Reality crashed in. The man.

She'd gone to help someone behind the firehouse, and he'd grabbed her. Choked her. Passing out from lack of oxygen left a massive headache. That had to be what she was feeling.

But who was the man?

An image of two twisting yellow snakes brought back her father's words. Had the hat triggered her father's reaction?

She thought back to what she'd learned in the hospital. Penny had said Sosa was dead. This had to be one of his men. The Brothers—wasn't that what Jude had called them?

But why go after her if Sosa was dead? Hadn't this ended with him gone? There was no more threat. No more danger—at least she'd thought so. Clearly, that wasn't the case. Where was he taking her?

The vehicle took another hard turn, and she heard shifting all around her. It sounded familiar.

Andi forced herself to slow her breathing. To listen—really listen—to what she was hearing. The rattling. The jouncing of metal clamps. The supplies.

With an intake of air, she suddenly knew where she was.

The back of an ambulance.

The sounds were so familiar they'd slipped into the background, but not when she focused on them specifically. The rattling was collars hooked to a railing. And the clamps that held the gurney down always sounded like that when someone was driving.

It had been almost a month, aside from a few shifts covering for Izan or Trace, since she'd been in the back of an ambo, and it felt right. Deep in her bones type of right.

Her mind supplied the look Jude had given her when he'd said she was talented. He'd meant his words as encouragement. He'd said them as someone *for* her, not against her.

Other worries crowded out the immediate danger. Worries like the fact she'd told Jude off and said she didn't need him when that was the furthest thing from the truth. It had been hard to admit at first—in fact, she *hadn't* admitted it to herself —but now she could see that she needed him. Not because she'd been trapped by a killer, but because he was right. And he was in her corner, maybe more than anyone else had ever been.

She'd done the most good as a paramedic. She'd saved lives. Not because she was strong or brave, but because she'd trained and followed the rules. Because she knew what the books said and followed them to the letter.

When she compared herself against her brothers, she fell short. But they weren't even on the same playing field. They never had been, though she'd forced herself to see it that way. The endless cycle of not matching up. Of wanting to belong in her own family. It had all been of her own making.

Tears slid past the blindfold covering her eyes. Would she ever see them again to tell them she was proud of them? She'd worked so hard to be equal to them that she'd never let herself see how incredible they truly were.

And Jude. She had to see him again. Had to have the chance to tell him he was right and she was wrong. That she loved him.

Love.

The word came as easily as breathing. And it was true. He had always been a calm presence in her life until the day her actions had driven him away for good. Regret streaked through her as she remembered how she'd thrown his kindness in his face.

She'd been the one to tell him to break the rules, to go out to the gorge for a party...just this once. She'd seen the look he'd given her. The one that had said he hated everything about her idea. And yet he'd gone along with it. For her.

Despair swallowed her whole as memories assaulted her. She'd dragged him to the high-school summer party where alcohol was plentiful and stupid ideas were the major draw. She'd known Jude hated it, but she hadn't let him leave.

And then, on a dare, Lana had jumped.

The ambulance went over a few thick bumps and tossed

her back and forth on the floor. Her hands tied behind her offered no leverage, and her face smashed into the lower cabinets. She tasted blood.

Still, her memories played like a movie she couldn't look away from. Lana laughing and dancing on the bridge one second. Falling through the air the next. Slamming into the half-submerged rocks below. The screams that followed.

Lana's body had surfaced moments later, but face down. Andi had wanted to dive in. She knew she could save the girl. She was a strong swimmer, and she was going to rescue her friend.

But Jude hadn't let her. He'd called the police and held her back as the voice of reason. Always so calm and decisive in moments of chaos. She'd resented him for that.

Then, when they were questioned by the authorities, Jude had claimed it was *his* fault they were at the party. He'd taken the blame that should have been hers, like she was too weak to bear the weight.

And, even worse, they'd believed him over her. Every single person down to her mother, the lawyer, who was supposed to be able to spot a lie a mile away.

But they'd never believed her.

She'd confronted Jude, much like she had earlier that night, and told him everything that was on her mind. She could've taken the punishment for underage drinking and trespassing if he'd admitted it had been her fault.

All he'd done was kiss her once, the softest touch of his lips to hers, and told her goodbye.

Lana's death had been an accident, one Andi always carried with her. Evidence that, no matter how hard she tried, she would always fail. The cherry on top had been Jude exiting her life just as quickly as Lana had gone from this world.

The motion of the vehicle slowed. Andi needed to do something. Fight, get away, anything. But her body protested.

Her head pounded in a constant jackhammer of pain, and her arms were tied. She was alone, and this was her moment of truth.

"I can't do it."

The admission ripped her inside out, but it was time to face reality. No matter what she did now, she couldn't save herself. Couldn't be her own superhero. She hadn't been able to run fast enough to save her grandpa. She couldn't have saved Lana. And she couldn't even save a cat without needing help.

God, I can't do it.

Humiliation mingled with defeat and gave way to fear. Deep, bone chilling terror that she was going to be killed in this ambulance. That she'd never see her family again. Never have another moment of clarity with her father. Never kiss Jude again.

"Jude." She whispered to the silence of the now stationary vehicle. "Goodbye."

This was where she would die, at the hands of a killer, and there wasn't anything she could do about it.

31

J ude hit the brakes and skidded the car to a stop in front of the firehouse. He raced from behind the wheel to the side door, noting both firetrucks in the engine bay were gone. They must have been called out. Where were those officers he'd told Penny to call?

He saw Andi's car but took only a moment to look inside. The doors were locked and everything looked normal. No sign of a struggle or damage to the car.

Maybe he was blowing this out of proportion. She could be inside and had chosen not to come home. That was all. It had to be.

Jude yanked open the front door and jogged down the hallway. His boot treads squeaked on the laminate flooring, but the sound of music coming from the direction of the kitchen pushed him deeper into the firehouse. The halls were empty. Had everyone gone on the callout?

"Anyone here? Andi?" He called out her name, got no reply. "Hello?"

"Hey, man." One of the paramedics—he thought he

membered Andi calling the guy Izan—came out of the pantry wiping his hands on a towel. "What's up?"

"Where is everyone?"

"On a call." He looked confused. "Why?"

"Have you seen Andi tonight?"

"I was just about to go looking for her. Not sure where she got to. She said she had to feed Ashes, the cat, and I assume she got distracted. She likes that thing, even if she tells you otherwise." His smile faded. "That was like...ten minutes ago, though."

Jude's heart rate sped at the simple words. Ten minutes. It could have been a lifetime. "Where did she go?"

"Uh, she usually feeds the cat out back. This way."

Jude slid to a stop behind the young man just outside the door.

"There's the food and the cat." Izan glanced around. "But where's Andi?"

Jude was busy reading the scene before him. Ashes eating the food at the edge of the light from the back door. Darkness surrounding the parking lot. No one else around.

He tapped his pointer finger against his thigh. It was so dark. She wouldn't have gone with anyone willingly, but there was no sign of a struggle. While the light didn't reach far into the parking lot, the ground near the back stoop was covered in dirt. There would have been evidence of another car or a set of footprints.

Then he saw a shoe print. Placing his hand near it, he calculated the size was about right. He pulled out his phone and, turning on the flashlight app, searched around him. Footsteps led toward the parking lot and the ambulance bay. Andi's footprints?

The dirt gave way to asphalt, and he lost them.

"Our ambo is missing."

Jude spun toward the young man. "What?"

"Our ambulance is missing. It's usually parked there, next to the one that's out of commission. Oh man, I've got to alert another house to take our calls and get Trace—"

"Hold on." Jude didn't wait for Izan to finish. He raced into the darkness, phone light bouncing as he ran. Beside him was one empty bay in the double garage with the door rolled up, the spot where he assumed the ambulance had been. Their second clue after the footprints.

Jude slowed to a stop at the sight of something under the broken down ambo next to the space. He knelt down and let out a frustrated breath. His fist pounded the ground despite the protest from his ribs.

"No!"

"What is it?" Izan stood behind him, careful not to get in his way. "What do you see?"

Jude took a pen from his jacket pocket and carefully pulled out what he'd found. "Andi's running shoe."

She wouldn't have gone off wearing only one. Someone— no, *Sosa*—had her in the back of an ambulance.

"You guys have a channel to the PD?"

"Yeah. Inside in Command."

"We need to get them here stat. Andi's been kidnapped by a very dangerous man."

"Follow me." Izan ran a hand through his hair.

They raced back inside, and Izan led him toward Command and Control but, just outside the door, the young man spun back toward him. "I just realized something."

"What?"

Izan bounced on the balls of his feet. "There's GPS in the ambo."

Realization struck Jude like a Mack truck. "Can you access it?"

"Verna will know how to do it. Come on."

Izan shoved the door open, and a woman who looked to be

in her mid-fifties spun around with a hand to her chest. "Goodness, Izan. You scared the living gumbo out of me!"

"Sorry, but we need Ambo 21 taken out of service immediately. Then we need you to trace it. Can you do that?"

"If you're not in it, where's it got to?" Her southern drawl spilled out like molasses left in the sun.

"Someone's taken it and—"

"Ma'am." Jude stepped in, seeing this was going nowhere fast. He flashed his badge. "I'm with the ATF, and I have reason to believe that there has been a kidnapping. This person has taken Ambulance 21, and we need to track its location. This is urgent."

"Well, bless my grits." Verna spun in her chair to face the bank of monitors. The minute her fingers touched the keyboard they raced across the keys, her inch-long, hot-pink nails clacking with the movement.

"I see Ambo 21 traveling north along Hillcrest. We have no callouts in this location at the moment." She'd switched from Southern belle grandma to professional dispatcher in less than a second. Jude appreciated her even more then. She continued, "If I were to guess—which, believe you me, I dislike doing—I'd say they're headin' to the gorge."

Every thought in Jude's mind came to a screeching halt.

The gorge. As in his teenage nightmare come to life again? That couldn't be it.

He leaned over the woman's shoulder and saw she was right. There were only a handful of gravel roads out that way, and the ambo registered on one with a single destination.

Jude held back a curse and jammed a hand through his hair. "I need you to contact PD. They should be here already but—"

"Oh, sugar, everyone's at that big to-do on the west side of town. Something involving multiple departments. Truck and

Rescue were both called out, but I haven't heard a report back yet. Havin' trouble getting anyone on the radio."

Jude knew before she finished her explanation that it was a smokescreen, but he didn't share those thoughts. Not with her and Izan.

"Can you send me the ambulance location in real time?"

"Sure thing, honey. Give me your number." She winked, but took no time in typing it into her system. "Okay, you're good to go. Call in if something happens. Want me to send PD to the location?"

"Yes."

"And I tell them what—kidnapping?"

Jude scrunched up his nose. "Talk to Chief Barnes first. Tell him Jude Brooks says it's an emergency. He'll know what to do."

"I'll be an alligator's uncle. Sounds serious. I'll get right to it. You do what you need to. And honey?" She placed a pink-taloned hand on his arm with a gentle squeeze. "God's got this in the palm of His mighty hand. Don't you forget that."

"Th-thanks." He met her gaze, one full of insight and wisdom, and for a moment he believed God was big enough to save Andi. And that He wanted to save her as much as Jude did.

"Now, get."

He didn't need to be told twice.

"Jude, wait." Izan chased after him, but Jude didn't have time for the kid to get in the way.

"Stay here and direct any PD that show up over to the gorge."

"But—"

Jude paused at the door and spun to face the kid. "You're helping me best by doing this."

Izan looked as if he wanted to say more, but Jude had no time for it. He gently but firmly pushed the young man back toward the firehouse and spun on his heel toward his car.

Behind the wheel, Jude jerked the car into reverse and sped backward, skidding to a stop in front of a truck that had appeared out of nowhere.

Logan and Bryce, here on their day off.

Both brothers jumped out and came to the driver's side window.

"You need to get out of my way."

"Not until you tell us what's going on." Logan looked deadly serious. Bryce even more so.

"I think Sosa has Andi and is taking her to the gorge." He held up a hand. "I don't know why. And I don't know how much time we have, but if we wait here any longer..." He shook his head. There was nothing more to say.

"We'll follow you."

There was no use arguing. "Then hurry."

They ran to their truck and backed up so he could get out. When he spun onto the main road, they tailed right behind him. Despite the circumstances, he felt better knowing they had his back, even if they were unarmed.

It didn't change the fact that he'd failed Andi.

Sickness swelled in Jude's gut as he sped through stop signs where there was no cross-traffic and broke every law he could afford to on his way toward the gorge. He couldn't have foreseen it. He knew better than to berate himself for lack of impossible foresight, but that didn't ease his guilt.

He'd let her leave without explaining what she really meant to him. Not only that but he'd let her believe that he'd undermined her, sided with her brothers against her, when nothing could be further from the truth.

He was in her corner, no matter what.

He'd thought he had time. Wasn't that always the way it went?

"God, keep her safe. I can't...I can't l-lose her." Hot tears blurred his eyes, but he willed them back. His emotions, no matter how valid, would only get in the way. He had to save Andi, and remaining calm was the only way to do it.

They escaped the more congested parts of town for the open highway, and Jude pushed ninety. Logan and Bryce kept up, but not as close as before. The road would soon narrow and turn twisty enough to rival a snake, but Jude knew the roads. Knew the ebb and flow and how to push just enough but not too much.

It came almost instinctively, but he wondered if there was something supernatural about it. Was this his chance to redeem what had happened at the gorge all those years ago?

He'd taken responsibility for Andi because he'd *felt* responsible. As the older party, he'd known better than to trespass with a bunch of drunk teenagers. He'd also known better than to stand by and watch Andi jump into the river to save someone beyond saving.

Those had been hard calls to make, but he'd learned that bad decisions often led to bad outcomes.

He knew Andi felt responsible for the girl's tragic death—as if she could have somehow become invincible and rescued her—but it was Jude who truly felt at fault. He had allowed it to happen by not stepping in sooner. By letting his feelings for Andi become bigger than what was right. He'd kept Andi from getting herself killed, but he hadn't prevented what happened.

Wrestling with what-ifs always ate away at a person, and Jude tried not to go down that road too often. Tonight was like facing his past and a potential future in one terrifying, uncontrollable moment.

If there was ever a time he needed God's guidance and help, it was now.

Otherwise, he wasn't sure Andi would be alive come morning.

32

The movement of the ambulance slowed as he made a turn. The tires abruptly left the pavement for the uneven ground of an unpaved road.

If they didn't stop soon, they'd be out of Last Chance County. Unless that was the point. What would happen after that she wasn't sure, but she told herself she was going to do everything she could to stop whoever had kidnapped her.

But what could she do when he had all the power and she was completely at his mercy?

Andi mentally ran through her sadly short list of options. Her wrists were tied behind her back with what felt like plastic ties. Her phone? She checked her back pockets, but they were empty. He'd taken it.

That left what was in the ambulance. The problem with that was a lack of anything useful that she could reach. Still, she had to try.

She rolled over to the storage bins at floor level. There wasn't much in them since they were often hard to get to quickly, but maybe she could find something.

After attacking it from every angle, she gave up. She wouldn't be able to do anything with her hands tied as they were. She had to get them in front of her.

Knowing it was going to be painful but that it was physically possible, Andi moved to the middle of the floor and tucked her knees to her chest. The pinch of her skin in the cuffs made her eyes water, but she stretched her arms and got her hands in front of her.

The blindfold came off first. The darkness was complete, but she knew her way around the ambulance. Andi rushed to the drawer where the industrial shears were kept, moving quickly and quietly so as not to alert her captor she was free.

The weighty scissors looked insignificant in her shaking hands, but they were something. Next she rushed to the cabinet where syringes and vials of medicine were kept. An injection of fentanyl would take the man down and—

The motion of the vehicle slowed. Her stomach bottomed out when it came to a complete stop, and she pressed herself against the back with shears in her tied hands.

She wasn't going without a fight.

Several seconds later, the back door opened and a man appeared, illuminated by the dim overhead light. His tanned features were sharpened into a menacing scowl. She instantly recognized him from the picture Jude had shown her.

Diego Ruiz Sosa. He was alive.

"*Hola, Señorita.*" His smile was cold, his lifeless eyes lit with a spark of hate. "Come here."

Andi shook her head, cowering as far back from him as she could. She used her wrist and palm to hide the shears.

"Don't make me do this the hard way." He pulled a gun from the back of his waistband and aimed at her. "I'd prefer not to shoot you, but I will. In the leg first. How about that?"

Andi weighed the pros and cons. There was a greater

chance she could get away if she was outside of the ambulance. That thought alone pushed her to the doors, where Sosa pulled her the rest of the way out into the darkness.

The sound of rushing water reached her and, with gut wrenching clarity, she knew where she was. The gorge. It was right behind them.

She hadn't been back since she was seventeen, and now here she was, zip-tied and with a drug lord. *God help me!*

"*Bueno*. Now, smile big." He leaned in and shoved her back so she was sitting on the tailgate of the ambulance.

A bright light shone in her eyes, blinding her. She winced and looked down. Was that a phone?

"Hello." When Sosa spoke the next time, his voice was clear and in command. The light from the phone reflected his evil grin. "I have your daughter, as you can see."

The sound of sobs hit like an arrow shot straight into Andi's heart.

"Mom?"

"Andi!"

The light shifted and he tapped the screen. "Listen to me, Mrs. Crawford." Sosa dropped his voice low. "You'll give me the account numbers or your daughter dies."

Andi inched to the side wall of the ambulance. If he turned far enough, she could make a run for it...

And he would shoot her in the back.

Sosa continued, "I will unmute you only if you agree to these terms. Nod if yes." Andi held her breath. "I see you. Go ahead."

"P-please don't hurt my baby."

Sosa's tone darkened. "Is that what I asked you about?"

"Sorry. I'm sorry." Andi heard her mother take a shuddering breath. "It's an offshore account. I...I have the password and routing numbers. Everything you need." Her mother's words tumbled over each other in her effort to get them out. "Don't hurt her."

"Send them now to this email." He rattled off a generic address. "Remember, your daughter dies unless I have what I want."

"Yes. All right. Please—" Elizabeth cut herself off before Sosa could. "Sending them now."

A loud *ding* sounded, and Andi guessed that was an email from her mother.

"If you've lied to me..." Sosa's tone held warning, but Andi had the feeling there was another part to this. Something more sinister. "I see them. Yes, very good."

The light shifted, and Andi sensed him coming closer. Would he be close enough that she could injure him with the shears?

"Andi?"

Her heart thudded in her chest at her mother's desperation. "I'm okay, Mom. I'm—"

"*¡Cállate!*" Sosa shifted the light so she could see the gun aimed at her forehead.

Andi flinched. He'd blocked her in with the ambulance doors and blinded her with the light. Not to mention the gun. If she tried to run now, her eyes wouldn't have time to adjust to the darkness. She'd be an easy target.

"Andi!" Her mom's scream cut off.

"That is all you get to say." Sosa's voice was ice. "I took my destiny into my own hands when I took over the cartel. And I'm taking it into my own hands now."

He flicked the gun in a gesture Andi assumed meant he wanted her to get into the back of the ambulance again. She wasn't going to submit to her own death.

Andi didn't move.

"I know you helped Camilo, Elizabeth. Esteban told me

everything. You see, I do not let debts go easily. You owed me my money, and now you owe me for the child that was stolen from me. My heir." Sosa pressed the gun against Andi's forehead. "You will know the sting of losing your child. Perhaps all three if I am ambitious. With Camilo dead, this is your penance. To watch your children die before I come after you myself—"

Something that sounded like a distant helicopter made Andi's eyes jerk to the sky. Sosa heard it too.

He muttered something in Spanish, and the light vanished in a rush of darkness.

The next moment, he slammed the gun against Andi's temple, disorienting her with blinding pain. She dropped the shears. Then, with a violent shove, he pushed her back into the ambulance. She heard the sound of the doors as they slammed shut, drenching her in darkness. Then the vehicle shifted forward. Toward the cliff overlooking the gorge.

Andi scrambled to her feet, wrists still bound, and rushed to the back doors, yanking at the handles. "Let me out! Help! Someone help me!"

She heard the driver's door creak open and a thud outside. The ambulance kept going—he must have wedged the gas pedal somehow.

She had mere moments before the truck went over the side and—

Weightlessness threw her against the back doors as the ambulance dove off the cliff. She was free-falling. Then the world came to a crashing halt. Lights flickered and the siren sounded once.

Andi slammed against the talk-through window and blacked out.

When she came to, the lights flickered off and on in an erratic rhythm. The movement of the truck was unsteady—she'd landed in water. Panic stole logic, and she fought to reach the back doors, but water filled in through the space under them. Every step on the slanted floor slid, stalling her progress and threatening to send her to her knees. She reached for a cabinet handle, but her bound hands gave her no way to latch on.

One of the metal supports had broken in the fall. The sharp edge stuck out like a rope to a drowning man, and she slammed the zip ties against the pointed edge. Her teeth clenched, and she stifled a cry when the metal met skin instead of plastic, but they finally broke, leaving her wrists bloodied but free.

Her victory was short-lived.

The truck rocked from side to side in the violent current before slamming down wheels first. She landed on her hip and whimpered.

Andi scrambled to the back door and yanked on the handle. It still didn't budge.

She turned and went back to the front of the ambulance and the talk-through window. Water flooded into the cab, dipping the nose where it pointed downstream. With a violent jolt, the ambulance slammed against a barrier of rocks and stopped moving. The lights flickered again, then went out.

Darkness enveloped her.

The sound of her heart thudded in her ears and erased everything else. All she knew was the fear of drowning in the back of an ambulance. The sensation of the ice-cold water already up to her calves.

Hopelessness triggered a memory. Running through the forest to get help for her grandpa.

His words echoed from the past. "You can do it. I believe in you."

But she hadn't saved him. Not on her own.

Andi slumped, the exhaustion of fading adrenaline making her limbs weigh a thousand pounds. This couldn't be how she died.

She'd been trying to escape being tied to an ambulance for

so long she'd forgotten what it was like to actually be *in* one. Sure, she'd only been a firefighter for a short time, but she'd mentally checked out of being a paramedic years before. But why?

Faced with her death, it didn't add up.

She'd compared herself to her dad at first. Thinking she'd be a nurse, but then she'd been able to jump right in as a paramedic, and that had seemed more heroic. Her brothers were always leaving for calls while she waited. Then, when the paramedics were called on, they took people to the hospital for someone else to save. At least, that was how she'd seen it.

"God, what am I chasing after?" Tears fell in torrents down her cheeks.

To be enough. But you already are.

The thought slammed her against the wall as if it had been a physical blow. She'd failed her grandfather so many years ago. She'd failed Lana by not saving her. She'd failed as a firefighter—saving a cat and putting others in danger. There were so many other mistakes.

How was a person supposed to live with them?

My flesh and my heart may fail, but God is the strength of my heart and my portion forever.

The verse dropped out of the air and into her mind as if she'd read it from the Bible at that moment. Her grandfather had quoted the verse often to her, but as she'd grown up, she'd forgotten it. What was it he used to say?

You'll fail, it's a sure thing. But God never will.

With a clarity that shocked her, she knew Jude had been right as well. She wasn't that little girl anymore, running scared. She was meant to be a paramedic—maybe even a nurse someday. She'd let herself be convinced she wasn't enough—for her family, for herself, maybe even for him.

But she was already who God had made her to be—and He had given her everything she needed.

The lights flickered back on.

Andi pushed off the side of the ambulance and took stock of her surroundings. This time she looked around with the eyes of someone who was going to fight to live.

No matter what it took.

33

Jude skidded to a stop at the edge of the cliff overlooking the gorge. His stomach twisted in knots until he thought he might be sick. He didn't know if it was the height or the lingering effect of the concussion. Maybe both.

From the light of his high-beams, Jude could just make out the ambulance at the base of the thirty-foot drop. It sat wedged between rocks, tipping forward and sinking fast as the current rushed around it. The taillights were almost covered.

A shape blocked out the light coming from inside the truck through the back window.

"It's Andi! She's in there!" He yelled the words.

Bryce and Logan ran to his side, and he didn't know which one said, "Dear God."

Logan groaned.

Bryce, ever logical, rounded on Jude. "How do you know she's in there?"

"I saw her." He paced back and forth once, then looked back at the vehicle sinking fast. "She's alive, but how do we get to her?"

Bryce pressed his lips together.

Logan pulled out his phone. "Verna, you get ahold of the chief yet?" He listened for a moment. "Patch me through." Another moment. "We need Rescue out here ASAP. It's...she's... Andi's in the gorge."

Jude blocked out the rest of what Logan said and focused. They didn't have time to wait for the rescue squad. Saving Andi was all that mattered right now. On a subconscious level, Jude knew Sosa was out there, and he would hunt him down. But first, he needed to get to Andi.

She was not dying tonight. Not at the gorge. "I'm going down there."

"Don't be an idiot," Logan said.

"What he means," Bryce said in a calmer tone, "is that you're injured and the rescue squad is equipped to do this. You think we don't want to jump right in and save our sister? It's safer for all involved if we wait for the truck and our equipment."

Jude hesitated. He knew they were right. Knew what the book would say. Wait for the squad. Don't create more issues to be solved—like another person in the gorge who needed rescuing.

But as he looked down on the ambulance bobbing in the rushing water, sinking lower every moment, only one thing mattered.

Andi.

"Send them down when they get here." Jude threw off his coat and gun, but kept his shoes on and approached the cliff. The water was deep—at least fifteen to twenty feet in places—which was why this area had become so popular with cliff divers.

But there were other dangers. The sheer cliffs of the gorge were unique in that they narrowed in some parts, boasting dangerous class-six rapids, then widened to create deep pools before narrowing again.

He could only pray that God would help him land in the deepest part.

"Jude, don't be stupid—" Logan shouted after him, but it was too late.

Jude held his breath and jumped toward the pool of darkness. The sense of weightlessness made his stomach flip. He sucked in air. Pressed his lips together. Closed his eyes and fell.

Icy water stole his breath as he plunged in deep. The impact sent knifing pain across his torso, but he numbed it by shoving the agony to the back of his mind. He was under a moment before the water churned him to the top. Sucking in a painful draught of air, he let the current take him down toward the ambulance.

He couldn't afford for any debris in the water to further injure him on the way there. It was so dark he wouldn't be able to anticipate anything. He shifted so that his feet went in front of him. The soles of his shoes kept stray tree limbs and smaller rocks from pummeling him when he drifted too close to the bank.

He wanted to call out. Wanted Andi to know he was coming.

But his voice would only be lost in the cacophony of rushing water.

The current brought him close to the ambulance, and he braced himself for the landing. His feet connected with the back first, but the force of the water was so great that he nearly went around the side. Jude grabbed a handle and slammed his face against the reinforced glass.

Andi appeared. Her blue eyes went wide in shock when she saw him. Then they shifted to fear as she looked around her. The water in the back of the vehicle reached her knees.

"We're getting out of this." He shouted the words, not sure if she could hear him. When he caught the glint of determination flash where fear once was, he knew she'd heard. That was the woman he loved. Strong until the end. No matter what.

He searched around for something to smash against the window and latched onto a floating log.

"Stay back," he shouted.

When the wood connected with the glass, it didn't even crack it. The water-soaked log splintered in his hands, and he floated away in the water. He needed something stronger. He searched around him as he swam back to her, but there was nothing but water and boulders.

Rocks! If he could get a small enough one, maybe he could use it to—

The sound of banging on the back door drew his attention. Jude pressed his face up to the window and watched as Andi, the water at her waist now, pointed to the front of the truck. Moving away, she hefted a cannister of oxygen and slammed it into the talk-through window, shattering it. It was narrow, but she could fit through.

He waited, curious about her plan, until she motioned to the front again. Then he understood. She wanted to go out that way. He wasn't sure how, but when his eyes met hers, he knew all he needed to. She had a plan. He was going to trust that.

One nod and he shifted to the edge of the ambulance, even though every move was a fight against the stabbing pain in his side. Bulbous emergency lights stuck out and made decent handholds, giving him purchase as he fought the current pushing him away from the vehicle.

He was almost to the front when a loud groan echoed against the stone cliffs. The next moment, Jude felt the ambulance tilt forward. The sudden shift almost forced him to lose his grip, but he held fast and searched the waters for the cause.

His breath caught.

Illuminated by the vehicle's submerged lights, Jude better

assessed the situation. The ambulance sat wedged between two boulders, but the entire front half had already made it past them before becoming high-centered on another rock beneath the surface.

The front half dipped forward into a deep pool and was almost fully submerged, making the back doors inaccessible now. If the ambulance shifted too far forward, it could topple over into the deep.

Jude pressed his palm to the freezing metal. He shivered, teeth chattering. His body temp lowered the longer he remained in the water, which was both a blessing and a curse. The cold and adrenaline masked his injuries but also slowed his movements. If Andi was inside when the ambulance went over, Jude wasn't sure he'd be able to get her out once it sank. She could drown before the rescue squad arrived.

He had no way to communicate what he saw to Andi. If he went to the front with her, could both their weights shift the ambulance enough to dislodge it?

But if he didn't go, would Andi think he'd abandoned her?

I need some guidance.

Admitting it wasn't easy, but Jude had tried things his way. He'd followed all the rules and done everything the *right* way, and still people had died. What happened if he broke the rules now and had the same result?

Andi's death on his hands wasn't something he could live with.

What do I do?

He asked again. This time, in place of the panic, peace settled over him. It was the type of calm he usually got in hectic, stressful situations. The calm he'd learned to hone in his years with ATF. But was this training or...God?

Okay, I'm letting You take the lead here.

Jude pressed his eyes closed for a moment—no longer than a second—but in that instant he knew he needed to move to the front. He didn't know how, but he knew it was the right course of action. So he did.

Jude kept one hand against the side, trying not to push too much against the vehicle. He reached the front in time to see Andi almost submerged in water.

His heart leapt at the sight. He needed to get her out—now!

Frantic, Jude pulled in oxygen, then dove to try the handle of the door. It was foolish with the weight of water pressing in, but he had to try something.

It wouldn't budge. He pulled. Once. Twice. Three times, but it wouldn't move. There was too much pressure.

Andi appeared, her image blurry and dim in the remaining cabin light, but he could see her. The sight infused him with urgency, and he tried the door again.

She shook her head, motioning for him to stop. Helplessness rushed through him like the water surrounding him. She couldn't give up. He wouldn't let her.

He slammed a hand against the window, and that's when he saw it. The oxygen tank she'd used to smash the talk-through window was in her hands. She was going to break the side window.

Relief coursed through him even as his lungs burned. Andi held it up but paused. Their eyes locked, and a dam of emotions burst from him. He loved this woman. Loved her courage and moxie.

He mouthed the words his heart beat to. "I love you." It felt silly, juvenile even, but he wouldn't waste another moment.

"I love you too." She said them back, precious bubbles escaping before she slammed the canister against the window.

It bounced back.

He pounded his fist against it in desperation, but she shook her head, then swam to the top of the cabin. There was barely any air left, but she drew in a breath, then came back. This time determination etched deep lines on her brow as she brought the heavy tank forward.

The laminated glass spider-webbed. One last hit sent the glass floating free.

His surprise sent the rest of his air outward in a stream of bubbles, but he felt Andi's hand in his and pulled them to the surface.

The sound of Andi's gasp for breath alongside his was the most beautiful thing he'd ever heard. Jude made sure he had a good hold against the ambulance and pulled her close, ignoring the burning in his torso as he kept them steady. Her arms wrapped around him, and she tucked her head against his neck.

"I was so scared." Her words, barely a breath, rocked him to the core.

"You and m-me both."

"Jude." Her arms tightened. "You came for me."

He laughed, the feeling surreal in such a moment. "I'll always come for you."

She leaned back to look at him and, right there, clinging to the side of the sinking ambulance moments away from being swept downriver, she kissed him. No apologies. No excuses. Just her lips on his; her arms clinging to him. She was all he knew. No pain, no cold, nothing but Andi.

A shiver that had nothing to do with the water streaked through him, and he pulled her closer, succumbing to the kiss. Her warmth was the perfect contrast to the frigid river swirling around them, and a reminder that they had made it—together.

This kiss meant the world to him. It *was* the world.

The woman he loved was safe.

"Come on." He pulled her close and maneuvered them to the back of the ambulance. "We need to move before this thing gets dislodged."

They made it as far back as they could, but he knew they still weren't safe.

"It could flip over any minute." His body was cold everywhere but where she pressed against him. He suppressed another shiver.

"Good thing I know a few people on the rescue squad."

Jude frowned. "What—"

Shouts made it through the din of the rushing current. High-powered lights ran across the water and came to rest on them. Jude turned, a stab of pain in his rib stealing his breath, but there they were. Rappelling down the cliff face.

The crew got them out of the water and onto dry land quickly, wrapping them in blankets and directing them toward a Westside ambulance. Logan and Bryce rushed up and enveloped Andi in a hug, their words a jumble he couldn't make out through the pounding in his ears.

She was alive.

Jude had expected her to push her overbearing brothers away as she usually did, but this time she allowed their attention. She accepted a bottle of water from Logan. Something had changed in Andi.

She caught him staring, and he looked away.

"Jude." She spoke his name, but her hand on his brought his gaze back. "Thank you."

"For doing my job?"

She made a face. "I'd say this was outside of your orders."

"I'm sorry I let Sosa get to you." The familiar weight of disappointment rested on his shoulders. Not only had he barreled past his boss's order to keep his personal life separate from the job, but he hadn't been fast enough. Hadn't caught the photo glitch or checked to make sure the body had been the cartel leader's. Surely he could have stopped—

"You did everything perfectly. By the book." Andi's hand

squeezed his. She knew what the words meant to him, and there was no trace of humor there.

"Did he hurt you?" Jude had taken visual stock of her when they were pulled free from the water. She'd looked okay aside from a gash on her forehead and her injured wrists. There would be emotional damage though. The things beneath the surface he knew wouldn't go away with bandages or pain medication.

"No, he didn't hurt me." She pulled the blanket more tightly around her shoulders. "He wanted account numbers from Mom. You don't think..."

"Mom's at the police station. She's safe." Bryce stepped up next to them. "Sorry, I was eavesdropping."

"So, eavesdropping runs in the family?" Jude shot Andi an amused look but sobered quickly. "She's safe. We're going to catch Sosa."

Lights flashed across them, and Jude turned to see another car pull up to the scene. He squinted but immediately recognized the woman jumping out of the driver's side.

"Penny?"

Izan jumped out of the car after her. He wore a haunted expression that sent Jude's senses to high alert. Something wasn't right.

"I'm glad you're both okay." Penny looked visibly shaken. "I got here as fast as I could. We need to talk."

"All right." His gaze shifted from Penny to Andi and her brothers and then back. They were as much a part of this now as he and Penny were. Rather than getting up and walking away to keep the information private, he shrugged. "Talk."

enny hesitated. Andi recognized it as concern over sharing privileged information, but Penny quickly refocused on Jude and said, "I was at the police station when they brought Elizabeth in. She was a wreck." Penny grimaced as if realizing who she was speaking to. "But she was okay."

Jude reached over and took Andi's hand. The strength of his grip helped keep her worry at bay, but thoughts of her mother's distress caused her stomach to cramp. "Has anyone told her I'm all right?"

"Radioed it in first thing, Andi Bear." Logan nodded at her, and she took a deep, calming breath.

"What happened, Pen?" Jude asked.

"She said Sosa called her on *Andi's* cell phone. Apparently Elizabeth has GPS access." Penny visually checked with Andi, who nodded. "I showed her how to track it, and Sosa isn't far." She held up a phone, and Andi immediately recognized it as her mother's.

"He's close." Jude's gaze met hers, and she saw the conflict there. He wanted to go, but he also wanted to stay. With her.

"You have to go after him." Andi pulled the blanket tightly around her. "You have to. And I'm going with you."

He opened his mouth to protest, but Penny beat him to it. "Only if you stay in the car."

Jude's head jerked to her, but he said to Penny, "She can't come."

Hurt mingled with frustration. Andi wanted to see the man apprehended as much as Jude, but the look in his eyes showed his words were guided by concern, not the rule book.

Penny took a step. "When we first heard that Sosa wasn't the body recovered, I called Denver ATF. They sent a team to work with local PD. We'll be supplemental. Sosa's going down, but I thought you'd want to be there."

Jude shifted back to Andi. "You'll stay in the car?"

She nodded, relieved. "Of course."

"Okay, then let's go."

"What about us? What can we do?" Bryce stepped a little closer to Penny, chest puffed out.

"Stay here," Penny said. "Recover that ambulance so we can get evidence from it. We'll keep you in the loop."

"Here." Izan handed Andi a radio. "In case you need us to help."

"You came with Penny?" Her question surprised him, but she was curious about his role.

"I couldn't stay back at the station. She stopped by and I got a ride." He shrugged but then looked away. Whatever he was holding back, it would have to wait.

Jude placed a hand on the small of her back as they headed toward Penny's car. She wanted to soak in the touch. Take all the comfort from him she could. But she also didn't want to distract him.

He paused at the car door, taking her hand again. "You okay?"

She nodded.

"You sure?" His eyes narrowed, but Andi felt the seconds ticking by.

"Put this on, Brooks." Penny tossed Jude a bulletproof vest.

He caught it but kept his eyes on Andi, waiting for her answer.

"Promise. We'll talk later."

"I look forward to it." His smile warmed her through.

Cradling the radio, she climbed into the back of the vehicle. Logan and Bryce offered a small wave she caught through the rear window. It was a sendoff she hadn't expected. Knowing them, she would have expected arguments and a refusal to let her go into danger, but they seemed to trust not only Jude but her as well.

It was an empowering feeling. One she wouldn't soon forget.

"Direct me." Penny pressed her foot to the gas, and the car shot forward.

"Take a right at the fork." Jude glanced back at Andi once, and she flashed him an encouraging smile. This was a big moment for him.

Radio chatter from a handheld device gave updates about arrival times. Someone said they had eyes on Sosa. The officer on foot. Running toward a forested area.

Andi's stomach clenched. She was certain that if Sosa reached the trees, this would get infinitely more difficult.

"Come on, Penny." Jude leaned forward in his seat.

"Can't go much faster." Her posture was stiff as she navigated the dirt road. "I turned in the rental SUV before this went down, and all I could find on short notice was this rusted bucket of parts."

Andi held in a smile. The car was nice, but maybe not as nice as the one Penny had been driving before.

"He's going to disappear if he reaches the tree line. You know it." Jude's words were terse.

"I know."

"Falcon to Control." The radio crackled to life as the helicopter called in.

"This is Control. Go ahead," the dispatcher replied.

"Be advised we're dropping altitude in front of the suspect." A burst of static followed the pilot's reply.

"That's going to turn Sosa in another direction." Jude leaned forward in his seat as the sound of the helicopter closed in overhead. "There are only so many boots on the ground."

"We're going to get him," Penny assured him.

When he didn't respond, Andi gently squeezed his bicep. He turned to her. She couldn't see much in the dark car, but the dash lights showed the depth of emotion in his eyes. She'd survived Sosa, and Jude would too.

"There he is!" Penny shouted. She hit the brakes, and the car skidded to a stop.

Andi shot forward with the momentum of the car. Her hands braced against the seat in front of her as she leaned forward to peer out the front window. A man on the road ahead ran in their direction. The helicopter's spotlight followed his movements.

Agents swarmed from the trees, farther away than Sosa. It was the perfect trap except for the fact that the other agents were still too far to catch him.

They were the only thing between Sosa and escape.

Jude jumped out. Andi's hand went to the door handle before Penny turned around.

"No you don't," she snapped. "You stay here. Let us do our jobs." The woman didn't stay to see if Andi followed her directions. She left the car, pulling a gun from a holster at her hip.

Andi let the handle go, her heart pounding. She leaned around the front seat and watched as Jude closed in on the guy.

Keep him safe. Please!

Her fingers clenched the seat as she watched. It was the worst situation she could imagine, watching someone she loved running toward danger. But she also knew he had to do this. Jude needed to focus on apprehending Sosa—not worrying whether Andi might be in danger. If she left the car, that was exactly what could happen.

She prayed and watched.

Time slowed. Jude drew closer, gun drawn. Fifty feet. Then twenty. Then he paused.

Without the benefit of being closer, all she could hear were the rotating blades of the helicopter. The wind whipped up a tornado of dirt and leaves around Jude and Sosa. An ATF agent pointed a sniper rifle down from the open door to provide cover fire, but it looked like Jude was in the way of his shot.

It was killing her not being able to see. Her hand went to the handle. If she stayed behind the door she'd be safe. She wouldn't leave the car.

The rotor wash blew her hair in every direction as she stood, hoping to get a better vantage. Above the noise, someone called over a megaphone for Sosa to stand down.

Jude took a step, then another, toward the drug lord and her heart stuttered. When he moved a few feet to the right, she gasped. Sosa had pulled a gun.

Crack!

A shot rang into the night and Sosa fell. Her fingers gripped the car door so hard the metal bit into her palm, but she was in shock. He'd been standing one minute and—

An arm encircled Andi's throat, roughly yanking her away from the car.

Her scream died as the grip tightened. Constricted. She reached up and clawed at him, desperate for a breath.

"¡Parada! Stop!" The cool metal of a gun pressed against her temple. "You are my ticket out of here, *cariño*." The raspy voice spoke into her ear. It had to be one of Sosa's men.

Her vision blackened from lack of oxygen. Terror paralyzed her. She couldn't think. Couldn't move.

His hold tightened as he yanked her toward the tree line, but her training took over. Kicking her legs out, she writhed against his ironlike grip. The arm around her throat loosened as he readjusted, and a scream ripped from her.

Through eyes blurred by tears, Andi saw Jude turn in her direction. She knew the minute he assessed the situation. Saw the determination in the set of his jaw. The next second, he exploded into a sprint toward her.

Andi wanted to cry out again. Wanted to tell him to stop. But that's who Jude was, the type of man who ran toward danger to save the innocent.

She wasn't helpless, though. And she wasn't letting this criminal steal her life or the life of the man she loved.

Despite her lightheadedness, she drew in every ounce of strength left and thrust her elbow into the man's side. She heard him wheeze and tucked her chin enough to get out of the slackened headlock. Without thinking, she turned to face him and sent a kick directly at his chest.

He flew backward, sending her off balance as Jude's footsteps drew near. But she stayed upright.

The man landed on his back but wasn't down. He rolled over. Aimed the gun directly at Andi.

She froze.

A hollow sound rang in her ears. She was distantly aware of steps pounding toward them. Jude coming to her rescue. She needed him to be safe. Needed to stop this man—

She watched his finger as it tightened around the trigger. Felt the instinct to turn away, but knew it was too late.

Her eyes closed, and she flinched as a shot rang out.

Then two more.

But Andi felt no pain.

Her eyes flew open as she tripped backward.

Jude was on the ground, red splattered across his vest.

No no no!

Dizziness pitched her to the side as she raced toward him. Tripped. Threw herself down next to him. There was so much blood.

"Jude!" His name ripped from her throat. He couldn't be dead. He couldn't.

He rasped a cough, and relief spiraled through her. *Thank You, God!*

Her focus shifted to his injuries, and her mind settled. She could help him; she knew what to do. Before moving him, she checked his pulse. Weak, but still beating. Good.

She was vaguely aware of Penny running toward her, agents trailing behind. Of the report over the car radio of officer down.

Andi moved around Jude so she could see his face. He lay on his side with his eyes closed. His hand gripped his shoulder where blood flowed from the wound. Confident she could lay him back without further injury, she gently rolled him over.

"Jude, can you hear me?" Her voice trembled as she cupped a hand to his face. His eyes flickered open.

"You're safe?"

"I—" She looked around. Her assailant lay in a crumpled heap. She could see blood on the ground and no sign of breath or movement. The shots—Jude's shots—had caught him in the chest.

"Yes."

"I'm glad it's you."

She frowned. "Do you know what happened?"

"I wanted it to be you last time. When I got shot. But it was Bryce." Jude made a face. "I like this better."

She didn't know what he was talking about, but his sense of humor was intact. That was good. "You've been shot. Looks like a through and through to your shoulder."

"Whatever you say, doc."

She couldn't help but smile, relieved that he felt well enough to tease.

"Ambulance is on the way." Penny stepped up, her anxious gaze going from Jude's wound to Andi. "Just hold on, Jude."

"I'm in good hands." Jude's eyes closed for a moment as pain wrinkled his forehead.

"He'll be okay." Andi tried for a confident, reassuring tone. "I just need to stop the bleeding."

Penny assessed the man who'd grabbed Andi. "Clean shooting, Book. Two in the chest."

He groaned. "By the book."

Penny laughed. "Exactly."

"Sosa?" he rasped.

"In custody. You've got matching wounds."

"N-nice." Jude released a breath, then reached up and gripped Andi's forearm. "Dee?"

"Shhh. You need to be still."

"I need to tell you something."

"Why don't you wait until we get you fixed up?" Andi quickly ripped the shirt she wore. It was still damp, but it would have to do.

"No. Now."

"So demanding." She tried for a smile, but her emotions were still too rattled. Moving his hand away, she pressed the cloth against his wound. He winced but didn't protest.

"I'll give you two a minute." Penny flashed Andi a smile and moved to join the other agents.

"I need you to know that—" He gasped in pain as she put more pressure on. "I'm sorry."

"Sorry for what? Running at me with a gun?"

He chuckled, but the action made him groan, and more blood appeared through the cloth she pressed against his wound. Her heart pounded a frantic rhythm. Where was that ambulance?

"For letting you leave the hospital without saying that I'm behind you, Dee. A thousand percent." He paused, taking in a labored breath. "I know you think I wasn't supporting your decision to be a firefighter, but if that's what you want, I know you can accomplish it."

"You really should be still." Her protest was weak. His words struck the soft spot of her heart.

"No." He shifted and his face contorted in pain. After a moment, he pressed on. "You're the strongest woman I know. The bravest. And the most talented. But I don't need you to be anything other than Andi Jayne Crawford. For me, that's more than enough."

Tears streaked down Andi's cheeks, but she couldn't remove her hands to wipe them away. Didn't want to. His words were a balm to her heart. While she'd already decided to go back to being a paramedic, she hadn't realized how much she'd needed to hear him say exactly this.

"Are you finished?" She sniffed, more tears falling.

"Almost." Despite the pain she knew he was in, he reached up with his free hand to wipe away her tears. His warm brown eyes poured into hers. "I also need you to know one more thing."

"What's that?"

"I said it before, but the water got in the way. I love you. In fact, I think I've always been in love with you."

She giggled. More tears falling, but this time in happiness. The warmth of his words erased some of the cold shock of what had just happened, though not all.

"Did you just...giggle?" He looked amused.

"I think I'm allowed, seeing as you just made my teenage self very happy."

"Yeah? And what about adult Andi? Is she happy too?"

Still keeping pressure on his wound, Andi leaned down and kissed Jude. Gone was the timid, shy teen girl. In her place, the young woman Andi had grown into reveled in the fact that this man cared for her. Loved her, faults and all.

"She is exquisitely happy." Andi kissed him again, then pulled back. "And she loves you too."

His smile stretched his infinitely kissable lips wide, and she took a moment to soak him in. He'd been shot while saving her, but his primary focus was telling her how he felt. How did she deserve this man?

An ambulance siren broke into her awareness, and her muscles relaxed. Help was coming. But more than that, this nightmare was behind them. It was time to move on. Time for new and better things. Together.

A shadow of doubt slipped past the glow of Andi's joy at the thought. She'd decided her career direction, but what about Jude's job in California?

eep. Beep. Beep.

Jude blinked several times until the room came into focus. He was in a hospital bed connected to monitors and IVs. There was a heaviness to his body that reached past the pain meds being pumped into his veins. When he tried to shift positions, a dull, painful stab radiated from his shoulder.

His head. His ribs. His shoulder. Everything hurt like—

He'd been shot.

The memory of facing down Sosa and then the man who'd held Andi captive flooded his mind. He'd sensed that same surreal peace rush over him as he raced toward the guy—Fausto, if his guess was correct. Watched as Andi took him down. Felt the shot meant for her.

Now fully awake, Jude blinked several more times. The room was empty. Disappointment coursed through him along with another wave of dulled pain. Where was Andi?

The last thing he remembered was her admission that she loved him. Yeah, he was sure a lot of other things had happened too, but that was the only thing worth remembering.

He wanted to see her again. Wanted to talk about all of this and what it meant for their future. Heck, he wanted to tell her he *wanted* a future with her.

He contemplated calling the nurse, but even the thought of sitting up made him dizzy. Maybe it was best to wait. She would come. He knew it.

He was fading in and out of sleep when the door opened. His eyes widened when he took in Paul Crawford, alone, coming into his room.

"Hey, Jude." The older man wore a goofy grin Jude hadn't seen since he'd known the man in his younger years.

"Paul. Hi."

Paul shuffled forward, a clarity in his eyes Jude hadn't expected.

"I need you to do something for me." Paul took Jude's hand, and Jude was overwhelmed with gratitude to the man who had been a true father to him in his younger years. Something he'd so desperately needed when his own father had abandoned him.

"Anything, Paul."

"Take care of Andi. Will you do that?"

"Yes, sir."

Paul held his gaze, then dropped his hand. Jude could tell by the fading clarity in his eyes that his moment of lucidity was gone. Jude instantly missed the connection he'd had with the once-great surgeon as he slipped back to something closer to a child. There were some things in life that wouldn't make sense this side of heaven.

"Hey." The soft words drew Jude's gaze from Paul to Andi, who stood behind him. Her look didn't betray whether she'd heard her father's words or not. "Charlotte said you were awake."

"I am."

Paul moved toward the window, and Jude held out his hand

to Andi. She stepped forward and took it, her gaze never leaving his.

"Feeling better?"

"Now that you're here." He loved the blush his direct words brought to Andi's cheeks.

The sound of a throat clearing drew Jude's attention to the door, where Bryce, Logan, Elizabeth, and Penny stood.

He grinned. "Looks like you brought the party."

Andi laughed, and her family joined her.

"You just had to get shot, didn't you?" Penny moved to Jude's injured side. "Always have to be the center of attention."

"Hey now." He feigned hurt. "I do not."

"Do too." She gave him a look that made him laugh. "But I guess in the end it worked."

"It did?"

Penny's smile widened. "We got him. Or, more accurately, *you* got him. You shot Fausto, the man who tried to capture Andi."

Andi's hand trembled in his, and he squeezed gently. The absolute terror on her face was burned into his memory, and he promised himself she'd never feel that again. Ever.

"And before that, we captured Sosa. But you saw that."

The tightness in Jude's chest released. "It's over."

"It is." Her confident words made him smile.

"What about the money?" Jude's gaze flickered to Elizabeth.

"Didn't have time to transfer it. His cell had all the information, but the area we captured him in was a dead zone for service. Pretty lucky, if you ask me." Penny's lips twisted into a smug smile.

"Not luck," Andi said.

Jude looked up at her and nodded. "Not luck. God was all over this."

Penny had never been fully comfortable with Jude's faith,

no matter how weak it had been when he'd first known her. Now she merely shrugged. "Maybe there's something to that."

"Anyone left to take over for him?"

Penny accepted Jude's change in subject. "Actually..." She turned toward the door and nodded.

Andi's brothers shifted to the side as Mick Perry and Keith Jackson stepped into the room, relief in their expressions.

"Cutting it close, Boss." Mick held out his hand to Jude, then pulled it back, remembering the injury.

"Glad you're okay," Keith said.

"You guys made it." Jude sent a questioning look to Penny.

"They've been all over this since they got here earlier today."

"To answer your question," Keith said, "it looks like the Sosa cartel is dead in the water."

"I think we're safe to assume any loyalty left to Sosa will dissolve with the criminal charges brought against him," Mick added.

"I like the sound of that." He was glad his team was there, taking care of things when he couldn't. Sosa was captured, and his cartel would be dissolved. Not only was he captured, but his ability to hurt Andi and her family was gone now too.

"We're still trying to tie up a few loose ends, though." Penny shifted, and Jude glimpsed someone standing behind her.

"We're gonna head back to the police department, Boss. Call us if you need anything." Mick nodded to him, and he and Keith left the room.

"Izan." Jude motioned the young man forward, remembering his quick thinking about the ambulance GPS back at the firehouse. "I'm glad I'm getting the chance to thank you for all your help. I wouldn't have known about the tracker in the ambulance without your quick thinking."

Izan nodded, clearly uncomfortable. He stepped past Jude's

teammates into the room with the Crawford family and Penny. "Sorry to interrupt."

"No way. You were an instrumental part of this."

Izan stiffened, which tipped Jude off to something deeper behind the young man's discomfort. He remembered the way Izan had tried to stop him, but Jude had been solely focused on rescuing Andi. There hadn't been time.

Jude looked around the room, but Logan and Bryce appeared just as surprised as he was to see the young man. Andi had welcomed him, but she took up a place next to Jude where she could hold his hand.

"What's going on?" Logan glanced around at each of them.

Jude's eyes landed on Elizabeth. She bit her lip, hyperfocused on the view outside the windows. It was easy to read her, but difficult to know where to go from there.

Their hurried conversation came back to him. How she'd always known more than she had shared. But there had been one question he hadn't had the chance to ask her. He looked back at the young man. Izan's hands clenched into fists, then released, and things clicked into place.

He wouldn't point a finger of blame at Elizabeth. He didn't have the right to judge her actions when they had only come from her concern about her family's safety. But there was one thing he knew to be true about this situation. One thing everyone deserved. If only she'd see it that way.

"I think it's about time everything came out into the open. Don't you, Elizabeth?" Jude said. His voice came out stronger than he expected, but it helped draw her attention.

Her shoulders stiffened, and she turned back toward him. "I—I don't know what you mean."

"Mom? What is Jude talking about?" Andi looked from him to her mother.

"What do you think, Izan?" Jude turned his question to the young man. "Isn't it time for the truth?"

36

Andi looked from Jude to Izan. What was Jude talking about?

Izan looked uncomfortable now, like he wanted to leave. She'd wondered why he was in the hospital parking lot, but she'd assumed he might have been there on a shift with Trace.

Her mother stepped forward. "He doesn't have to say anything if he doesn't want to."

"What are you talking about, Mom?" Andi's attention snapped to her mother, who wore her "lawyer face."

"No, it's all right, Mrs. Crawford." Izan swallowed—hard—then took a step. "I, uh, need to get this off my chest."

"What is going on?" Andi turned to Jude, but he shook his head.

Izan shifted from one foot to the other, and then resolve hardened his features. He took a deep breath and reached into the pocket of his jacket. What he pulled out looked like a stack of letters.

"I should have told you. Before." Izan met Jude's gaze. "I

just...I wasn't sure if I should, and Mrs. Crawford said it was better to wait."

"I'm sorry, Jude." Emotion flickered across Elizabeth's face. It looked a lot like shame. "It was my fault he didn't speak up sooner. He wanted to, but I convinced him it would be a bad idea. Besides, I was keeping a promise."

"I think I understand." Jude looked from Elizabeth to Izan.

Izan nodded. "These are letters. From my dad."

Andi had met Izan's father on several occasions.

"My biological dad," Izan said, as if reading her thoughts. "I always knew I was adopted. That was pretty clear from the start—I mean, you guys know my family—all blond and blue-eyed, and me clearly Hispanic." Izan offered a half smile. "But what I didn't know was who my biological parents were. I didn't really want to know. The parents who raised me are great. Really great."

"But the letters?" Jude prompted him when Izan paused.

He closed his eyes. "It was several months ago. When I got the first one in the mail from the prison, I almost threw it away because I thought it was a hoax or a mistake. But it had my name on it and...I opened it."

"What was it about?" Logan spoke up, breaking some of the spell in the room.

"I didn't realize until later that Elizabeth had transcribed it." Izan looked up at Andi's mother for a moment. "It explained that Camilo claimed to be my father. He told a...crazy story."

"That your father had worked for a drug lord named Diego Ruiz Sosa."

"Yeah." Izan met Jude's gaze. "And that he'd fallen in love with my mother, and they'd escaped only to be found in Denver, where my mother died. He told me that everyone said he had killed her, but he hadn't."

"He told you the truth." Elizabeth spoke up now. "He

dictated it to me, and I wrote it down word for word. Plus, I knew of your father's innocence firsthand."

"I believed him." Izan shrugged. "But what I have to say is about more than that." Izan looked guilty now, avoiding eye contact with them all.

"It's okay, man. Just tell us what happened." Jude's tone was gentle.

"I guess you could say I had an identity crisis when I got that letter. I mean, finding out that your biological dad is in prison for killing your mom is a big blow. But then to be told it was actually some guy named Sosa's fault..." Izan shook his head. "It was a lot to take in."

Andi couldn't imagine. His life had been turned upside down by the admission.

"I tried to find this Sosa guy." Izan's admission sucked the air from the room. "My dad's letter made it clear he was bad news, but I didn't care. He killed my mom, you know?"

Andi's mouth dropped open. Izan had known about Sosa this whole time?

"I asked around. I don't know how I thought I could get information, but I did. Met a few unsavory people that way." Izan met Andi's gaze, and she thought back to the day when she'd been on duty with him.

The woman at the house where the man had overdosed. Was that one connection he was talking about?

"I finally started taking trips to Denver, and that's where I made headway. I found out about Sosa's operation and got in close with a few people who worked distribution for him locally. And then I fell into some information about where he was going to be. In California."

"It was you." Jude shifted, and Andi saw the pain the movement caused.

Izan seemed to know what he meant. "I called in the tip about his villa. I thought if he were apprehended, maybe he would confess to killing my mom and...I don't know, my dad could get out of prison. It sounds ridiculous saying it like that, but I wasn't really thinking clearly. And it didn't matter. Camilo—my dad—died in prison."

Elizabeth stepped forward and placed a hand on his shoulder. Andi could see the compassion in her mother's gaze. "He didn't need to be cleared of the crime. The way he saw it, as long as you knew he was innocent, that was all that mattered. He stayed quiet to keep you safe."

"What do you mean, Mom?" Andi searched her mother's blue eyes, so like her own.

"Izan's parents were on a date the night his mother was killed. He was only four. They left him with a woman who watched him for several weeks after his father was arrested." Elizabeth turned the young man so he faced her. "When I took your father on as a client, his first order of business was for me to ensure that you were safe and cared for. And I did." She cupped his cheek for a moment before stepping back.

"Thank you." His words were barely above a whisper.

"Then Paul was in an accident—one meant to scare me—and that's when I knew I had to continue to protect you, just as if you were one of my own. No one could know who you really were."

Izan took in a shuddering breath. "I...what did you do?"

"After your father went to prison, I arranged a private adoption to your parents, the Collinses. I knew they were good people looking for a child, and you were so young. Your father signed off on it, which also sped things along. But I passed him updates about you often. He knew of your life, even if you knew nothing of him."

Izan roughly wiped tears from his face and turned to look out the window. Andi's shoulders sagged like the weight of her friend's sorrow rested on her now too. It couldn't be easy hearing the truth like he was—and with an audience.

She looked at her mother. Really looked at her. The woman who always had the answers, who never missed a training run in the morning or getting breakfast on the table for her and her brothers. That same woman had taken on an impossible weight. Not only to keep her family safe, but to preserve the family of another.

Her mother had watched her dad succumb to the traumatic brain injury that had changed his personality. Then she'd had to keep the information she had about Sosa quiet. And Izan. And any number of other things that could have changed their lives for the worse had the information gotten out.

"Mom." Andi's voice cracked.

"Oh, sweetie." Elizabeth looked at Andi, then her brothers. "I'm sorry I didn't tell you everything. I saw what happened to your father, and I was terrified. I did what I could to ensure that Camilo went to prison as he wanted. I kept his secrets for him, but also for Izan because I wanted everyone to have a life lived without fear. Parents take on the bad so you kids only get the good. That was what Camilo did."

Andi nodded, wiping her own tears.

"And the money?" Penny looked reluctant to bring it up.

"Camilo confided in me about the money he'd taken from Sosa during a privileged meeting. He was relatively safe from outside influence in the prison, especially since there were members of a rival cartel to Sosa's inside. But Camilo thought Sosa would find a way in eventually. He specifically said the money was for Izan. For his future."

"That's why he sent the letters." Izan sounded as if the pieces were falling into place for him.

"He wanted you to know he loved you." Elizabeth's eyes were glassy.

"I didn't need his money. I needed him." Andi could see Izan hadn't meant to say it out loud, but it was the truth.

"What will happen to it?" Bryce asked, his eyes on Penny.

"It's drug money." She shrugged. "More than likely it will be seized by the feds."

"I never wanted it." Izan said it again, but this time he made eye contact with Jude. "And I was only ever trying to help."

"I get it. You did what you thought you had to, and your tip was helpful. It led us to the surveillance photos, which led us here before it was too late. Just don't go after a drug lord again, okay? You're not alone. You've got friends here."

Izan offered the hint of a smile and nodded.

Jude looked up at Andi, and his expression radiated warmth through her. His words held wisdom for them all. Her mother had tried to handle everything on her own. Her brothers were always in competition with one another. Andi had placed herself in the same type of competitive arena against everyone in her family, isolating herself.

Together, they could all accomplish so much—and had done so much already. But separately, they would only work against each other.

"Izan." Elizabeth spoke up. "I'm sorry I didn't come forward sooner. I've always cared for you, though, like you were part of the family. You have the Collinses, but you have us too."

When she held out her arms, he accepted her hug immediately, and everyone took a collective breath. They would spend months working through the ramifications of this. Andi knew that much. But she also knew something else. She wanted to leave the competition behind and work toward collaboration.

What could she do now that she was ready to embrace her gift of practicing medicine?

Maybe the better question was, what *couldn't* she do?

37

Jude watched the emotions cycle over Andi's soft features. It was so much to take in. About her mother, her co-worker, the drug lord who had disrupted all of their lives. But she processed it head on. He wouldn't expect anything less from her.

He squeezed her hand, which drew her blue-eyed gaze to his. The responding smile she offered sent warmth through him. Oh, how he wished he could get up out of this bed and wrap her in his arms and—

"I think it's time we give these two some *space*." Logan's dramatic suggestion distracted Jude from his thought of kissing Andi.

Logan winked, and Jude laughed. He had to hand it to the brothers—for as annoyingly competitive and protective as they were, they truly loved their sister.

"Why don't we get some lunch? Andi, Jude, we'll bring something back for you." Elizabeth smiled at Jude, and he could see the apology behind it. She'd held things close to the vest, but there were fine lines when it came to confidentiality. He wouldn't be seeking any legal ramifications against her regarding this case.

With Sosa dead, the bulk of his money frozen in an offshore account accessible to Jude's team, and the other members accounted for, this had wrap-up written all over it.

"Thanks, guys." Andi ushered them out. It seemed she was just as eager as he was for a chance to talk.

When the door finally closed and she turned back to him, his heart thudded in his chest. She was beautiful. The minor cuts on her wrists were bandaged, and she had a purple bruise near her temple, but nothing affected her beauty.

"Hey, come here." He held out his free hand, and she came forward, gently settling on the hospital bed next to him. "How are you doing?"

Andi took a deep breath. But rather than anxiety or worry at what was to come, he saw something different. Peace.

"I think I'm finally doing okay."

"Finally?" He smiled and traced the shape of her face with a finger.

"You were right."

His finger stalled at her chin. "Can you repeat that?"

She laughed, and he reclaimed her hand. "You were right, Jude. I wanted to keep up—with my family, with my brothers, with some invisible standard I have for myself. I thought that being a firefighter was the way to do that, but I was wrong."

He waited, giving her the space to collect her thoughts.

"In the back of that ambulance at the gorge, I came face-to-face with all of my failures. I remembered that moment when Lana fell and..." A tear slipped down her cheek, and Jude reached up to catch it. "I was so angry."

"At me?"

"I thought so at first, but the more I considered it, I realized I was angry at *me*. Why had I been the one to insist we go to that party—against your better judgment? Why didn't I stop her from going out on that bridge? Why wasn't *I* strong enough to save her? Just...everything."

"I know you don't believe it"—he tapped her knee softly—"but I truly felt responsible. For all of it."

"But I forced you—"

"I went with you, and that's ultimately why I took the blame."

They held each other's gaze before Andi took a deep breath. "I think God spoke to me. In the back of the ambo. Well, maybe not so much Him but His word. It reminded me that *God is the strength of my heart.* Jude, no matter how hard I try, I will always fail. But that's when I'm relying on my strength, not His. And I'm done doing that."

He could see it now. Her transformation. The set of her shoulders and the confident peace that came over her.

"I'm going back to being a paramedic." She said the words with a smile. "I may even continue working toward a nursing degree, because it's what I want. I convinced myself that it wasn't good enough if I couldn't be a surgeon like my dad, but that's so wrong. I see that now."

"I'm happy for you, Dee." He cupped her cheek, and thoughts of her lips on his flickered through his mind.

"And there's one more thing." She looked down, overcome with uncharacteristic shyness.

"What's that, Super?"

She grinned at the nickname and then met his gaze. "I'm going to need a study partner."

He waited for the rest of her request.

"What I'm saying is, I want you to stay in Last Chance County. With me."

And there it was, laid out in front of him. The chance at forever he'd always wanted. He weighed his response. "I think that scripture is for me too."

"How so?" Andi leaned forward, accepting his non-answer,

and her sweet strawberry scent washed over him. He wanted to pull her close, but he needed to get this out.

"I've always wanted this." He swallowed, the thought choking him up even now. "Something that feels effortless. With you, Andi, it's always been easy. You push me to be better, but you also accepted me as I am. I was convinced that no matter what I did, it would never be enough. I saw my dad leave, and I thought I wasn't enough to keep him around. I watched Vanessa die, and I wasn't enough to save her. But looking back on those things—even the gorge—I realize that, no matter how many rules I follow, I'll never be perfect. And it's not my place to be. Otherwise I wouldn't need Jesus in my life."

The realization was a breath of fresh air in his lungs. He didn't need to be perfect. He believed in a heavenly Savior who already was. His eyes closed for a second, letting the truth wash over him. When he opened them, the weight of compassion in Andi's gaze crushed him.

"The right thing to do for my career—the by-the-book answer—is to stay in San Diego. I want to say it could work. I could fly back and forth to see you. I could come on weekends and holidays, but that's not enough." He cupped her cheek again, pulling her forward. "It won't be enough unless I'm here. With you."

"What are you saying, Jude?" The budding smile on her pink lips enticed him closer.

"I'm saying"—he nuzzled her nose with his—"that I think"—he kissed the corner of her lips—"I'll be requesting a transfer." He kissed the other corner. "Against my superior's recommendation."

"Really?"

"Really." He pressed his lips to hers and went to pull her forward, but the IV and cables got in the way. "Hold on." He pulled back, and she looked at him, pink-cheeked and breathless.

In one swift movement, he yanked the IV out and then the other cords. Loud beeps filled the air.

"Jude, what are you doing?"

He turned to her. "I'm going to kiss you properly."

He shifted and came to his feet, somewhat unsteadily.

"You're crazy. You know Charlotte is going to rush in here any minute thinking you're dead."

"Let her come."

Jude pulled Andi to his chest. He wrapped his injured arm carefully behind her back, then slid his fingers into her hair and kissed her with abandon. The fear he'd lived by for so long, governed by the rule book of his life, was gone.

The only thought he had was of marrying this woman. He'd promised her father that he would take care of her, and he'd meant it.

He pulled back, his senses filled with Andi. Her sweetness. Her confidence. Her unrelenting spirit. Pressing his forehead to hers, he said, "I love you."

Andi kissed him again, her lips so soft and gentle on his they were like a whispered prayer. "I love you too." Then she pulled back. "And you know what?"

The cacophony of beeping behind them had faded to the back of his mind as she took center stage. "What?"

"I've never seen you be so reckless." She pointed to the dangling IV and sensors hanging from the bed.

Jude laughed, the feeling loosening something in his chest. "You haven't seen anything yet."

WHAT'S HAPPENS NEXT...

EMT Trace Bently leaned against the wall at the back of the chapel and crossed his arms. The cellist's notes filtered above excited chatter as people took their seats and prepared to celebrate Allen Frees and Pepper Miller's wedding.

He'd tried to get out of coming today, but none of his co-workers would take no for an answer. They claimed it was a way to deepen friendships outside of work hours. Except he didn't need another elated bride and groom to remind him of what no longer existed for him. He'd rather deal with a severed limb than his broken heart.

Police Chief Conroy Barnes and the rest of the groomsmen made their way to the front of the altar.

Trace sighed and checked his watch. If he snuck out now, he might get away unnoticed.

Allen wheeled in and spun in a three-sixty, a frown pulling his brows together. His sage bow tie accentuated the rest of his suit. His quick scratch at the base of his neck told Trace it wasn't the most comfortable.

Allen found the wedding coordinator. "We've got a slight hold-up."

Trace straightened and held his breath. Pepper couldn't have gotten cold feet. No, she wouldn't do that moments before they exchanged vows. He'd seen the two of them together more than enough times to know that.

"Can you prolong the prelude for a few minutes?" Allen asked.

"Happy to." The wedding coordinator spun to the sanctuary. "Anything I can help with?"

"I have just the man for the job."

Trace frowned as well when Allen wheeled over to him. "Can you help me for a minute?" Allen leaned in. "Everyone else is seated, and I don't want to make a big deal about this."

"What's going on man?" Trace scrunched his brow.

A tint of red colored Allen's cheeks, but nothing else indicated he was in distress. "Victory is complaining of a stomachache and says she won't make it down the aisle. Can you talk with her? Maybe she needs something to hold her over until the ceremony is finished."

Trace didn't have a medic bag with him, but a stomachache would be easy to treat. He might only need a kid-friendly can of something bubbly for Pepper's niece—the child she and Allen were adopting right after the wedding. "Sure thing. Where is she?"

He pointed at the end of the hall. "In the bridal suite. I can't go in, you know." He winked. "Waited this long to see my bride. I don't want to ruin it now."

Trace kept his mouth shut and rapped on the door.

"Who's there? Allen, you know you can't come in!" a woman exclaimed.

His stomach flipped. Maybe something was going around. "It's Trace Bently. I'm here to talk with Victory."

The door opened and Trace stood frozen, unable to move. Memories flooded to the forefront. How quickly midnight struck and what that hour had taken from him far too soon.

"Victory won't get up from the couch." Pepper waved her hand in his face and pointed behind her to a small loveseat by the window. "Says her stomach hurts too much."

Trace swallowed and pulled in a breath. "I'll see what I can do."

Pepper and the bridesmaids went back to adding their final touches while he walked over to Victory and knelt beside her.

"Not feeling too good today, kiddo?" He scanned her face, but a healthy color remained. They'd met before, so she knew he helped people.

"My stomach feels nausea." She pouted.

Trace bit his tongue to hold back a laugh. "Feeling nauseous is never fun." He placed the back of his hand on her forehead. *Not warm at all.* "When was the last time you ate?"

Victory slid up a fraction, and she scrunched her forehead. "I was hungry, so Auntie Pepper gave me some trail mix. Those raisins and pretzels tasted great."

He glanced at the bride, who mouthed, *About an hour ago.* Trace nodded. "What about water?"

"Auntie Pepper says we needs to stay hydrated so we can dance tonight."

"You've got a special aunt who's taking care of you. And I think I know what the problem is." Trace waggled his finger and raised his eyebrows.

The girl's eyes widened, and a smile formed. "You do?"

Trace could spot the problem a mile away. "Are you nervous about the wedding?" he asked softly.

Victory puckered her lips, and she swung her foot under the chair. "Maybeeee a little." She leaned close. "I has to walk in front of everybody."

"Well, I think it's completely normal to be scared. It's a big day, and you have a big responsibility. Sometimes that makes our stomach twist in knots and makes it hurt."

Victory sat up on the sofa. "I don't know how to make it go away."

"I have an idea." Trace snapped his finger. "When you're walking down the aisle and throwing those petals, why don't you pretend everyone is a cat and you're giving them treats? Just like when you help Auntie Pepper at the vet."

Victory let out a giggle. "That's so silly."

"Do you think you can do that?"

Victory nodded and hopped off the sofa and picked up her basket. "I'm ready to go, Auntie."

Trace stood.

The bride came over, and it had to be said. "You look amazing."

"Thank you." Pepper beamed. "I don't know what you did, but thank you."

Trace followed everyone out of the room and watched as, one by one, the bridesmaids made their way to the front of the sanctuary.

Victory turned back to him, and Trace gave her a thumbs-up. She dipped her hand in the basket and threw rose petals perfectly until she got to the end of the runner. "One for you." Her singsong voice trailed down the aisle. "One for you..."

"Thanks, man." Brett Filks, the local vet and Pepper's boss, gave him a fist bump before he tucked his arm under Pepper's and the music changed. On cue, everyone stood to their feet.

Trace rubbed his fingers across his chest, trying to get rid of the painful ache. He needed to get out of here. As Brett escorted Pepper toward her happily-ever-after, Trace turned and made a beeline for his car. In order to save his broken heart, he needed to leave.

He'd had that joy once.

And lost it.

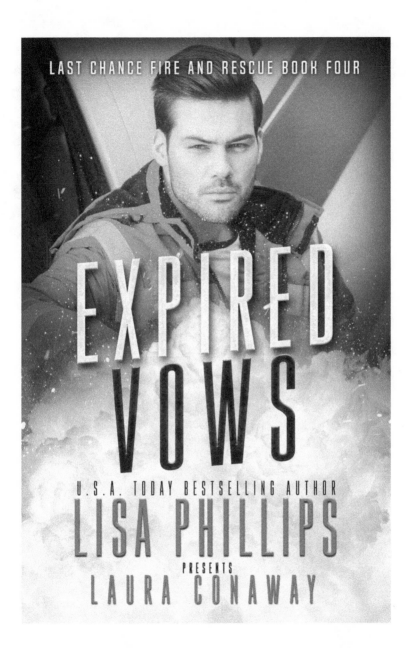

LAST CHANCE FIRE AND RESCUE BOOK FOUR

EXPIRED VOWS

U.S.A. TODAY BESTSELLING AUTHOR

LISA PHILLIPS

PRESENTS

LAURA CONAWAY

Turn the page for a sneak peek at the next Last Chance Fire and Rescue novel, *Expired Vows*...

EXPIRED VOWS SNEAK PEEK

LAST CHANCE FIRE AND RESCUE #4

CHAPTER 1

Trace Bently wasn't going to let anyone die on his watch—not today.

"You ready to go, partner?" Andi peeked her head around the driver's side door of the ambulance. Her voice echoed in the enclosed garage area of the Eastside firehouse.

"All set." Trace hit the side of the truck and jogged to the passenger side.

The tires squealed against the pavement as they made a sharp turn out of the station. Sunlight streamed through the windshield, and he pulled down the visor. Andi leaned forward and flicked the sirens on. Traffic steered to the shoulder, and they were given the right of way.

Trace spoke into the radio. "Rescue 5 is on the way. Any updates on the situation?"

Static crackled through the line as he waited for a response. Hostage situations could get ugly fast, and he hoped a negotiator was already enroute. Time was always of the essence. With no telling what would tip the captor over the edge to do something stupid. He'd seen it too many times when he'd been a cop. Standing around, powerless to do anything.

Now that he was an EMT, he could focus on the victims rather than just who needed to be arrested. Saving lives was his job—and that's exactly what he was going to do.

He leaned forward and tapped his foot against the floorboard before sneaking a glance at Andi. A knowing look crossed her face as she raised her eyebrows. She was going as fast as possible. He knew that. But he didn't have to like how slow it felt in the meantime.

"We've got a male holding two kids at gunpoint," the commander on the other end of the line stated.

Trace winced. "Copy that."

"Kids?" Andi hissed.

Trace gritted his teeth. "I know."

"The wife escaped and is with an officer now but needs immediate medical attention. Gash to the forehead and cuts along her arm. Possible broken bone," the commander said.

"ETA seven minutes." Trace let go of the button.

Despite the clear skies and sunny morning, the flash of their blue and red lights illuminated the surrounding neighborhood and trailed down the street to encircle the corner property as they pulled in. Bystanders shifted their heads in an attempt to get a closer look at the commotion while officers blockaded the area.

Before Andi even rolled to a complete stop, Trace hopped out and scanned the area. As soon as she parked, he grabbed his bag, Andi not far behind.

Suburban neighborhood. The house had a front porch with a swing, dotted with several decorative pillows. It could comfortably seat two. The front lawn was meticulous. Shrubs trimmed with precision, and the hanging plants vibrant with color.

Patches of brown grass were the only indication of trouble

beyond the exterior of the property, though Trace knew that was simply from the cooler temperatures making way for winter weather. To the outside world, the family who lived here had a good life.

Lieutenant Basuto stood on the sidewalk. He waved them over. "Husband hit her on the head with the butt of his gun."

Trace looked over at the woman, her hand propped against her head.

"On her way out, she tripped over an uneven sidewalk and slammed into the pavement with her arm." The lieutenant averted his gaze to the woman. "We already took her statement, so she's all yours."

Andi led the woman to sit on the curb.

Trace stayed with Basuto. "And the kids? Any injuries?"

"As far as we can tell," he lowered his voice to a whisper. "They're unharmed, though they're still inside with him. We're working to get them out."

"You'll need blueprints of the house layout to know the best route in. I wonder if one of the side windows has open blinds. Maybe a drone would work to see in through the skylight." Trace took a few steps back and pointed in the direction of the roof.

Basuto's eyes scanned him up and down. "We've got it under control."

"Right." Trace nodded. "Keep it that way."

He'd slipped right back into "cop" mode. *Old habits.* Some things were ingrained, and he'd been a police officer for almost six years. But he would never go back. That season took too much of what he loved, and he'd never get it back.

Trace clenched his hand.

Now he had the power to save people on the front lines every day as a medic. This new job gave him purpose.

"If you're good to take over here, I have a patient to see to."

He grinned, playing it off like a joke when nothing about this situation was funny. *Get your head straight.*

Lieutenant Basuto's eyebrows rose. "Sure thing, Bently."

Trace walked over to Andi who had her stethoscope out and a blood pressure cuff around the woman's arm.

"Alice, this is my partner Trace. Trace, Alice." Andi released the valve, and air whooshed out before she packed up the cuff. "Glad you could finally join us." She shot Trace a look.

"Had a few things to tend to with Basuto." Trace waved his hand and crouched along the curb.

Alice had a cloth pressed against the side of her head and cradled her right arm against her chest. Tinges of white peeked through, but the majority of the cloth was saturated with hues of red.

The woman looked between the two of them and burst out in tears. "My kids. They're still in there with Gerald. He said he was going to take them." Her shoulders heaved with each sob.

"These officers are here to make sure that doesn't happen. They will do everything they can to keep the kids safe, Alice." He gave her a reassuring smile.

Inside, his stomach churned. He wanted to pray those kids made it out safely, like that would actually help. God had stripped him of those he loved. Why trust Him when the outcome here might not be any different?

Trace trusted that law enforcement here in Last Chance County had the training to resolve this peacefully. They'd find a way to take the guy down and reunite the kids with their mother.

Trace pulled back on his insecurities and focused. "Right now, we need to get that cut on your head taken care of." And make sure Alice didn't have a concussion.

Her sobs slowly eased up until only silent tears trickled down her face.

"BP is elevated, but everything else is good," Andi said.

"I'm going to move my finger, and I want you to follow it, okay, Alice?" Trace said.

She nodded and focused her gaze on his finger. He moved it side to side and up and down. Her eyes tracked, which was a good thing. But he didn't like how heavily her head wound bled.

Trace pulled out gauze and bandages. "Alice, can you hand Andi the cloth so I can take a look at your head?" Trace donned a pair of gloves. The elastic snapped against his skin.

Blood trickled in a steady stream from the wound. The woman's hair was sticky and tangled, and it took a minute to clear the area to assess the cut. As he did, he glanced back at the cops, who stood around, waiting.

"Wishing you were over there with those tough guys?" Andi asked.

"When I can be here doing the real work? Nah." He chuckled.

Resolve stirred in him as he probed Alice's wound gently. *This* was where he was supposed to be.

"That's going to need sutures. Here." Andi handed him alcohol swabs. She cut some gauze and gave it to him.

The bandage would suffice for now, but they needed to get her to the hospital soon. Get a CT scan ordered to make sure there wasn't internal bleeding. The fact that she was coherent was a good sign. He didn't want that to change before the police resolved the situation and got her kids out of the house.

Trace watched the way she held her elbow. "Can you move your arm for me?"

"I-I don't know." Sweat beaded on her brow. "It hurts."

"That's okay." He held out his hands. "I'm just going to touch different areas and you tell me if you feel any pain."

Alice nodded. "I can't believe I tripped on my own front walk."

He worked his way from the shoulder down. When he

applied pressure to the radial bone, she winced. "All right. I'm going to add a little more pressure. Bear with me." His fingers connected with her skin. She let out a hiss before biting her lip. "You've definitely got bruising at minimum, but only an x-ray will tell how bad the damage is."

A tear rolled from her eye. Trace carefully placed her arm in a sling, and Andi put the supplies back in the bag.

A scream pierced the air.

"My babies!" Alice pushed herself off the curb with her good arm and managed a few steps before swaying. "What is he doing to them?"

"Whoa. We can't have you passing out now." Trace gingerly took hold of the woman's left arm as Andi held the other.

"He's hurting them!" She pushed against their grip.

"Hold up, okay?" Trace looked at Andi. "Can you look after her?" He turned to Alice. "I want you to sit, okay? I'll see what's going on."

"Trace." Andi's eyes held an edge of reluctance.

"I'll be right back, okay?"

He spotted Alex Basuto and figured the lieutenant would be able to fill him in a little on what just happened. Trace couldn't help it. Even though he wasn't a cop anymore, the instincts were still there. If someone was in danger, it was his responsibility to make sure others were safe—no matter what job he did.

Trace jogged across the street and weaved around several patrol cars. The scene commander yelled into his radio. Adrenaline hit him like electricity trying to find a circuit and catch a spark. The rush of running into a deadly situation, not knowing what would be on the other side of the door.

The child's scream still rang in his ears.

He just hoped no one else got hurt and the negotiator's skills proved infallible.

Trace approached Basuto. "Did they get the negotiator in there yet?"

It seemed like law enforcement was at a standstill. No one moved. Several heads were lowered in conversation—the scene commander, Chief Conroy Barnes, and a couple of other officers.

"The guy refuses to see one." The lieutenant frowned. "He said he'll only talk with his counselor."

That wasn't the "cop" way to solve a problem. "They could end up getting everyone hurt."

"Right now, it's the only option we have to work with if we want this resolved with those kids safe." Basuto's radio crackled to life and someone shared intel. "We're in a bind right now, Trace. None of us can do anything." Basuto spoke into the device. "What's her ETA?"

The radio crackled. "Five minutes out."

"Copy," Basuto said. "We'll continue to hold down."

The blinds on the house were shut. From this angle, Trace could see a tan fence enclosed the backyard. There was no way to get a look at what was going on inside. The gunman had the upper hand, and he likely knew it.

A few minutes later a gray Impala pulled up to the opposite corner of the house. Officers waved the crowd back and a woman got out of the car. Trace couldn't make out who it was, other than that she had long, auburn hair.

A counselor empathized with someone's feelings. They weren't trained to de-escalate someone who clearly had other intentions in mind. She wouldn't know where to position herself in case any bullets went flying. There was no way he could sit back and do nothing.

The whole situation was crazy. "This woman could end up getting everyone killed."

His legs started moving before his mind caught up. He

needed to talk some sense into this crew and brainstorm a plan B that didn't involve this counselor stepping in the crossfire.

"Dude, you can't go over there." Basuto called out.

Trace made it as far as the fire hydrant several yards from the front walkway before Basuto was in front of him, palm up, legs positioned in a defiant stance.

"They should really have a better plan in place. Or at least think through another option than this." Trace waved his hand in the direction of the team suiting up a woman who had no clue what she was doing.

He raised his heels and strained to see past the entourage of officers.

"You're not a cop anymore." Basuto crossed his arms. "And if you were, I'd be your superior. So back off."

The words sliced through the air and stabbed right at his heart. Being a cop hadn't helped him to save the one person who needed him. He'd vowed to never let that happen again, so he'd become an EMT. Yet here he was, stuck in a quandary.

He hated being useless.

Trace winced. "But..."

"Places everyone. We'll be ready to go in five." The chief's command came through loud and clear on the radio.

Basuto waved him off. "Go do your job, Trace. Let us take care of ours."

Trace shut his mouth. He looked over once more at the team assembling and let out a sigh. He made his way back to Andi who was still with their patient.

"Kelsey!" The name echoed through the air behind him.

Trace turned to see what the commotion was about. That is when the counselor turned. She took something from an officer and slid her hand up to her ear to fit it in place. She gave a thumbs up.

Kelsey.

She was the counselor? His heart beat faster against his

chest at the realization that she was here at the scene. The roof of his mouth dried like flames licking up the heat. He'd moved here to escape his past, not come face to face with it again.

His mind spun with thoughts, but one question rang loudest. What was his dead wife's best friend doing in Last Chance County?

ACKNOWLEDGMENTS

Every book takes on a life of its own. No matter how many I've written, each book stretches me and grows not only my ability to write, but also my approach to writing. *Expired Promise* is no different. This is my first traditionally published adult novel and I have Sunrise Publishing and Lisa Phillips to thank for that. Thanks to Lindsay and Susie for taking a chance on me and Rel for being an absolute rock star. And thanks to Lisa for your amazing support—you are crazy (in the best way) and I love it!

Thanks to my amazing Book Ballers Group! Natalie, can you believe I finally did it? I wouldn't be who I am as a writer without you. Christen, you're the best motivational kick-in-the-behind a girl could ask for. Your "throw it at the wall and see what sticks" approach is invaluable to me. Steffani, we're really doing it—we've achieved the dreams we had as little girls and we're doing it *together*. I couldn't ask for a better sister-friend to be on this journey with.

A huge thank you to Dr. Matt and Corrine. Some of these final scenes wouldn't be half of what they are without the insight of you both! Any medical errors are fully mine.

This book is in your hands in part thanks to Tamela Hancock Murray, my amazing agent. You've stayed with me through my wild-ride of ideas and I am grateful for your unwavering support.

Readers, whether this is the first book of mine you've read, or you've been with me from the start, thank you for your support! I endeavor to create books that you'll enjoy and that will leave you with this simple truth: you are loved and you are enough.

Having a book traditionally published is a dream I've had since I was young and that is in part thanks to my mom and dad. Thank you both for my love of books, for reading everything I write, and for always always *always* supporting my dreams, no matter if they seemed impractical or impossible.

Alex, the dedication says it all (and might be the only thing you read in this book—LOL). I love you and am so thankful for your support!

Lastly, I write for an audience of One. Jesus, may my works glorify You, and You alone.

CONNECT WITH SUNRISE

Thank you so much for reading *Expired Promise*. We hope you enjoyed the story. If you did, would you be willing to do us a favor and leave a review? It doesn't have to be long- just a few words to help other readers know what they're getting. (But no spoilers! We don't want to wreck the fun!) Thank you again for reading!

We'd love to hear from you- not only about this story, but about any characters or stories you'd like to read in the future. Contact us at www.sunrisepublishing.com/contact.

We also have a monthly update that contains sneak peeks, reviews, upcoming releases, and fun stuff for our reader friends. Sign up at www.sunrisepublishing.com

ABOUT THE AUTHORS

Lisa Phillips is a USA Today and top ten Publishers Weekly bestselling author of over 50 books that span Harlequin's Love Inspired Suspense line, independently published series romantic suspense, and thriller novels. She's discovered a penchant for high-stakes stories of mayhem and disaster where you can find made-for-each-other love that always ends in happily ever after.

Lisa is a British ex-pat who grew up an hour outside of London and attended Calvary Chapel Bible College, where she met her husband. He's from California, but nobody's perfect. It wasn't until her Bible College graduation that she figured out she was a writer (someone told her). As a worship leader for Calvary Chapel churches in her local area, Lisa has discovered a love for mentoring new ministry members and youth worship musicians.

Visit Lisa's Website to sign up for her mailing list to get FREE books and be the first to learn about new releases and other exciting updates!

Connect with Lisa: https://www.authorlisaphillips.com/sunrise

Emilie Haney grew up in the Pacific Northwest and has a love for the outdoors that matches her love for the written word. She turned her passion for stories toward writing at an early age, finding entertainment and adventure in made-up worlds fed by the books her parents read to her as a child. Now, she's still getting lost in those worlds but they are of her own making. Emilie writes contemporary fiction with strong themes of romance and suspense and believes that–no matter what–love fights for what's right.

Connect with Emilie at emiliehaney.com.

Join Emilie's newsletter!

https://view.flodesk.com/pages/63d98cadecc67819006271ff
Support Emilie on Patreon:
https://www.patreon.com/eahcoalition

OTHER LAST CHANCE COUNTY NOVELS

Last Chance Fire and Rescue Collection

Expired Return

Expired Hope

Expired Promise

Expired Vows (September, 2023)

Last Chance County Series

Expired Refuge

Expired Secrets

Expired Cache

Expired Hero

Expired Game

Expired Plot

Expired Getaway

Expired Betrayal

Expired Flight

Expired End

Expired Promise: A Last Chance County Novel
Published by Sunrise Media Group LLC
Copyright © 2023 Sunrise Media Group LLC

All rights reserved. No part of this publication may be reproduced or
transmitted in any form or by any means without written permission of the
publisher.

This book is a work of fiction. Names, characters, places, and incidents are
either products of the author's imagination or used fictitiously. Any similarity
to actual people, organizations, and/or events is purely coincidental.

Scripture quotations marked TPT are from The Passion Translation®.
Copyright © 2017, 2018, 2020 by Passion & Fire Ministries, Inc. Used by
permission. All rights reserved. ThePassionTranslation.com.

For more information about Lisa Phillips and Emilie Haney please access the
authors' websites at the following addresses: https://authorlisaphillips.com &
https://emiliehaney.com

Published in the United States of America.
Cover Design: Ryan Schwarz, thecoverdesigner.com

CPSIA information can be obtained
at www.ICGtesting.com
Printed in the USA
BVHW040201020623
665276BV00004B/94